EASY MOTION TOURIST

Leye Adenle

Abuja – London

First published in 2016 by Cassava Republic Press
Abuja – London
www.cassavarepublic.biz

ISBN 978-1-911115-06-9
eISBN 978-1-911115-07-6

A CIP catalogue record for this book is available from the British Library.

Printed and bound in Great Britain by Bell and Bain Ltd, Glasgow.

Distributed by Central Books Ltd.

Prologue

Florentine wasn't her real name, neither was Florentina, but she answered to both. She was a second year mass communications student at Unilag. And even though her parents were not paying her tuition or her living expenses, they were still disappointed when she didn't score high enough to study medicine, or engineering, or law.

In her first year in school she couldn't afford to stay in the hostel, so she lived with an aunt, a distant relative who made her sleep on the floor in the sitting room, next to the driver and the house girl, who were on intimate terms. The aunt also paid her school fees and gave her a little extra to take a bus to school. In that first year Florentine lost twenty kilograms and failed half of her courses.

Then she met an old friend in school and moved in with her on campus and the aunt stopped sending money.

The tokunbo cars, expensive jewellery, and latest phones owned by students at Unilag makes it hard to believe there is poverty in Nigeria. Florentine's friend, for instance, bought Brazilian hair from another student who regularly travels to Dubai to buy clothes, jewellery, and human hair to sell to her schoolmates. Florentine's friend paid two hundred and fifty thousand naira for the hair, and a week later she had it taken out because other girls now had virgin Peruvian hair and she didn't want to be unfashionable. She gave Florentine the discarded weave, and when Florentine had it fixed everyone said she looked more beautiful than the current Miss Unilag.

Not that Florentine objected to the way other girls made money, but she never went clubbing with them. They would go out on Friday, usually to one of the expat clubs on Victoria Island, and they would either come back the next morning or be away all weekend and only return to school early on Monday morning, sometimes dropped off by chauffeured luxury cars. Monday was when they settled debts, bought airtime for their phones, or sent money home to parents and siblings.

But Florentine was not brought up to sell her body. That's what she told her friend, and that's the reason the girls stopped inviting her to parties or to clubs.

Unlike them, Florentine had found friends who looked after her. One was her boyfriend, Nosa, a banker on the island. They would meet at a hotel near school where they would spend the whole weekend together. They couldn't go to his house because of his wife.

Another friend, who was even more protective over her, was a much older man. A chief, in fact: Chief Ojo, a well-known businessman in Lagos. He was more generous than Nosa, and he took her to better hotels and even let her stay there alone for the weekend after spending Friday night with her. He was also married, but unlike Nosa he was old enough to be her father - so she could never think of him as a boyfriend, even though he introduced her to his friends as his little wife and he constantly asked if she was cheating on him.

With just these two steady friends, and occasional men she met through friends, Florentine was able to pay her school fees, eat three times a day, and soon enough buy her own Peruvian hair. Even her grades improved. And when there was no hope of passing a paper, she could afford to pay the lecturer to overlook the fact that she hadn't taken the exam.

It is easier on one's ego to receive charity when you don't need it. When Florentine's income was sufficient enough and steady as well, she was able to go clubbing with the girls without a thought for the judging eyes that would follow her all the way there, whispering 'prostitute.'

It was at a club that she met a boy. He was about her age but he was also a student at university so that made him a boy. While the other men there were older and richer, and bought champagne for their dates, he sat with a group of girls who paid for his drinks. He kept looking at her, and when she got up to go to the toilet he got up too. When she came out he was outside the door. He said, 'Hey,' and handed her a business card as if he was someone important. She wanted to tear the card and throw the pieces at his face, but he had started walking away and the girls he was with were looking at her with resentment, or perhaps it was envy.

Back in school she showed her friend the card and learned that she had hit the jackpot. She sent the boy a text but he did not respond. She called and he rejected the call. She sent three more messages over the week and had given up when he called her two weeks later and invited her to his house in Victoria Garden City.

He asked if she wanted to make money. She did. He told her about a place called the Harem. It was an exclusive club owned by his brother, Malik. If she wanted in she would have to have an HIV test first. He would pay for it. She couldn't tell anybody about the club, and once she became a member she would have to stay there for weeks at a time and wouldn't be able to contact anyone outside. While she considered it, he added, 'You will make one million naira in a month.'

She told the banker that she was pregnant, and as she expected, he gave her money for an abortion and was busy anytime she called. She told Chief Ojo that she was going to Ghana with a friend; they were going to buy gold to sell to their mates in school. He praised her entrepreneurial spirit and gave her money for her new business.

Three months later, on the day after the results of her second blood test came back, the boy picked her from school and took her to his house in VGC. There was another girl there who didn't talk a lot and was constantly looking about: at a door opening, a door closing, the boy standing up.

At midnight a man came to the house with a policeman walking behind him. The boy introduced the man as Mr Malik, the owner of the Harem. Malik told the two girls that they would be blindfolded for the journey to the club. Florentine wanted to object; the other girl began to cry and beg to be allowed to leave. Malik told her it was too late.

The girls got into the back of Malik's white Range Rover Sport which had blackened windows and he collected their phones. The policeman tied clothes around their faces. They drove for hours and when the car stopped and the blindfolds were taken off, they were in a large compound surrounded by a twelve-foot fence topped with barbed wire. Dense forest grew beyond the compound. The house was huge and unpainted, but otherwise complete and elegant; it had the double height columns that had become trendy in Lagos. About twenty cars were parked in front. Some had drivers waiting in them. A generator was rumbling in a corner by the gate, and as they walked up to the building, they could hear music coming from inside.

A woman opened the front door and greeted Malik with a hug. She was in pink lingerie. She had a glass of wine in one hand and a smouldering cigar in the other. Other girls in lingerie were strolling about or sitting on sofas with men, drinking and talking or cuddling and laughing. The men, about ten, wore masks like the ones people wear to fancy dress parties.

'You cannot know who your client is,' Malik said as he led Florentine and the other girl up the staircase. 'They are regularly tested for HIV and other STDs, just as you were. You cannot ask them for money. You cannot ask them to use a condom. If a client shows you his face, you must look away. And you must tell me. If you think you recognise someone, you must keep it to yourself. If your client is a woman, you cannot refuse. You cannot speak to anyone about what happens here. At the end of the week, Sisi will pay you two hundred thousand.'

The girls were taken to different rooms and given lingerie to try on. Florentine got dressed and was going downstairs when Sisi, the lady they met at the door, stopped her on the stairs.

'I have an important client coming today,' Sisi said. 'He always wants to be first to try the new girls.' She took Florentine's hand and led her back up the stairs. 'Malik didn't tell you something; sometimes a client will give you money. You can keep it so long as you didn't ask for it, but you must tell me about it. This guy who I have for you, he is going to settle you big time. You can thank me later.' She led Florentine into the room. 'By the way, what is your name?'

'Rolake, ma.'

'That's too local. From now on you are Florentine. OK? And don't call me ma.'

As Florentine waited on the bed, changing her position

a dozen times, unable to make up her mind which pose was most seductive, or for that matter whether she should go for sexy, or for the good girl look, she contemplated her luck and smiled at how she would soon be richer than the banker and would no longer need the chief either.

Someone knocked and she said, 'Come in.' She had decided to sit up, stretch out her legs and lay them one on top of the other, with her arms spread over the headboard.

He stepped in, clutching a bottle of Moët in one hand and two champagne flutes in the other. He looked comical in a glistening mask with gold discs and green feathers at the edges, and a long white tunic, stretched in the middle by a protruding belly.

He raised the hand in which he held the glasses and lifted the mask off his face.

'Rolake!' he said. His mouth remained open and his eyes bulged.

Her legs retracted towards her body and she pulled a pillow to cover herself. 'Oh shit! Chief!' she gasped.

1

To start with, going alone to a pickup joint in Lagos wasn't my idea. Well, that's not entirely true. Nigeria was where Melissa – my half Nigerian, half Irish ex-girlfriend – was born and I wanted to have stories to tell her when I got back to London. I also wanted to get out of Eko Hotel to see this country I'd heard so much about.

Anyway, Magnanimous – that's what he insisted his name was – the concierge at the hotel, said it was safe and that many other white people would be there. Looking back, he did say it with a grin. At the time, it looked like a smile: one of his perfunctory ones that he would switch on the instant he looked up and noticed you. But now I'm sure it was a grin; a knowing grin and a wink, which I almost missed when I turned to look at a slender African woman walking past us in the hotel lobby. She smelt like vanilla ice cream.

I'm not blaming him for what happened at Ronnie's, only setting the record straight, which is to say that I was not out looking to pick up a girl.

I make this point upfront because every time I've told the story, I've been stopped at this moment by someone who thinks it's hilarious that I was at the bar in the first place, then they totally miss the reason why I start telling the story from the bar, and I stop telling it altogether. Their loss. At least you will hear my story.

I strolled out onto the streets of Lagos alone that night and I found 'the big signboard with plenty lights' where Magnanimous said I'd find it. In the end, it was a short walk from the hotel and not one Nigerian looked at me with as much as a passing curiosity, or for that matter the glare of someone about to rob a foreigner.

At Ronnie's bar, shirt clinging to my body, I walked through the open gate with the swagger of a regular – a totally put-on show. I was still anxious, to tell the truth. 'Whatever you do, never go out alone and especially not at night' the Nigerian taxi driver who dropped me at Heathrow had said.

A large man standing in front of the entrance held out his hand and I shook an enormous, moist palm before he stepped aside and pointed to a sheet of A4 paper taped to the door: GIRLS FREE. MEN N1000. Inside, the room was packed, engulfed with smoke, and the music was loud.

It appeared to have been someone's front room at one time. You could see where walls had been knocked down and plastered over. A solitary disco-light hung from the ceiling, looking out of place like a display fixture in a DIY store. Massive speakers were set on rusty metal chairs, next to giant fans oscillating like robots watching over the crowd. The air con was either broken or just not up to the task, and unlike Magnanimous had promised, mine was the only white face there.

It made me think of the first time I was in a room alone with black people: a church in Lambeth, a short drive from the family home in Chelsea, not long after my mum's divorce. I was ten. She left me surrounded by strangers and went to the front to the pastor who spoke patois. He made her take off her shoes and stand in an inflatable pool. Then he made her sit in it before placing his hand on her head and pushing her into the water, holding her down until she emerged again, water running off her, gasping to applause and hallelujahs and cymbals, and a spontaneous rift from the church pianist.

Nevertheless, I was in an actual Nigerian nightclub in a Nigerian city, surrounded by Africans and the endearing strangeness of their accents. I loved it. I loved that I would have this to tell Mel when I returned home. We hadn't spoken in two months. I was giving her the space she asked for when I called on what would have been our anniversary and asked to take her to Rodizio Rico in Notting Hill where we'd had our first date. Maybe she thought I was making my comeback bid, but after our talk I'd accepted that we were over. I was even self-aware enough to know that the maturity with which I was handling the entire affair was just the period before the novocaine wears off after a visit to the dentist. Of course, it broke my heart that after eight years she didn't want to be with me anymore, and I knew at some point I would probably get past the initial numbness, go on a bender, and end up on the floor in my flat, crying to Whitney Houston's I Will Always Love You. For now at least, I was cool. And I was even mature enough to want to stay friends. Funny how she was the one who remembered the anniversaries – until she suggested we take a break. I'd sent a BBM from the airport telling her about the trip to Nigeria, after weeks of no contact. She read it but didn't reply. I was about to fly to her country of birth, where her father still lived in his hometown Ibadan with his new wife and her half siblings who she hadn't met, so it seemed okay to message her. Thinking of how I'd tell her about 'this girl I met at a club in Nigeria who reminded me of you,' I pushed through the dance floor, squeezed past couples, danced for a few seconds with a girl who took my hand and began grinding her bum against my crotch, and eventually made it to the bar. As soon as I sat down, another girl with a cigarette sat next to me. She was wearing a pink tank top, a pair of blue jean shorts, black tights, and knee-length black leather boots that looked suspiciously shiny. She pouted her red glistening lips to exhale a long jet of smoke, then turned and asked if I wanted to buy her a drink.

I wanted to buy myself a drink, if only I could catch the barman's attention, but he was too busy looking down the dress of a girl sitting at the bar, who in turn was nodding to whatever was playing through the earplugs of her phone while flicking her fingers over its screen. I'd given up on the scrawny fellow, as I wasn't yet sure that I wanted to stay, when the girl who wanted the drink leaned over to shout into my ear again, her breasts pushing into my shoulder. I looked at the barman, waving at him lamely, then I shrugged helplessly. The woman turned round and raised herself over the bar by kneeling on the stool. Her arse in my face, she bent over and shouted the barman's name: Waidi, or, Waydi, or, Wady. He hissed, shuffled over and, ignoring the girl who had called him, asked me, 'Are you being served?'

He was the only one behind the bar. I asked for a double brandy – any brandy they had. Seeing the bottle he was reaching for, I shouted at the back of his head, 'No, not Three Barrels. Hennessy. No ice.' The girl said she wanted the same. Waidi waited for me to nod, then he glanced at the girl whose cleavage had fascinated him so much.

Without looking at me, he said, 'That is three thousand five hundred for the two.' This ticked off my new friend. 'Did he ask you for the price?' she said – loudly enough to attract attention. I was already fumbling in my pocket for the money. I'd done the maths: it was about fourteen quid and sounded about right – I'd been told that Lagos was expensive.

Waidi said something to her in a language I didn't understand and it must have been rude. She began poking her finger in his face, looking around for support as she cursed, screaming, touching the tip of her tongue with the index finger of her right hand and pointing the wetted finger to the ceiling over her head. The barman just stood there grinning. At one point, it looked as if she was going to reach over and slap the smirk off his face.

I counted out the money. He took the notes and counted himself, and then he went about fixing the drinks. The girl in the pink tank top sat back down, her face gathered into a snarl. She said something like 'wait for me', then stood up and started off through the crowd. I didn't like the look on her face when she turned back to look at him. He didn't see it, but I'm sure if he had, he'd have been alarmed like me. I'd seen the look before: the look of a lad going off to find a bottle during a pub brawl.

Waidi brought the drinks and my change. I was already standing up. I downed the brandy in one go, immediately regretted it, and left him the dirty, crumpled notes he'd placed on the bar with my receipt. I only made it halfway to the exit.

Like fans invading a football field, a mass of people rushed in through the entrance. I stopped for a moment, not sure what was going on. People were being pushed to the ground by the newcomers who ran in screaming and shouting. I was almost knocked off my feet but I managed to sidestep the mayhem and backtrack to the bar. From there I watched as even more people hurried in looking shell-shocked. Bodies quickly piled up on the floor and others were climbing on them. A profound chill came over me when I saw a head rolling over the backs of the fallen; then I realised someone had only lost their wig. The shouting got louder, and I became acutely aware of my situation: I was a white boy in Africa for the first time, on assignment to cover a presidential election that was still weeks away, the outcome of which was a foregone conclusion. This was only my second day in Lagos and the first night I'd gone out alone – exactly what I'd been advised not to do.

'Hey!'

The barman turned round from placing bottles on the top shelf. He scanned the commotion with the excitement of one reading IKEA instructions, and dismissed it all with a hiss that folded his upper left lip.

'Prostitutes,' he said. His face was sufficiently animated to show his disapproval, as if the place he worked in wasn't a pickup joint for all sorts of working women, and maybe even men; as if his wages didn't depend on their patronage. 'The police are doing a raid and they think they'll be safe in here,' he added.

I looked around to find the bouncers for reassurance but they too were staring helplessly at the gatecrashers.

The large speakers kept blasting out R&B songs at near deafening decibels but no one was dancing. Scantily dressed girls and young men in colourful outfits gathered in groups, talking loudly and with urgency, and prodding the people who had rushed in for information.

Waidi took another stab at reassuring me: 'Anytime the police raid them outside, they always run in here. The bouncers will soon chase them away.' He sounded confident.

It's funny how the mind works. In those few seconds when the frightened people ran in, I'd already concluded that war had broken out in Nigeria and I was caught in the middle of it. Or something equally dreadful. Then, just when I decided to sit it out and trust the chap who looked genuinely amused at my fear, a shapely tall girl with blond hair down to her waist – not hers obviously – came to the bar and started telling him what had happened. I tried to listen but she spoke her broken English so fast, and with so many foreign words, that I was lost. She glanced at me and the fear on her face reignited mine.

When the blonde was done, Waidi fetched a large red handbag from under his counter and handed it to her. All across the bar, other girls were collecting different shapes and sizes of bags that they'd obviously deposited for safekeeping.

The blonde left and Waidi stood still, watching her go, hands on hips and eyes wide open with fear, or disbelief, or both. She had told him something that spooked him. I wanted to know what it was.

'What happened?' I asked. He didn't answer. I reached over and shook his arm. 'What happened?' Just then the music died and my voice boomed over a hundred other frantic voices.

'They just dumped a girl outside,' he said. 'They removed her breasts and dumped her body in the gutter. Just now.'

2

Amaka examined her watch just as the man she was stalking did the same. She was at the bar in Soul Lounge. When she walked in, she counted four girls to each man, staff included. The girls were much younger than the men who they kept company. They had Gucci and Louis Vuitton bags on display on their tables, next to bottles of Moët. Some of the bags had labels that spelled GUSSI. She was the only woman in office clothes: a black skirt suit and a red silk blouse. She slid her hands down to her sides and pulled her skirt up to reveal more of her long legs.

'Anything for madam?' said the boy in an oversized black jacket standing behind the bar. She looked up at him and her eyes settled on his yellow teeth. His black clip-on bow tie that was slanted to one side looked like a propeller stuck to his neck. Earlier, when she arrived, he had placed a menu next to her but she pretended to make a phone call. Then he returned and started to say 'madam' but she picked up her handbag and searched in it.

'Can I get you anything?' he said, louder this time. She noticed he hadn't bothered with the 'madam.'

'Coke, with a lot of ice and a slice of cucumber.'

He gave her a puzzled look but she turned away and looked at the man in the white dashiki, alone on a sofa, throwing nuts into his mouth from a bowl on the table in front of him.

The man checked the time again, then he picked up his phone and made a call, all the time looking at his watch. He frowned, placed the phone back on the table and spread his fingers into the bowl of nuts for another fistful.

The barman placed a coaster next to Amaka and began fiddling behind the bar. He had packed the glass full of cucumber. She resisted the urge to make him repeat what she asked for. Instead, she dipped two fingers into the tall glass and removed all but one of the thick slices, which she then deposited into an ashtray for him to see. She turned back to the man in white. He frowned through another short phone call, checked the time, and leered at a girl walking past. He sighed, placed the phone on the table, and continued with the nuts.

Amaka looked around to make sure no one had noticed her watching him. Someone tapped her shoulder. It was a man she had noticed when she came in. Their eyes had met, and he had tried to take it further by smiling but she looked away and hurried to the only empty space at the bar. He was next to her now, on the stool vacated by a slim girl whose face had been hidden behind an enormous pair of black and gold Versace sunglasses.

'Sorry to startle you. Do you mind if I sit here?'

He had a British accent. It explained his cargo pants, worn trainers, and 'Mind the Gap' T-shirt. 'If you want to.' She turned back to the man in white.

'So, what do you do?'

'I said you could sit next to me, not talk to me.'

'Someone seems to be in a bad mood today.'

She watched the man in white end another call and go for another helping of nuts then she turned to the man by her side.

'Let me get this,' she said, 'a girl tells you she doesn't want to talk to you, and of all the possible explanations you think she must be in a bad mood?'

'Well I...'

'Well what? You just felt like saying something stupid?'

'You're a feisty one, aren't you?'

'There you go again. I'm feisty simply because I don't want to talk to you?'

'Hey, I'm only trying to buy you a drink.'

'I've got mine.'

'OK, I'm sorry if I came on strong'

'You didn't. You came on weak.'

He smiled. 'Fair enough. I guess I set myself up for that one.'

'You did. Look, give me your card and maybe I'll call you.'

She checked on the man in white. He was munching away.

'Here. Do call.'

She took the card and without looking at it put it into her handbag. 'I will. And you're right, I'm not in a good mood tonight, so understand if I don't feel like talking.'

'Does it have anything to do with that bloke?'

'Who?'

'Him.'

He thrust his beer hand in the direction of the man she'd been watching.

'No.' She turned her body away from him.

'I'm Ian. What's your name?'

'Iyabo.'

'So, Iyabo, what do you do?'

'I'm a prostitute.'

He choked on his beer, and before he could recover, she was walking towards the man in white. She'd just found her opening.

3

It was the craziest thing I'd ever heard. They removed her breasts? 'What the fuck?' I didn't realise I'd shouted it till everyone stopped to look at me.

'They removed her breast. Just now. Outside,' Waidi said. Surely he'd heard it wrong, whatever that girl told him. I looked for her and instead I saw petrified faces all around.

'They did what?'

He held one hand cupped under an imaginary boob and did a slicing motion with the other. 'They cut off her breasts,' he said.

'Who cut off her breasts?'

'Ritual killers.'

'Ritual who?'

'Killers. They removed her breast for juju, black magic. It is those politicians. It is because of elections. They are doing juju to win election.' He wrapped his arms round his body and hunched his shoulders upwards, burying his neck.

'They're out there?' I said.

'No. They just dumped the body and ran away.'

I fetched my phone and realised my hands were shaking. I pulled out a cigarette, lit it in a hurry and burnt the tip of my finger. Then, staring at my brand new phone with a Nigerian SIM card in it, I wondered who to call.

The morning I checked into Eko hotel, Magnanimous had, with a knowing smile, given me his card and said to call if I needed anything. I pressed the home button and realised I'd meant to store his information but never got around to it. I searched every pocket on me – twice, even though I could picture the card on the bedside table in my hotel room.

The only number I'd stored was for a bloke called Ade, a stringer my company hired to be my fixer in Lagos. So far, he'd sent two text messages to say he was held up in Abuja, the capital, and every time I called him his phone just rang forever and he didn't return the call. I tried again all the same. It rang once then I got a busy tone. Then the phone was switched off.

'Fuck.'

'Yes,' Waidi said.

I looked up from the phone. He was staring at me and nodding emphatically. He looked so serious that I almost didn't recognise him from before when he'd been so blasé.

'Every time there is election we find dead bodies everywhere,' he said. 'They will remove the eyes, the tongue, even the private parts. Sometimes even they will shave the hair of the private part. Every election period, that is how it happens.'

The faster he spoke the poorer his grammar became and I had to struggle to make out what he was saying. 'This has happened before?'

'Yes,' he said matter-of-factly. 'They will take the parts they need and dump the body anywhere. Every election period like now.'

'Hold on. They dumped a body and fled?'

'Yes. That is why all these people ran inside.' He waved at the packed bar.

'Why?'

'The security outside have called police. When they come they will arrest everybody they see.'

That explained the sudden influx. The taxi driver who picked me from the airport in Lagos described them as underpaid, ill-trained, semi-illiterates who used the authority of their uniforms to extort the citizens. He swore that some of them even rented their guns and uniforms to armed robbers. This I found very unsettling. I couldn't help feeling sorry for these people around me, who appeared to be as scared of their police as they were of killers. Then, still staring at his befuddled face, adrenalin rushed into my veins and I almost cried out. This time it wasn't fear; the journalist in me had just kicked in. I made for the door.

'Where are you going?' Waidi said. He ran alongside me on his side of the long counter. 'If you go outside, they will arrest you o.'

'It's OK,' I said, 'I'm a journalist,' and I instantly heard how stupid I sounded. I pushed past the bouncers, who had made it to the door but were understandably more concerned with not letting more people in than stopping those who wanted to leave.

I inhaled warm air as I stepped out of the bar. It was maybe midnight, but the heat was impressive, shocking you in an instant as though you'd walked into a sauna. My armpits went from dry to wet.

Earlier when I arrived, I had pushed through young boys selling cigarettes, cigars, sweets, even condoms, and girls in miniskirts who called me darling. They were all gone now. An unnerving silence had replaced the hustle and the hustlers. Other than the smell of exhaust fumes, dust, and other indiscernible odours mixed together into a faint ever-present reminder of pollution, every other thing about the night had changed.

A small crowd had gathered on the other side of the road. That was where the news was. I'd left my camera at the hotel. If indeed there were a mutilated dead body there, I would have to use the camera on my phone. I was thinking: Breaking news. Not that the audience back home cared much about the plight of ordinary people in Africa, but a ritual killing captured on video a few minutes after the incident was bound to be worth something.

Ronald would chew his pen lid off when he learned of my scoop. He was first to be offered the job and the minute Nigeria was mentioned I wished I'd been picked instead. Then Ronald moaned about his allergies, complained about his sensitive belly, and reminded everyone of his easily burnt skin. It wasn't the first time I would put myself forward for an assignment but thus far I had not been entrusted with anything more serious than picking the bar for the Christmas party. The real jobs were reserved for the real journalists. Ronald would hate my guts.

A man who had seen enough walked away from the crowd shaking his head. I caught him by the arm. 'What happened?'

He stopped and looked at the people standing by the gutter. He was old, easily in his late seventies. He was gaunt and wrinkled, but still standing upright. He had the same sort of ill-fitting khaki uniform I'd seen on the guards at the hotel. His creased face looked close to tears.

'They jus' kill the girl now-now and dump her body for gutter,' he said, his voice quaking with emotion. It didn't seem right to point a camera in his face but I was going to capture everything I could. I pressed the record button on my phone.

'They call the girl into their moto and before anybody knows anything, they slam the door and drive away. It was one of her friends that raised alarm. She was shouting 'kidnappers, kidnappers', so I run here to see what happen. One boy selling cigarette find the body for inside gutter. Jus' like that, they slaughter her and take her breast.'

He spat as if he could taste the vileness of it.

None of what he said made sense, and it wasn't because of his pidgin English. I just couldn't believe any of it had happened on the kerb outside the bar. But then, this was Lagos: a city of armed robbers, assassinations and now, it seemed, 'ritualists' had to be added to the list.

'You saw everything?'

'Yes. I am the security for that house.' He pointed to a three-storey building on the other side of the road. 'I see everything from my post. The moto jus' park dia. Nobody commot. The girl go meet dem and they open door for am. I don't think she last twenty minutes before they kill am and run away.'

'What kind of car?'

'Big car.'

He spat again and started walking away to the building he guarded, all the while talking, but this time only to himself.

I turned back to the crowd looking down into the gutter shaking their heads. Flashes from camera-phones intermittently illuminated the ground beneath them. There was something awful down there.

I covered the distance, got shoulder to shoulder with them and then I saw it too.

4

'Is anyone sitting here?' Amaka asked.

The man glanced up, scanned her body, shook his head, and turned back to his phone.

She tried to read what he was typing as she placed her Coke on the table. He looked up and their eyes met. She sat in an armchair facing him and he continued tapping into his phone. He looked up again and she was staring at him. 'Can you imagine what that man told me?' she said before he could return to his phone. She nodded at the bar. Ian glanced over at them.

'Was he disturbing you?'

'You won't believe what he said to me. He must think I'm one of those ashewo girls who hang around clubs looking for men.'

He looked at her. She crossed her legs, pushed out her chest and turned away to let him get a good look. She moved a strand of her braids away from her face.

'What did he say?' he asked as he went for more nuts.

'Imagine. He asked me how much it'll cost to take me back to his hotel.'

He chuckled through another mouthful of nuts, looked at Ian, and managed to say, 'What did you say?'

'I just picked up my drink and walked away.'

'And he didn't try to stop you?'

'He's lucky he didn't. I would have slapped him. Purely on principle.' He laughed. 'He's looking at you.'

'Oh God. Why won't he just give up? If he comes here, please tell him we're together. I hope you don't mind?'

'No, not at all.'

'I mean, if you're expecting someone...'

'No, not at all. Don't worry about it.'

He checked the time. She took a sip from her Coke then looked to the bar. Ian was still there, looking in her direction. She pursed her lips into a kiss and turned back to the man in white.

'Can't a girl just enjoy a drink on her own anymore?' she said. 'Why do men automatically assume any girl alone in a bar must be a prostitute?'

He scanned the bar. 'Well, what are you doing alone in a bar at this time?'

'Having a drink.'

'Are you expecting anyone?'

'No. Should I be? Can't I just have a drink on my own?'

He shrugged. She leaned towards him. 'You know, there are single girls like me, girls who have good jobs, who have their own money, who can go out to a bar alone and buy a drink for themselves. And if they end up sleeping with a guy they meet at the bar, it would be because they want to sleep with him and not because he's paying them for it.'

'And you're one of those girls?'

'Well, let's just put it this way – if I fancy you and I want to do you, I will. And it won't be because you're paying me for it. It'll be because I want to.'

He shifted forward, the sofa creaking under his weight.

'Who are you?' he said.

'Who am I? Who are you?'

'What do you do?'

'I'm a lawyer. What about you, what do you do?'

She knew what he did. The only thing she didn't know about him was what he weighed. He was a professional 'big man' in Abuja where he used his contacts to engineer deals and claim 10 per cent or more 'commission.' He had married into class. His wife was the daughter of a respected second republic senator; without her family name to throw about, he was nothing.

'I'm a businessman.'

'So, what are you doing here all alone?'

He checked the time then picked his phone. He looked at the device as if weighing a decision.

'I'm meant to be meeting someone,' he said.

'A date?'

He smiled. He held the phone for a moment, testing its weight. Then he placed it down and she tried to hide her relief.

'Not really, just a friend,' he said.

Lie.

'I hope your friend won't mind that I'm with you when she arrives.'

'No, not at all. It's nothing like that.'

'By the way, I'm Iyabo. What's your name?'

'Chief Olabisi Ojo. You may call me Chief, for short.'

'So, Chief-for-short, who's this girl who's so rude to keep a man like you waiting?'

'Believe me, it's nothing like that. She's just an aburo of mine.'

'Aburo? Sister? Real sister or the other kind of sister?'

'Na you sabi o. What other kind of sister is there?'

'You know what I mean. My own brother no dey meet me

for club.'

'I swear, you are funny. What did you say your name was?'

'Iyabo.' It was her fake name for the night. Together with her hazel contacts, it completed her disguise. 'I hope this sister of yours won't feel threatened that I'm here with you.'

'No, not at all. I'll tell her you're also my sister.'

'Chief, Chief. Chief player. Don't worry. Once she arrives I'll excuse myself.'

He smiled at someone behind her and began to struggle with his weight, trying to get up. For a moment, she thought his date had arrived. But that couldn't be. She turned to check.

The girl dropped her big yellow Chanel bag on the empty chair next to Amaka and sat with him on the sofa. She was young, mixed-race, tall with large breasts. Her thin waist made her wide hips appear even larger. She was in a long, body-hugging, yellow evening gown to match her monstrous bag. 'Debby, meet my friend, Iyabo,' he said when the girl paused, her palms placed one on top of the other on his lap.

Debby looked at Amaka just long enough to flash a quick smile and offer a weak 'Hi' before she turned her attention back to Chief Ojo. She placed her hand on his shoulder and threw her breasts around under her dress as she asked him, rather rhetorically, how long it'd been since they last saw each other.

Debby. Mixed-race. Could it be? Amaka ignored them and fetched her phone from her handbag. She switched it to silent then scrolled through the contacts till she found the entry she was searching for: Debby Christina Okoli.

To be sure, she pressed the call button and pretended to be clicking through the phone's menu.

D'Banj's hit track, Why Me? started playing in Debby's handbag.

Without looking up, Amaka ended the call. The younger girl reached for her handbag, but realised to get to it she would have to stand, so she waited for Amaka to hand it to her. Amaka picked the bag, was surprised that it wasn't heavy, and handed it to Debby. The girl rifled through it to find her phone then she stared at the missed call: 'Number withheld.' She placed the mobile on the table and returned her hands to Chief Ojo's lap.

Amaka continued toying with her phone, careful not to let her face betray the coup she had executed. She knew the girl. She knew her name – her real name. She knew how old she was, when she first came to Lagos, where she lived, where her parents lived. She knew the names of her siblings, when she got her periods, she also knew the result of her latest HIV test, and yet, sitting opposite each other, competing for the same man, Debby had no idea who Amaka was.

Amaka studied her. She was chatting, fluttering her eyes, swinging her boobs, and running her palm up and down his lap. So, this is what she looks like. The voice should have been a clue, but like everyone else, she sounded different on the phone. She was a threat. She had to be disposed of and fast.

5

In the open gutter by the road, flourishing with wild vegetation and an assortment of discarded plastic bags, lay the body of a girl.

She was on her back, her head turned to the side, her eyes wide open, her mouth frozen in a gasp. One arm was above her head and the other somewhere behind her back. Her legs lay one on top of the other. Someone had covered her torso with a white shirt. It was red in the middle and the blood was slowly spreading.

I turned away, took two steps, then hot chilli from the fish pepper soup I'd tried at the hotel burnt my nostrils and I puked. The world tilted to one side.

Whatever foolishness cajoled me out of the safety of the bar at Ronnie's vanished with what I threw up. My senses returned with a loud ringing sound. I'd never seen a dead body. What the hell was I doing here?

The ringing grew louder until it parked next to me in a flurry of red and blue flashing lights. I looked up and saw patrol vehicles spewing out police officers onto the road. They held AK-47s.

The crowd scattered as cops took charge of the scene by rounding up onlookers. Men, who a minute ago had been standing next to me, were manhandled into open-back vans. Uniformed security guards were spared, but anyone else without a valid reason to be out on the road at one in the morning was being frog-marched into waiting police cars.

A shirtless man in white trousers and white shoes tried to protest. The dull meaty thud of a rifle's butt striking his face made me sick all over again. He didn't go down with the first strike. He raised his arms to defend himself but only managed to attract more officers. They rushed at him like piranhas to flesh and efficiently beat him to the ground where he curled into a protective ball. He took blows to his head from leather boots and metal butts. He was going to die.

Before I could stand upright, wipe my mouth and restore my dignity, someone pulled me up.

'Who are you?'

The bright beam of a torch followed my gaze wherever I turned, trying to avoid it. I put my hands up to protect my eyes then I saw who had spoken; it was the muzzle of a rifle, and it spoke again: 'Who are you?'

'I was at the bar,' I said, and pointed across the road to Ronnie's. I didn't dare take my eyes off the menacing metal cylinder.

'What are you doing here?'

'I'm sorry,' I said, 'I'm sorry, I'm sorry.'

I was talking to a gun.

'Geraout,' it said, and I gratefully turned to get out of there.

'Wait,' a different voice said. 'Bring him here.'

The man who had received a beating was being dragged away by his legs. His bloodied arm brushed against my ankle and I saw up-close the extent of his punishment. He was bleeding from his nose and his mouth and his ears. His face was swollen all over, and his lips had erupted into mashed-up pink flesh. He offered no resistance to the two men dragging him over the hard ground. His silence scared me.

I cursed myself for my stupidity. I cursed Ronald for not taking the Nigeria job. I cursed myself for asking for it, and I cursed the dozens of friends who said I was going to have the time of my life.

6

Debby had found her man for the night and she wasn't going anywhere. With her big breasts, her long eyelashes and her hands that she wouldn't keep to herself, she went about sabotaging Amaka, one flirtatious giggle at a time. There was also the fact that she was mixed: something that men in Nigeria could not resist and this irritated Amaka more.

From what she knew, Debby's mother was British. She left Debby's father and three kids when Debby, the last child, was only two years old. She lived somewhere in London, claimed she was an artist, explained to her abandoned children that their father had tried to stifle her creativity, and further alienated them by refusing to help them get British passports because, as she said, 'You are African children. Africa is your home. England will corrupt you.' The father married again, an African woman this time, and left the upbringing of his mixed-race kids to a childless relative in Lagos. So it was that when Debby turned looks-old-enough, she was unleashed upon the men folk of Lagos, both as manipulator and as victim.

Amaka watched as Debby laughed at something. The girl's presence threatened everything. If only girls would learn to work together. Amaka came up with several plans, mentally played each one out, then discarded them one by one till she finally had the perfect strategy, and the perfect accomplice.

She sighed heavily and leaned forward. 'Is he still there?' she said. She had checked, seen Ian still waiting at the bar, and had blown him another secret, silent kiss.

Chief Ojo looked and grinned. 'He won't leave without you tonight. Maybe we should invite him over.'

She frowned.

'I'm just joking o.'

'Can you believe he even showed me the one thousand dollars he wants to give me?'

Debby looked across to the bar, then, catching herself, her eyes shifted back to Chief Ojo who had not noticed her reaction. She inspected her nails.

'A bundle of crisp hundred dollar notes,' Amaka said. 'I'm sure it's counterfeit.'

Chief Ojo looked at the man and Debby followed his gaze.

'How do you know? What if it's real?'

'Real or not, I don't care. God only knows what he'll want me to do for all that money. One thousand dollars is not small money o. That's almost a hundred and fifty thousand naira. Just to follow him to his hotel room? I think not.'

'I think you should go with him. I'll be your pimp. I'll collect the money for you and make sure it's real.'

'Very funny. I'll lay my back on the bed and you'll put the money in your pocket, abi?'

'We'll share it. Fifty-fifty.'

'Really?'

'Yeah. Go for it. As your pimp, I say go for it.'

She swept her right hand over her head, snapping her fingers once as she did so. 'God forbid bad thing.'

She turned to look at the man. He was still there. She winked and he blew a kiss at her.

'Oh my God, did you see that? What will I do? I have to go and get something from my car but I'm afraid he'll follow me if I get up.'

'Do you want me to come with you?'

Debby's hand shot to his lap.

'I'll be fine. If I'm not back in five minutes and if he follows me, call the police.' She smiled and stood up.

'Good luck.'

'Argh.' She shuddered and rolled her eyes then turned to leave. As she walked past Ian, she mouthed 'Follow me.' She continued to the door, hoping he could lip-read.

A bouncer pushed the door open and held it for her. A few seconds later, she heard footsteps behind her. She kept walking – away from the view of anyone inside the bar.

He caught up with her and touched her arm. She turned, smiling.

'I'm so sorry I came onto you like that,' he said, 'I didn't mean to imply that you're a… I mean, I just wanted to buy you a drink.'

'Listen,' she placed an arm on his shoulder, 'its OK. You don't need to apologise. I really am a prostitute.'

'But, you sound so…'

'So educated?'

'I guess.'

'Too educated to sell my body?' He looked at her suspiciously.

'You are a little bit new at this, aren't you?'

He nodded.

'How long have you been in Lagos?'

'Six months.'

'I see. OK, listen. Let me teach you how this is done. Did you see that girl at the table with me?'

'Yes.'

'I think she's more your type.'

He was about to say something but she continued. 'Did you get a good look at her?'

He nodded.

'Would you like to take her home tonight?'

He hesitated. She nodded to encourage him.

'The problem is, she's already with someone else,' she said.

A few minutes later, Amaka was back at the table. Chief Ojo was no longer checking his phone or the time. His palm was on Debby's lap and hers was on the back of his neck. The young girl pressed her body against his arm to whisper something into his ear that made him smile. A waitress came to the table with three champagne flutes and a bottle of Cristal in an ice bucket. 'The gentleman at the bar sent this,' she said. She managed to avoid knocking over the glasses on the narrow table as she set down the treat she had brought. She picked up the bottle and began peeling off the foil at its neck before anyone had accepted the gift.

Amaka gasped. 'This guy must be super horny tonight,' she said. 'He tried to talk to me when I went outside. I told him you were my date, and now he sends champagne?' Chief Ojo laughed. Debby looked back at the bar. The cork popped. 'Oh well, what the heck. If he feels like wasting his dollars, let's help him.' She shrugged and waited for her glass to be poured.

The waitress filled each glass and left, but instead of returning to the bar, she walked out through the exit. Ian stood up and headed towards the spiral staircase that led to the mezzanine level. On the way, he nodded at Chief Ojo who had raised his glass to him. He waited for a couple to descend then he climbed the stairs, looking over to Amaka as he did so. Chief Ojo's eyes followed him.

'I have to use the ladies,' Debby said.

The toilets were outside the bar, just beyond the entrance. Debby picked her bag and walked out, looked back at Chief Ojo, then stepped into the toilets. A minute later, she came out with the business card that had been cupped in the waitress's palm as she poured the champagne. She walked out to the car park and dialled the number written on the back of the card.

7

The voice that stopped my escape belonged to a tall officer in a uniform that looked like it had been freshly ironed. He was by the gutter, walkie-talkie in one hand, the other tucked into his pocket. The end of a pistol peeped through the bottom of a black leather holster attached to his belt. He appeared calm even though he was standing inches away from a freshly butchered corpse.

'Good evening' he said.

'Good evening,' I replied. We were about the same height and build, but I suspected from his exposed forearms that he worked out more.

'What is your name and what is your business here?'

'Guy, Guy Collins. I was at Ronnie's.' I pointed at the club.

'Guy Collins. You sound British.'

I wasn't sure if it was a question. He spoke in a casual, easy manner that was unsettling. I suspected that through this calm composure – his hand casually tucked into his pocket and his gentle voice – he was taking me very seriously, and how I responded was going to be important for me. I tried to appear as calm as him.

'I am. I'm a reporter with the BBC,' I lied, knowing the broadcaster was meant to be known and respected all over the world and could be my get-out free card. It seemed better than telling him I worked for a start-up internet TV news channel that had managed to find more venture capital than talent. Or that I was one of a paltry team of twelve operating out of a tiny office in Old Street where most of the staff spent their working days sending out job applications. Even I hadn't heard of it until I decided to give up on law and pursue my passion and it became obvious I wasn't going to get into any of the major media houses with nothing but my winning smile and an embellished CV. Then I remembered something else the Nigerian minicab driver had said about the police in here: 'They hate foreign journalists.'

'A journalist,' he said, and carried on as if we just had to get through some routine questions. Had he been brash and unruly like the rest of his men, communicating with shoves and blows, I would have known how to react: with grovelling and begging. But he was civil – too civil, and I sensed it was only a prelude to nastiness to come. 'So, what are you doing out here?'

'I was at the bar.'

'Yes, you told me. But now you are here and we have this dead body. So, what are you doing out here?'

'I came out for a smoke.' I thought it was a clever lie until I remembered that Lagos, unlike London, had not banished its smokers outdoors.

'You couldn't smoke inside?'

'I wanted fresh air.'

'Were you drunk?'

'What?'

'Were you drunk?' He pointed his walkie-talkie at the vomit on the road.

'No, I wasn't.'

'But you saw the dead body?'

'Yes.'

'And you wish to report this on the BBC?'

'No. I only came out to have a smoke.' I dug into my pocket for the pack of Benson & Hedges.

'Do you have any identification on you, Mr Collins?'

I didn't. I'd been advised not to carry any documents or valuable stuff on me when out and about in Lagos. The pickpockets, I was assured, were as crafty as the ones in London, and more brazen, often confusing their vocation for mugging. All I had on me was the money I'd planned on getting drunk with, my phone, and the key card to my room at the hotel. I wished I were there right then, tucked under the light duvet, enduring deathly boredom and the constant hum of the air con. Or better still, back home in my flat in Fulham, doing nothing more exciting than waiting for a Chinese takeaway to arrive and trying not to be bothered by the large stained patch on the cream rug – the result of a red wine spillage that was sure to eat up my rental deposit. Suddenly, the boredom that led me out on what was meant to be a little adventure now seemed like a conspiracy of all the unpleasant forces of the universe.

'I don't have any ID with me – its back in the hotel,' I explained.

'That's a pity, Mr Collins. I need to verify your identity before I can let you go. We need to talk to all the witnesses and take their statements. A nameless statement isn't worth much, you understand?'

I understood that I'd gotten myself into a mess and I was at his mercy.

'You will come with me to the station and we'll take your statement there. Is that OK?'

I wanted to protest but I remembered the guy who had received a beating and I decided it was wise to keep schtum.

'OK.'

'Do you have a phone?'

Perhaps he wanted me to call someone who could tell him I was Guy Collins, reporter with eCity TV, and not the BBC.

'Yes.'

'Can I have it, please?'

I handed it to him. He took one look at the Samsung phone and slipped it into his breast pocket. Shit.

I watched the vans filling up with people picked off the road.

'Don't worry,' he said, 'you'll ride with me in my car.'

I didn't know if I should be grateful for this privilege or even more worried. Somehow, in the space of a few minutes I'd gone from watching young African girls dancing, to seeing my first brutally murdered corpse, to being questioned by the Nigerian police, to having my phone stolen or seized – I didn't know which – and finally to being arrested.

8

Debby returned to the table and sat quietly. She ignored her champagne, kept her hands to herself, and did not join the conversation. Either she had taken out her contact lenses, or her eyes, by themselves, had gone a shade darker. Missing the absence of her attention, Chief Ojo discovered the sullen expression on her face. 'What's wrong?' he asked.

'It's my mum,' Debby said.

'Your mum? What's wrong with her?'

'She's been in hospital since last week. She has high blood pressure. I just called my sister to ask how she's doing and she told me they've discharged her.'

'So she's better?'

'No. The doctors have refused to continue treating her till we pay them. The drugs are expensive and we already owe them. I have to go home.'

'Now?'

'Yes. She's home alone with my little sister. I have to go and take care of her.'

Tears gathered in her eyes. Chief put his arms around her and drew her into an embrace. Her shoulders began to quiver.

Amaka felt a tinge of pity for her. After that performance, she would have offered to drive the poor girl home to her mother herself, if she didn't know that would mean driving to the UK. She clenched her teeth, trying not to chuckle or let her cheeks inflate.

He patted Debby's back and rocked her in his hands. Between sobs and dabbing her face with his handkerchief, she lamented how she didn't know what to do. Where was she going to get the money to help her mum? Why did bad things always happen to her? She had to go home straight away.

He placed his hand under her chin and lifted her face. He looked into her teary eyes and told her that everything was going to be all right.

Amaka was impressed with how she managed to cry without doing significant damage to her make-up. That was amazing.

'I'll take you home,' he said and put his phone in his pocket.

'My aunt lives close by,' Debby said. 'I called her and she said I should come and meet her so we can go to my house together.'

'I'll drop you at her place.'

'No. She'll be waiting for me outside. I don't want her to see me with a man.'

'I can drop you close to her house.'

'It's not far. She stays in Oniru Estate. I'll walk. Don't worry.'

'You are in no condition to walk, and not at this time. I'll take you as close to her place as I can.'

'Don't worry. I don't want anyone to see you dropping me.'

'My driver will take you. You shouldn't be walking alone at this time. It's not safe.'

'I'll get a taxi.'

'OK. Let me see if they can arrange a taxi for you.' He held his hand up to attract a waiter.

'Chief, don't worry. In the time it'll take them to find a taxi

I would have found one myself. There are taxis waiting in the car park outside.'

She dabbed tears from her eyes before they could roll down her powdered cheeks. He ran his hand over her head and squeezed her shoulder.

From his pocket, he produced a folded bundle of one thousand naira notes held together by rubber bands. He snapped the bands off, and without counting, split the bundle in two. He took her arm and pressed one half into her palm. She did not look at the money, on account of the tears she was tending to. He closed her fingers over the cash and dismissed her attempt to thank him.

'Keep me informed on her progress,' he said. 'Whatever you need, don't hesitate to call me. Do you understand?'

She sniffed, mopped her eyes and nodded.

'Let me get a waiter to call you a car.'

'Don't worry. I'll be fine.'

She gathered her things and stood to leave. She seemed broken.

He got up, with much effort, and held her for a few seconds in an embrace that looked fatherly, and then Debby was on her way.

Amaka felt compelled to say something. 'I'll pray for your mother,' she said.

'Thank you,' Debby said and left.

'Poor girl,' he said as he dropped back into the sofa.

'Really sad,' Amaka said. She made a mental note of Debby's performance – talent like that might come in useful someday.

Chief Ojo looked over Amaka's shoulder. 'Your lover has given up on you.'

'What?'

'Your boyfriend, he's leaving empty handed.'

She turned in time to see the man's back as he descended the stairs and made for the door. He handed the bouncer what must have been a generous tip because with it he bought an energetic salute.

Another satisfied customer, Amaka thought and smiled. 'What a pity. I was actually considering taking him up on his offer.'

He looked at her questioningly.

'Not for the money, of course, but after watching you and your friend touching each other up in front of me, I must confess, I've become quite horny.'

His eyebrows lifted. She leaned toward him and lowered her voice.

'Let me tell you a secret. I imagined you and Debby having sex and it turned me on so much that I started fantasising about the three of us...'

She stopped mid-sentence, fixed him a look as if she was considering something, then she shook her head and withdrew into her chair.

'What?'

'What?' she said, as if she had lost him.

'You were fantasising that the three of us were doing what?'

'I don't want to think about it.'

'What? Why?'

'Well...' she paused, like she was searching for the right words. 'I've never done this before.'

'Done what? A threesome?'

'No. Talk to a stranger like this, you know, about sex.'

'Well now, aren't you the one who said she could have sex with anybody she wanted to on her own terms?'

'I know what I said, but...that's just talk. I've never really done that kind of thing before. Oh no, this is so embarrassing. Sometimes I just open my mouth and say what's on my mind without thinking.' She hid her face in her palms.

'We're both adults. No need to feel embarrassed.'

'You have to excuse me,' she said and stood up.

His hand shot up to stop her. 'Where are you going?'

'To the ladies.'

She walked away, head down. She took her phone but left her bag so he would know she was coming back.

Outside, she walked around to get good signal strength then she dialled a number. 'Now,' she said. She waited for the person on the other end of the phone to say 'OK' then she ended the call.

Chief Ojo's phone beeped with a new message. He saw that it was from the girl he was waiting for. He expected her to be sending him a message to let him know she was close by, but the message read 'Cannot make it tonight. Goodnight.'

He frowned and dialled her number. Her phone was now switched off. He began to send her a message, mouthed 'fuck' when autocorrect didn't detect that he was trying to type the word 'ingrate', then he kissed his teeth and deleted the message.

From the entrance, Amaka watched him trying the girl's phone. Her plan was back on track. She walked over to him and picked up her bag, avoiding his eyes.

'Are you leaving?'

He sounded desperate. She shrugged.

'You don't have to go. Come.' He patted the cushion by his side on the sofa.

She closed her eyes and slowly shook her head.

'Come, please.'

She looked up to the ceiling, held her gaze for a while then she looked into his eyes. She dropped her bag onto the table.

'I really don't know about this,' she said. She settled down next to him. 'I've never...' she let her sentence trail. He waited. She looked at him.

'You've never what?'

She placed her palm under his chin and lifted his head. She tilted his face to one side then the other and held her head back to study his features.

'Hmm.'

'What?'

She took her hand away from his face and tried to figure out which champagne flute was hers.

'Iyabo, talk to me. What's on your mind? You've never what?'

She lifted a glass to her lips and took a sip, set the flute back down, placed two fingers on its base and pushed it to the centre of the table, then she threw her head back and watched him through slanted eyes.

'I've never been this horny. I think it must be the champagne.'

'Me too. What should we do about it?'

She motioned with her index finger and he brought his ear to her face. She leaned to whisper, pressing her breasts onto his shoulder just like Debby had done. She smelt a whiff of Christian Dior's Fahrenheit.

She told him the things she wanted to do to him, how she would do them, and for how long. She let her lips graze his ear lobe as she spoke. His breath became shorter. He moved his hand on to his lap, just below his belly, and adjusted himself through the folds of his white outfit. She told him that her only regret was that Debby could not join them, but if tonight went well, there would be other chances to do it with the other girl.

She turned her attention to her glass of champagne and lifted it to her mouth. Her plan was working. It had to.

He looked around for a waiter.

'Only one condition,' she said. 'You must not treat me like a prostitute. You must not offer me any money. If you do, you will never see me again.'

He reached for his drink. His fingers were shaking.

'You are not a prostitute.'

He downed his glass of champagne.

'Good. I expect that you are married and you have a wife at home?'

'Yes.'

'So we can't go back to your place. I stay with friends so you can't come back to mine.'

'I'm staying at a hotel tonight.'

'Which one?'

'Eko Hotel, I'm staying in the presidential suite.'

He watched to see her reaction. She was neither impressed nor surprised. She already knew where he was staying that night, and she knew that the suite had originally been booked for a Congolese diplomat he knew and had arranged to meet. The man's itinerary had changed at the last minute and Chief Ojo had asked what plans the diplomat had for the already paid-for hotel suite.

'Nobody can know about this,' she said.

'Nobody will know.'

9

Our ride was a single-cab pickup truck. Its cargo bed had been rigged with a metal bench welded onto the floor. Policemen climbed in from the sides not bothering with the tailgate. I sat in front between the boss and his driver, a dark fellow who responded 'yesha' to everything. The smell of stale sweat radiated from him. Thankfully, the windows were down.

I thought 'Bakare' was the word for slow down, or watch out, or fuck, or something like that, until the senior officer shouted 'Sergeant Bakare' when we were about to clip the rear of a motorcycle ferrying three souls and a black goat slung over the neck of the rearmost passenger.

Bakare swerved with a second to spare. I'd already seen the collision in my mind. I was still pressing down on my non-existent brake when he took his hand off the steering wheel, stretched it out of the window, and spread his fingers at the startled biker zigzagging to regain balance. This apparent rude gesture earned him another 'Bakare.' He grinned, floored the throttle, and my body shot back into the hard seat. There were no seatbelts. He attacked a bend without slowing down. Why was he in a hurry?

Perhaps to take my mind – or his – off Bakare, the man who arrested me began to talk. 'Do you watch EastEnders?' he asked.

Of all the things, why that? Did he once live in England? Was that where he got his slight London accent? Was he reminiscing? Was it a test? I told him I didn't, and for the first time I wished that I, like eight million other zombies, followed the damn soap.

But maybe it wasn't a test. Maybe he really wanted to talk about it, because when he looked at me, I swear, I caught a hint of regret on his face. He switched topics. I don't recall what to but I do remember that was when Bakare used his brakes – only after the front wheels had gone over a speed bump – then he down-shifted while the truck was still bouncing, and I looked in the mirror to check on the men in the back. That was the moment when a terrifying thought crept into my mind.

You see, when my head hit the roof, and my body rolled into Bakare, and his elbow – without releasing his grip on the steering wheel – shoved me away, I remembered with horror the story a Scotsman I met in the queue at the Nigerian High Commission in London had told me. He'd once lived in Nigeria; he still had a business there: tyres. He made friends with the family of a Nigerian professor of mathematics at MIT. The professor flew home to go to his village to bury his mother and he got snatched from the funeral procession, midway between the church and the cemetery. They found him two weeks later, tied to a tree in a place his people called the Forbidden Forest. His luck was that the gang were wrong in assuming he was rich. His family, unable to raise the money demanded, reported to the American Embassy that an American citizen had been kidnapped. The police had to act and act they did. Within days they knew who the inside guy was – the professor's young nephew studying to become a lawyer, and he, the nephew, fingered the policemen who provided the guns used for the kidnapping of his uncle.

Let's face it, I'd got into the car with men who didn't exactly say they were the police, didn't read me my rights, I hadn't asked for ID, we were racing to God knows where, and no one knew they had me. It would be a perfect kidnap. I thought of my boss getting a ransom demand and replying with a letter telling me I'd been sacked.

In the dark cabin, I tried to see the face of the man talking to me and I listened to his voice: not to what he was saying, but to how he was saying it. Was he keeping me calm till it was time for the blindfold? Was he weighing up whether I already suspected that I was in the middle of my own abduction? I was alert like I'd never been before – the thought of being kidnapped, I discovered, does that to you. I studied him, and finding nothing on his face to interpret as a clue, I listened to what he had to say.

He told me that the dual carriageway on which we travelled, Ahmadu Bello Road, was once a beautiful beach dotted with palm trees. Bar Beach, he called it. Over many years, he said, the Atlantic Ocean crept towards the city. Man and water lived in harmony for a period, until a pyramid shaped glasshouse sprouted on the coastal road. 'We just passed it,' he said. The 'sons of the soil' warned the bank that built it but the architects and the managers had foreign degrees and qualifications, so they disregarded the hocus-pocus stories of those who knew their ocean.

When the sun rises each day, its rays reflect off the pompous building and gather in a strong beam directed at the water. This dazzles the water goddess's eyes, the natives warned, which is why even little children know better than to play with mirrors close to the waves.

The goddess was angry. The bankers wouldn't tear down their building or replace its splendid glass with sheets of wood. The goddess decided to take the matter into her hands.

With a regularity that could only be spiritual, the ocean began to flood its shores. Violently. The government hired engineers who called it encroachment. To stop the problem, they replaced what remained of the beach with an unsightly chain of concrete barriers. It didn't work. Apparently, the water goddess demanded a sacrifice of appeasement, but either someone didn't pass the message on, or they did but the people that mattered didn't believe it.

He finished his tale and stared straight ahead. I didn't ask if he believed it himself. It sounded like a bullshit story. Exactly the kind of bull crap stuff you'd tell someone to keep their mind off the fact that you were kidnapping them.

10

The same car had driven past her twice, slowing down to a stop the second time. But when Kevwe smiled at the driver, he looked away and drove off down the road, past all the other girls. When she saw the Toyota Corolla turning onto Sanusi Fafunwa Street again, behind a black Land Cruiser with tinted windows, she turned to Angel, the new girl she had just met that night, and nodded that she could have the SUV. Kevwe left the group of much older girls they had been standing with and walked up the road so that she wasn't close to anyone. The Corolla pulled up onto the pavement. She looked down, away from the beam of the headlights that the driver had left on full beam and walked to the car.

She stopped by the passenger door and waited for him to roll down the window. She bent down, giving him a good view of her cleavage, and said 'Hi, honey.'

'Hi,' he said. He sounded like he needed water.

She smiled at him. His eyes moved between her breasts and her eyes. She waited for him to say something but he stared out his front window, at cars driving by, and he sank into his seat.

'Where do you want to take me, honey?' she said. She spat out the gum in her mouth and flicked her head to throw her braids back.

'How much?' he said.

'Short time or long time?'

'We will just go to my hotel.'

'Do you want me to spend the night, honey?'

'No.'

'OK, honey, just give me ten thousand.' She waited for him to haggle her down. A car slowed down by them. She stood up from the window and used her finger to draw back a strand of braid. The other car stopped parallel to the Corolla and she bent back into his window.

'Let's go,' he said.

She looked closely at him. The same men usually came to Sanusi Fafunwa Street but she had never seen him, or his car.

'Where are we going, honey?'

'Federal Palace Hotel.'

'I hope you will be nice to me, honey.'

He reached over and opened the door for her.

'One second, honey.' She placed her phone to her ear; she'd been holding it all the time. She took a few steps to the nose of the car and glanced at his plate number. She pretended to end the call she'd not been making and began typing a message before she got in next to him.

'What is your name, honey?' she said without looking up from her phone.

'Bayo. Use your seat belt.'

'What do you do, Bayo?'

'Why do you want to know?'

'I'm just asking, honey.'

'I'm a banker.'

'Which bank is that?'

'Why do you want to know?'

She finished composing her text message and sent it off. She dropped her phone on her lap, placed her palm on his thigh, and began stroking, letting her fingers touch his crotch to check if he was hard. Normally she wouldn't go with someone she didn't recognise without telling one of her friends and letting the man know that the friend had seen his face, seen the car he drove, and seen the licence plate number. But the young man looked too nervous to be dangerous. She decided right then to take advantage of him, but she still had to check.

He kept his eyes on the road as she worked on his zipper. As soon as she felt him getting hard, she removed her hand and checked if her text had been received.

Amaka's phone vibrated in her handbag. Like a mother programmed to her child's cry, she could hear the phone vibrating in another room. It was one of three mobiles she always carried with her. One was her personal line, as she called it. The second one had a new pay-as-you go SIM card in it – she always had new SIM cards in her bag. A few hundred girls had the number to the third phone; none of them had met her or knew her name. It was this phone that had received a new message.

The text was from a contact that showed up as KEVWE. She looked up and saw Chief Ojo watching her. She blinked at him and continued. The message read 'Evening ma. Young man at Sanusi Fafunwa. He said he is a banker. He is driving a black Toyota with number LA333KKJ. His name is Bayo. Going to Federal Palace. Thank you ma.'

She looked back up from her phone and caught him looking down her shirt. She smiled and he looked away at something on the ceiling. 'Work,' she said. 'Give me a minute.'

She got out a notebook from her handbag and switched it on. She had left it on hibernate – a trick her friend, Gabriel, taught her, so that the computer booted up faster.

Her fingers dashed around the keyboard, keying in her long password. An Excel spreadsheet filled the screen. She selected the 'Find' option and typed in the licence number from the text message. The number appeared several lines down. She clicked on the row to highlight it and read across. She was interested in the last column where the entry read SAFE.

In the car, Kevwe looked down at her phone. The message simply read: 'OK.'

She deleted it and placed her hand back on the driver's groin.

They got to Federal Palace Hotel quicker than if he'd been observing speed limits. He walked ahead of her and when the elevator doors slid open, he let other people waiting to get in first, including her, then he stepped in on the other side away from her.

His room was one of the smallest she'd been to in the hotel. She wondered if perhaps she should have taken the Land Cruiser she gifted to the new girl. She dropped her bag on the bed and kicked off her shoes. She had charged him a good price and had decided to get even more but she couldn't afford to waste time; she had to get back to her spot before another girl stole it.

She undressed. She had no underwear. His eyes moved from her breasts to her shaved crotch. She placed her hands on her hips and waited.

'Where you wan' do am?'

His face shot up at her sudden switch to broken English.

'Won't you shower first?'

'I don shower today.' She felt like smiling at her luck. She knew he wanted her to wash away the last client she had been with; she had picked up that he wasn't very used to this the minute he agreed to the price she asked for without first halving it. She'd decided to make him pay extra for anything other than plain sex with her lying on her back. If he wanted her to take a shower, he would also want to limit body contact and thus ask to take her from behind. She would tell him that doggy costs more.

'Just go and shower.'

'To take shower go cost three thousand extra.'

'You want me to give you an extra three thousand?'

'Yes.'

'For what?'

'To take shower, now. I tell you, I don shower today, but if you want make I go shower again, you go pay me three thousand on top the amount we agree.'

'Why?'

'Na time e go take.'

'A five minute shower? That's what you want three thousand extra for?'

'Time dey go o.'

'So, you won't take a shower?'

'You go pay?'

'OK. Don't bother with the shower. Just give me a blow job.' He undid his zip and pulled himself out.

'Ehn? Blow wetin? We no discuss that one o. I don't do blow job for ten thousand. That one is fifteen thousand, and you will use condom.'

As he stared at her, still grappling with the fact that the same girl who had called him honey and stroked his cock in the car was now hissing at him and refusing to look into his eyes, as if they had already had a fight. It dawned on him that he was being conned. He gradually grew limp. He zipped up his fly.

'You can go.'

'You want make I go?'

'Yes. You can go. I'm not interested anymore.'

'But you never pay me.'

'Pay you for what? We didn't do anything.'

'You are not serious. Shebi you brought me here? Na me say make your prick no stand? Abeg, pay me my money.'

'Money for what?'

'See me see trouble. If your dick refuse to stand, na my fault? Oya, come and fuck now. You no fit? If I know say you be time waster, I for no follow you. Give me my money. Yeye man.'

'Look, just leave.'

'Wey my ten thousand?' Her voice was sufficiently raised so that anyone on the corridor outside could hear her.

He looked down, shaking his head and smiling a regretful smile. He put his hand in his back pocket and counted out ten thousand naira. He held the money out to her.

She snatched the cash and counted it.

'Wetin be this?'

'Your money.'

'How will I get back to the place you pick me from?'

'I don't know. Take a taxi.'

'Make I take taxi?'

'Yes.' He could barely look at her.

'By this time, taxi will cost four thousand. That is even if I find one.'

'So what do you want me to do?'

'You this man, you are vexing me o. I for no follow you if I know say na like this you go dey do. Give me money for taxi.' She held out her hand.

He looked at the outstretched palm, saw the calluses, the dirt under her nails, her discoloured cheap rings, and he felt shame like he had never felt before, and loathing.

'I am not giving you anything. I will drop you back where I found you.'

'Where you find me? I be dog wey dem dey find? Just because of the work I'm doing does not mean you should be insulting me anyhow. If not for condition, you for see me carry? After all, I get men like you for my family.'

He doubted that she came from anything other than a family of blackmailers but he kept his opinion to himself. He fetched his keys from his pocket and waited for her to dress and leave his room, then he led the way back to his car.

Two policemen stood by the gutter while a third, handling a Polaroid camera with a separate flash held in a different hand, took pictures. This was the extent of evidence gathering.

A white Peugeot 504 station wagon converted into an ambulance was parked diagonally across the road. Two men in crumpled white overalls and yellow kitchen gloves stood by its open boot waiting for the photographer to be done.

The driver of a police van next to the Peugeot pressed his horn in one long blast and exchanged dirty looks with the photographer. People watched from the safety of the other side of the road.

Kevwe saw the police car up ahead. 'Stop, stop, stop,' she said, but he had also seen the cars and the policemen, and he had seen how the sight of them had made her jump. He continued driving until he was as close to the officers as he could, then he pulled his handbrake. 'Get out,' he said.

Kevwe sank low into her seat until her head was below the window line. As they passed by, she had noted that there were no girls on the road and that the only people watching were security guards and bouncers from the many clubs on the street. The police raided this area less than a week ago, so no one expected them to be back so soon. Several girls were still working longer hours to make up for the money they had lost to the last raid – including her. It had cost her sixteen thousand naira to 'bail' herself – all the money she had on her – and not before a drunken officer had pulled her into a lightless room that choked her with dust and pushed her hand down the front of his trousers. She had not been able to eat with the hand for two days.

'Bros, please now, please. Just take me down there, to the end of the road. Please. It is the way you will pass as you are going. Honey, please.'

'Get out now.'

'OK, let us go back to your hotel. I will shower. We can do anything you want. Please. Ehn, bros? Please. I beg you with the name of Jesus.'

'Get dafuck out of my car.'

She sighed, checked that they hadn't attracted the attention of the officers, then she climbed out. He pressed his horn twice as he drove off.

She scampered on the tips of her high-heeled shoes to the other side of the road, almost falling into the gutter as she bent down behind a parked Mercedes. She clutched her handbag to her chest and held her breath. Her ankles ached in the stooping position but when she tried to kneel, gravel bit into her skin so she had to stay crouched and endure the pain.

She thought of rolling up all the money she had in her handbag, putting it inside a condom and hiding her loot in the bush covering the gutter. She was searching the growth behind her for a good spot she would remember later when she heard engines revving, tyres screeching, and sirens screaming then fading away. Even then, she stayed where she was, peeping onto the road several times before she finally stretched her legs and shook the numbness out of them.

The police car had left and people were walking across the road to the front of the ambulance where someone was still taking pictures of something in the gutter. She did not see the two policemen standing there, surrounded by security guards and other onlookers. She moved towards the crowd and by the time she noticed the uniforms it was too late. She locked eyes with an officer who looked her up and down before taking a picture of what was in the gutter using his phone.

She edged around the group, staying as far from the policemen as she could. She pushed past security guards and looked down to see what they were all looking at.

As she saw, she lost her balance and had to grab the arm of the man standing by her side. She looked again and her worst fear was confirmed: it was the new girl who had gone for the Land Cruiser while she took the Corolla.

Her knees felt weak. She looked at the people around her; their bodies swayed disconcertingly. She wanted to scream out the girl's name, Angel, but she knew she would only get herself arrested, so she drew her lips in and walked away from the crowd, her heart pounding.

'No o. No be say they kill her for another place come bring am here. No. It is here that they kill her, inside jeep,' a man in a security guard uniform said to a group of the onlookers.

Kevwe stopped next to the people talking but as they turned towards her she continued walking away from them. She got her phone, and with shaking fingers, she called the one person she knew she had to tell.

Amaka was finishing her champagne and Chief Ojo was paying the bill when her phone rang. She asked to be excused and let the phone continue ringing as she walked out of the bar. Anytime that particular phone rang, the one the girls sent her messages on, she always answered it in private, if she could.

The caller didn't wait for her to talk. 'Hello? Aunty? They have killed her.'

'Killed who?' She took the phone away from her ear to see the caller's name but the screen had gone dark. 'Who is this? Who killed who?'

'She is dead, aunty, she is dead.'

'Who is dead?'

'They have killed her. Oh my God. Aunty, they have killed her. It is me Aunty, it is Kevwe. They have killed her. My friend, Aunty, she is dead.'

'Who killed your friend? What are you talking about?'

'Aunty, they have killed her, she's in the gutter. The police are here.'

'Where are you?'

'I dey Ronnie's. I just return from Federal Palace. Aunty, her body dey inside gutter here. They cut her open, Aunty. Oh my God, Aunty, she is dead.'

'Calm down. You say you're at Ronnie's?'

'Yes, Aunty, na here they dump her body.'

'Who killed her? What is her name?'

'Aunty, wetin I go do? Police dey for here.'

'Listen to me. Take it easy. What is your friend's name?'

The girl did not respond.

'Hello? Kevwe? Kevwe?'

Kevwe was still holding the phone to her ear, silent tears rolling down her face.

Amaka tried repeatedly but couldn't get her to respond. Against herself, she ended the call. She knew that the girl would soon switch her phone off and leave town for some time while the police rounded up prostitutes in the name of investigating the murder. She closed her eyes and took a deep breath. Her mind conjured up images, each one more gruesome than the last. She shook the thoughts away. She didn't have time for that. She called eight contacts from her phone and four more from memory. She asked each person she spoke to whether they had heard anything about Ronnie's bar that night. A few girls had heard a rumour but no one knew for sure. She considered calling Kevwe back, maybe she would answer. No. She had to go to Ronnie's herself. She bit her lips. Damn it. Not tonight.

Chief Ojo was exchanging looks with a group of chatty girls who had settled at a table next to him. Amaka stood at the entrance and watched. She contemplated turning round and walking away. One of the girls looked at him and did a little wave. She decided that she had come too close to give up. She walked up to him and sat on a different chair so that he had to turn his back to the girls.

'Something came up,' she said, 'I have to go somewhere quickly.'

He shook his head. She placed her hand on his shoulder.

'Listen, I want you. I want to fuck you. Tonight. And I will fuck you.' She said it with so much conviction that she was surprised when he cast a doubtful look at her then glanced at the girls.

She pulled his head to face her.

'I really have to go and sort this thing out. Give me your phone number, go to the hotel, and wait for me. Once I'm done I'll call you and I'll come and meet you.'

'What do you have to go and do at this time?'

'I can't tell you. Trust me, I will be back.'

'You can't tell me?'

'Listen, I don't have time to explain. I'll tell you all about it when I return. I promise. It doesn't have anything to do with another man, if that's what you're thinking.'

'Give me your number.'

'OK. Let me call myself with your phone then we'll both have each other's numbers.'

She took his phone and dialled her phone with the new SIM in it. She pressed her palm against the side of her bag and killed the connection when she felt a vibration.

'Now, go to your hotel and wait for me.'

'How do I know you'll come back?'

She looked him in the eyes while he waited for her answer. She turned to the girls. They were giggling their way through a bottle of Hennessy. They were young and pretty, and obviously on the job. She returned her gaze to him. Her face was expressionless. Looking straight into his eyes, she pushed her hands under her skirt, shifted on the chair and reached up. She found the strings of her underwear and twisted her fingers round the silk fabric.

He watched. She pulled her white thong down her thighs

to her knees then down to her ankles. She reached down and stepped out of the underwear. She gathered it in a fist, took his hand, and squeezed her knickers into his palm.

'Those are my favourite ones. I got them from Agent Provocateur in London and I want them back. Go to your hotel and wait for me.'

11

Bakare criss-crossed his hands over the steering wheel as we approached another bend. I braced and held my breath. The van was balanced just on two tyres as we rolled onto a narrow muddy road. There were no pavements. A wall covered in overlapping posters stood on the left while the right side was a row of deserted market stalls. He slowed down now because the terrain wouldn't let him speed. Up ahead, the headlights briefly illuminated what at first seemed to be nothing but blackness but turned out to be blocks of flats standing in eerie silence like a ghost town. Clothes hung from laundry lines strung across grey balconies.

He turned hard, braked harder, and figures appeared in the beam. I jumped when a head materialised in the window to my right. The door opened and my captor climbed out. I quickly followed him, preferring to be close by. Now that the wind was not blasting my face, I began to sweat at a terrific rate. We were surrounded by officers who seemed drawn to us. I was the only one sweating. Everyone else just had faces that glistened as if a coat of Vaseline had been applied to them.

Policemen jumped out from the back of our van and more cars screeched to a halt next to us. We had come to a rundown bungalow with a single light bulb illuminating its front porch. A signboard to its right said BAR BEACH POLICE STATION.

Officers dashed into the station or to our vehicle and stiffened to do chopping, sharp salutes at the man by my side. He was indeed the boss. I stayed close to him as he spoke to his men who kept casting glances at me. He turned to walk into the building and I followed, and behind us, a dozen other men. He fired off instructions in a local language and several people darted to carry them out.

Inside, the station was crowded, hot, and choking with the stench of body odour. A concrete counter divided the front room into a waiting area and a 'police' area. The wall behind the counter had three framed pictures hanging from strings that extended to nail hooks. The middle one was the President. I did not recognise the other two. The upper parts of the walls were blue, the lower parts and the counter were green. A foot-thick yellow line separated the two colours.

There were girls everywhere: tall, short, slim, plump. All dressed up and made up, all looking upset. Some sat behind the worn counter on a row of low wooden benches; some were standing with their arms folded across their bodies. Some leaned against the walls of a dark corridor that surely led to some darker horrors within. Those not frowning with upturned noses were pleading frantically, others, sensually, with police officers who appeared to enjoy the attention. Others were making calls on their mobile phones, or sending text messages. There were lots of them, and more were arriving, escorted in by men holding AK-47s battle-ready and absolutely unnecessarily. It looked like a whorehouse filled with disgruntled staff and unyielding pimps.

With a wave of his hand, the boss got someone to take me down the frightening corridor through the throngs of women.

They stretched out their arms and called me 'customer'. One was determined to get my attention. 'Johnny, it's me, Rose,' she kept repeating, until the officer threatened her with a slap gesture and she recoiled into the line of girls. I wondered if, like me, she found it difficult to tell foreign faces apart and she had mistaken me for a white boy she knew, whose name was Johnny. Then it hit me, the meaning of 'customer'. I was a John. It made sense, there in a rowdy noisy 'joint', surrounded by desperate hookers.

I was led to a room that smelt of dust. It had a single two-foot-square window with dirty glass louvres that looked like they had never been opened. Iron bars set about one foot apart protected it: enough gap for a slender man like me to squeeze through. The door was a flimsy plywood ensemble that was coming loose at its hinges and had lost most of its bottom bits to decay. It was even hotter in there; I was drawing in more dust than air into my lungs. I heard and saw the mosquitoes that flew straight at me. There was no chair, no bed, nothing.

'Wait here,' the officer said, and while I did, I had the time and solitude to evaluate my situation. I concluded that I was well and truly fucked. The Nigerian police had arrested me, my phone had been seized, I had lied to the police about my employer, and nobody who cared about me knew where I was.

Someone had told me that in Nigeria, there's nothing a bribe cannot fix. I calculated how much money I had on me. At the hotel, I'd changed fifty pounds into naira at the rate of two hundred and fifty naira to a pound. I also had an extra hundred pounds in twenties hidden in my socks. I wondered how it would go down. Do I make an offer first? Would I be told how much to pay? Was there a going rate for this sort of thing? Was it going to be a negotiation? I desperately wanted my phone back. Would that cost me extra?

If I got the phone back, who would I call? Sure, my boss could bark all day long in the office in Old Street, but what could he do for me now? I had listened to him scream at people on the phone, even watched him reduce colleagues to tears, but somehow, I didn't think his bullying would move the folk here. Nah. As bad ideas go, calling the Walrus – that's what we called him – would be the worst.

I could call Mel. At least she was half Nigerian. But then again, what could she do from her flat in Maida Vale? She didn't even speak a Nigerian language. Then there was Ade, my fixer, a man who had proven to be as reliable as a campaigning politician. He was meant to have picked me up from the airport, but just before the last boarding call for the Virgin Atlantic flight from Heathrow, he called to apologise and explain that he would be in Abuja on some official assignment. Thankfully, he arranged a car to collect me and deposit me at the hotel. He promised to see me in the morning once he got back from Ghana. It was only later while watching an air hostess point out the exits that I realised his gaffe.

There was no one to turn to, so I waited and counted the mosquitoes I killed while the blood they sucked stained my palms.

The door flung open and a plain clothes officer stood in its frame. That was when I realised it hadn't been locked. He grunted something, which I understood to mean he wanted me to follow him. He led the way deeper into the dark belly of the building and the mosquitoes followed, not done with the blood of a foreigner. He stopped, and in the darkness, I bumped into him. We were in front of the last door on the corridor. He knocked softly, almost cautiously, three times, and waited. Cool air wrapped around my ankles and slipped up my trousers. It came from under the door where there was a slither of light.

I didn't hear anyone respond but my escort opened the door, stuck his face into the crack, and barely audibly said, 'He's here, sir.'

'Bring him in,' someone said from the inside. It was the voice of the boss.

Sweat on my forehead turned icy as I stepped into his office.

'Sit down, please, Mr Collins,' he said. He was behind a cluttered table, elbows on wood, perusing some open files in front of him.

As I sat, I spotted a name plaque on the desk: INSPECTOR IBRAHIM. Now we knew each other's names.

'What a night, eh?' he said.

I wasn't sure what I was supposed to say to that – or if I was expected to say anything, but in my mind I agreed: what a screwed up night.

'You must wish you were back home right now.'

This time he smiled and it felt OK to respond. I nodded.

'Well, we also want to get you back home quickly. We just need to clear up a few things.'

I wondered if by home he meant England.

'Where are you staying?'

'Eko Hotel.'

'Yes? Nice hotel. I've stayed there myself. So, what are you doing in Nigeria?'

Good question. Why was I here? It was a bullshit assignment, to be honest, not the sort of thing I had in mind when I changed careers. We could have hired a local stringer; that was Ronald's first attempt to get out of it. But then the Walrus wouldn't have been able to let it slip at his club that he had a team in Nigeria covering the election – 'the team' comprising a grand total of me.

The initial excitement of getting the job had waned before I collected my visa at the Nigeria High Commission – the Walrus might soon have milked the bragging rights and then the trip would no longer be 'workable'. I didn't start getting excited again until I was strapped into my economy class seat, being instructed to 'switch off all electronic devices'. Then it was suddenly all too real, and the suppressed thrill burst out in one unrestrained moment marked by an unconscious smile that I caught in my reflection in the aircraft window. After that I was sober – enough to question myself.

I was going to Nigeria, a country sufficiently dangerous to warrant a Foreign Office travel warning and I was going in election season when political parties would be at war. And I'd asked for the job. When I was showing off my Nigerian visa in the office, Jen, my best buddy at work, took one look at my passport and asked, 'Are you going because of Mel?' We had drinks later that evening, and we talked about the Mel situation. I was being honest when I told her yes, I wanted to go to Nigeria because of Mel, but not in the way she thought. It was over. I had accepted that. But I felt I knew the country like one knows an old relative, and there was nothing wrong with taking the opportunity to go there.

There was another reason that also had to do with Mel, but I didn't tell Jen because she wouldn't have understood. Early, when we started dating, Mel asked how many countries I'd been to. I counted fourteen. 'Only Europe,' she said and she looked at me with a deadpan stare, as if she'd just discovered something significant about me. I asked her how many countries she'd been to: four continents and fifty-two countries. A month later she was going to Cambodia and she asked if I'd come. When she returned she didn't talk about the trip and I knew that at some point she had concluded that I wasn't 'that kind of person.' That would have been fine, only that a week later, at her friend's retrospective at the Barbican, an art professor we met there asked if we'd be able to come to a new exhibition he was curating in Cairo and Mel said 'I'll come.' In the cab back to her flat I asked why she'd assumed I wouldn't go and she said, 'But you never leave Europe.'

Well, damn her. Here I was in Africa. And as I contemplated the policeman's question, I realised I'd already started blaming her for the mess I was in.

'I'm here to cover the elections,' I said.

'Are you married?'

'No. But I have a girlfriend. She's half Nigerian.'

'Really?'

'Yes.' Maybe I could get him onside. Melissa was doing her bit.

'You met her here, in Nigeria?'

'No. England.'

'Oh, I see. You said she's half Nigerian.'

'Yes. Her mother is Irish. White.'

'So, she's half-caste.'

'Sorry?'

'You said her mother is white.'

'Yes. She's mixed.'

'What is her name?'

'Melissa Iyiola.'

'Iyiola,' he said, using the correct pronunciation, I guess. I'd said it the way Mel says it, which was surely the wrong way.

'You said you work for the BBC?'

'Yes.'

He pulled a laptop from a drawer and set it upon his desk.

'So, if I Google your name I'll be able to confirm this?'

He plugged a wireless dongle into his laptop and started

working the keyboard.

'We just need to match your face to your name, then we can take your statement, and then we can let you go,' he said. 'By the way, is your profile on the BBC website?'

Noise from the corridor made him look up from the screen. It sounded like a fight had broken out. He stopped to listen, then as quickly, he continued to prod the Internet.

'W, w, w, dot, b, b, c, dot, co, dot, UK,' he read out as he typed. 'So, where would I find you on here, Mr Collins?'

I was still trying to decide whether to continue lying or to come clean. The noise from the corridor grew louder until it was possible to make out words. There were shouts of 'congratulations' and 'fire for fire,' and loud slaps. He looked up again.

Whoever knocked did not wait to be invited in. The door flew open and men in uniforms that looked more military than police poured in. There wasn't enough space for all of them so some stayed outside in the corridor. They were shaking hands and slapping one another on the back. Their automatic weapons dangled from straps slung over their shoulders; extra magazines bulged from pouches on their belts. They looked tough and dangerous.

The shortest of them, still a considerably tall fellow at that, shared the good news with Inspector Ibrahim who had risen from his desk. 'Fire-for-Fire has done it again, sir,' the man said. 'We have rounded up every member of the Iron Benders gang. No casualties, two fatalities.'

12

Inspector Ibrahim yelled and I jumped in my chair. Maybe it had something to do with the 'two fatalities.' What the heck did that mean, 'No casualties, two fatalities'? But then he grabbed the officer's hand and shook it like he wanted to tear it off. It was good news. So good, that the inspector called someone on his mobile to share the news: 'Sir, we have just captured the Iron Benders… Sorry sir. I didn't check the time… The Iron Benders… Yes, sir. No, sir, those ones are from Benin Republic. Iron Benders, sir. They used to be iron benders. They worked at a mechanic's yard in Ajegunle.'

It turned out that the Iron Benders gang was a group of novice robbers who compensated for their inexperience with violence. Their speciality was carjacking. In the few months since they took up their new trade, they had become the most wanted robbers in two states. They shot and killed for no reason, raped and tortured for sport. Ibrahim told the person on the phone a story of how they once relieved an elderly pastor of his S Class Merc. They made the terrified man of God pray for them and bless them, before shooting him in the leg and asking him to pray for a miracle that would instantly heal the bullet wound. They left him bleeding on the road and sped off in his car. A few kilometres into their getaway, the car stopped. It had an anti-theft immobiliser. They set it ablaze, snatched another car, and went back to find the pastor – to teach him a lesson for deceiving them. The pastor barely survived the beating. They told him they only spared his life so that his congregation would buy him a new car, which they would in turn return to collect. They were a bunch of disillusioned, disaffected, drug-crazed, violent gangsters.

The gang had been on a crime spree that night. They had snatched several cars, probably to order, and then driven their loot in a high-speed convoy, picking up more cars on the way, heading out of Lagos. The men of Fire-for-Fire were out on their nightly patrol and the gang drove into them. The gunfight that followed saw motorists abandoning their cars to flee on foot. In the end, two of the criminals fell and the rest were arrested.

Ibrahim asked for details and shook hands with the officers. He wanted to know who fired the fatal shots: it was Sergeant Hot-Temper, as usual.

Hot-Temper, a lanky fellow with deep lacerations that spread from the corners of his mouth to his cheekbones, was standing straight, arms folded across his chest, grinning toothily through glazed eyes.

Ibrahim slapped a loud handshake onto his palm.

'Hot-Temper, why didn't you waste all the bastards?'

'Oga, my bullets finished. Before I reload, they don surrender.'

The men burst into laughter.

This man, this Sergeant Hot-Temper, who stood less than a metre from me, had just come back from ending two lives. I shouldn't be here.

A short man with a tiny face like a squirrel's eased his way into the room. He tried to catch his boss's attention amidst the taller, harder looking combatants. He waited until the inspector noticed him and beckoned. I listened to their conversation while pretending to admire the plaques on the wall.

Squirrel-face told his boss that a woman had trekked barefoot to the station and asked to see the officer in charge. Her car had just been snatched. She 'spoke well' and looked like a 'big woman,' so the constable thought it wise to inform his boss rather than ask her any further questions.

'Where is she?'

'She is at the counter, sir.'

'Has she written a statement?'

'No, sir.'

'OK. Ask her to write her statement and when she finishes, bring her here.' He turned to me. 'Mr Collins, as you can see, we are very busy here tonight.' I nodded. More than one of the terrifying-to-look-at officers had given me the once-over. I really didn't want him drawing attention to me right then.

'What you witnessed tonight, at the club, I advise you to forget. These things happen in our country, but even worse things happen in yours, we see it on TV all the time. My boys will take you back to your hotel and you will forget everything that happened tonight. Understand?' I nodded.

'As you can see, we the police are doing all we can to get rid of the miscreants in our society. What you witnessed tonight will not go unpunished. The life expectancy of armed robbers in this country is less than thirty. We will catch the culprits, and when we do, we will bring them to justice. You do not need to worry about it. This is a local problem and we will deal with it locally. Understand?' I nodded. 'Just forget everything, OK?'

I'd been so busy dealing with my own predicament that I had

actually forgotten about the girl in the gutter. I wanted to believe that this man would do something about it. That he would find the bastard who did that to her and turn Sergeant Hot-Temper loose on him. I suddenly felt a strange sense of responsibility for the girl.

'OK,' I said.

'Good.'

His phone rang. He checked who was calling and told everyone to be quiet. All eyes were on him. He answered the call.

'Hello, sir,' he said.

In seconds, his face dropped and a frown formed. When the call was over, he looked scary. When he spoke, he sounded dangerous.

'Everybody, clear out,' he said.

Everybody began to leave. I followed them.

'Not you.'

I turned to look.

He walked past me and his shoulder brushed mine so that I had to step back to remain standing. He slammed the door. It hit its frame and bounced back. He rough-handled it again and this time it stayed closed. What the hell did that call have to do with me?

He went to his desk and picked up a remote control. He pointed it at the TV set on top of a rusty filing cabinet. A few clicks later and we were watching CNN.

I recognised the road in front of Ronnie's and my apprehension moved up a notch. The picture was grainy, probably filmed with a mobile phone. A female voice spoke over the shaky video, reporting what I already knew: a woman had been murdered in an apparent ritual killing, organs had been taken from her body, and it happened right outside a busy nightclub in Lagos.

His face creased and contoured with every frame.
'You people. Sergeant!'
A policeman came running into his office.
'Lock him up. Cell B.'

13

Cell B. I didn't like the sound of it.

The summoned officer looked at his boss. If he was worried, so was I. He stepped towards me with one hand showing the way to the door.

'No.'

Inspector Ibrahim looked surprised. 'What?'

I don't know how I got the courage. Perhaps it wasn't courage. Perhaps it was just desperate, cowardly determination? Whatever it was, I wasn't going to walk willingly to the images of killers, violent cellmates, and brutal sodomy that filled my mind. Not that I would have physically resisted if it came to it. I still remembered the clubber who'd been beaten to silence in front of Ronnie's, but Cell B didn't sound like a place you simply allowed yourself to be led to.

'I haven't done anything wrong. What are you detaining me for?'

I considered telling him about my law degree and my past life as a solicitor but I calculated that it would only infuriate him further, and that was not the point of my outburst.

He didn't say anything so I continued.

'I'm a journalist. I came here to cover the presidential election and nothing more. If you want to confirm that, I'll give you my work number. Either that or you can call the British High Commission.'

He just kept staring. What was he thinking? Was it the mention of the British High Commission? Like playing the race card, it was cheap, it was manipulative, but if it worked, what the heck.

Someone knocked. A skinny officer opened the door and stayed there.

'What is it?' the inspector said.

I wished CNN would go to commercials or something, anything but the images of the breaking news they kept repeating.

The little man seemed scared. 'There is a woman here to see you, sir,' he said. 'She said she knows you. She said the Minister of Information sent her. She gave me her card to give to you. She's just arrived.' He took a step into the room and held out a business card with both hands. 'She says it is urgent.'

'What is her name?'

'Amaka, sir.'

He looked at the messenger and at the same time pulled out his handkerchief.

'She's out there?'

He cleaned his face and the back of his neck then folded the cloth and used it again, then he straightened his collar. On the back of the business card I recognised the red eagle, black shield, and two white horses of the Nigerian coat of arms.

The inspector turned his attention to the card. 'I thought you said she gave you her card?'

'Yes, sir.'

'This is not her card. This is the minister's card.'

He turned the card over and saw the handwritten note.

'Bring her.' He turned to me. 'So, you think I do not have a right to arrest you?' He stood and tended to his uniform.

'On what grounds?'

'You're very funny, my friend,' he said, smiling a smile that was neither pleasant or friendly. 'You people think you can just come to our country and do as you like. You think you're above the law here. So, you are a reporter, does that give you diplomatic immunity, eh?'

'I've done nothing wrong and you know it. The shit that went down tonight, it had nothing to do with me. I was in a bar and I came out for a smoke, that's all. I don't know why you brought me here, and quite frankly, I don't think you do either. I suggest you let me return to my hotel and we can all forget this ever happened.'

'What shit? Do not use that kind of language here. You might be undisciplined in your own country, but over here, we have morals. And by the way, who are you to tell me what to do?'

'I don't mean to tell you what to do, but let's face it, you and I both know I'm not a criminal. I did not film that shit on CNN and I sure as hell didn't kill that girl, so what the hell am I doing here?'

I didn't mean to be rude, but by now I was more angry than rational. What was he doing keeping me there? The thought of Cell B had triggered the fight or flight response and pumped more adrenalin into my system. I could not run – or fight – so the stimulant worked instead on the muscles that controlled my mouth. I was not thinking before talking; someone would later tell me that in Nigeria this is called 'running your mouth'.

'You keep using these dirty words. Perhaps a night in the cell will wash them out of you.'

'Fuck it. Lock me up if you want to, but be ready to answer to my High Commissioner. I am a British citizen.'

I smelt her perfume before I saw her. She walked in as if she owned the place. Her long thin braids were like a mane that scattered over her shoulders, framing a slim dark brown face punctuated with slanted piercing eyes. I immediately noticed she wasn't wearing makeup. Till this day I don't know why I did what I did next. I got up, held out my hand, and startled her a bit.

'Hi, I'm Guy.'

'I'm Amaka.'

As we shook, she looked at me as if she was trying to remember me.

'Amaka, long time. Please, come and sit down. I'll be with you in a minute,' Ibrahim said.

She was about to say something but he placed his palm on her back to lead her to a chair.

'Please, just wait one minute,' he said, and to me: 'Please, go with the officer. We'll finish our conversation after I've seen my guest.'

He spoke with such a civil tone that you'd think we'd been discussing the latest Test Match at Lord's. She stood by his desk, looking at me. I was not going to beg for my freedom in front of her. I left with the man waiting at the open door. I already had the inspector on the defensive, anyway. Cell B – bring it on.

Ibrahim held the chair for Amaka then skipped round to his, cupping a palm over his mouth to check his breath when his back was to her. He sat and pulled his chair forward until the desk bit into his belly, and then he leaned forward placing his elbows on his files, bringing his body even closer to her.

'Madam lawyer, you have come to cause trouble for us again?' He smiled.

'I see you guys have been busy tonight.'

'And you have come to bail them all, abi?'

'There are so many tonight. Have you guys started raiding the mainland too?'

'Very funny. Actually, there was a murder tonight. A girl's body was dumped in front of Ronnie's Bar.'

'Really?'

'Yes. In fact, I just got back from the crime scene now.'

'And so you arrested all those girls? Are they suspects?'

'No. We only brought them back for questioning.'

'So, they are not under arrest?'

'No.'

'So, they will all be released tonight?'

'Yes, of course.'

'Without paying bail?'

'Amaka, you have come again.' He smiled to douse the tension.

'They will all be released tonight?'

'Yes, of course.'

'And since they haven't been arrested, your boys won't harass them for bail?'

'The boys won't be happy with that o,' he said, and then, seeing her unrelenting face, he added, 'I'm just joking. You have my word: they'll all be released tonight and nobody will harass them.'

'Thank you.' She smiled for the first time since entering his office.

'Are you going to give me your number now?'

'Oga Ibrahim, I already told you, I don't give my number to married men.'

'You mean there is not one married man you've ever given your number to?'

'Not the ones who ask to take me to dinner at Protea Hotel.'

'Amaka, I told you before, I didn't mean it like that.'

'You did. Anyway, I'm here about something else.'

'Yes, I can see that.' He picked the business card from his table and looked at the note scribbled on its back. 'What are you doing with the Minister of Information?'

'It's a long story. Something to do with the charity.'

'I see. And how do I fit in?'

'You don't. I actually came about someone you arrested tonight.'

'Someone I arrested? Is the person related to the minister?'

'No. It's a journalist. The minister wants him to do a story on the Street Samaritans. I think it might be that man who just left.'

'That man?'

'Yes. Well, I can't be sure. But it's a white man; a reporter who was arrested by your men at Ronnie's.'

'That man?'

'Like I said, I'm not sure. I don't know what he looks like. But, that man who just left – is he a journalist?'

'That man? He said he is.'

'What's his full name?'

'He said his name is Guy Collins.'

'Yes, that's him, Mr Collins. I'm coming from a meeting with the minister, at the Sheraton. He sent me to go and get the man. I tracked him down to Ronnie's. That's where they told me he'd been arrested. I wanted to know what he did before reporting back to the minister.'

'Nobody arrested him. He was found in the vicinity of a crime and we brought him here for questioning, that's all.'

'That sounds like an arrest.'

'It's not. I just need to take his statement and then he can go.'

She shook her head. 'I need to tell the minister something. I can't just return and say "the man you sent me to get is at the police station being questioned." Why have you detained him?'

'I told you, we have not detained him. We picked him up at Ronnie's, and once we take his statement we'll let him go.'

'You picked him up? Why? Was he involved in the crime?'

'I didn't say so.'

'So, why have you brought him here? You know what? It's late and I need to go to bed. I'll call the minister and you can explain the situation to him.' She opened her bag and fetched her phone.

'No, that won't be necessary.'

The short officer, who I could easily have held in a neck choke until he stopped moving, led me to Cell B. Stale urine wafted from the darkness beyond the iron bars. I could just make out where the murderers stood waiting for me. The policeman worked the locks and pulled the heavy door. My ears ached at metal scrapping over concrete.

He waved me in and I obliged, determined not to appear scared. The plan was simple: I would promise anyone who tried to pick on me, that once I got out I would get the lawyers and staff and even the British High Commissioner himself to help them get out too. I would promise to take a personal interest in their case and to not only make sure they were released without charge, but also to help them get permanent asylum in Britain – and even get them compensation for the hardship they had suffered.

The door squeaked and clanked shut behind me and I got ready to swing a defensive punch.

Pulse racing, I surveyed my new digs. Something was wrong. I had not attracted the attention of all the hoodlums in Lagos. They were silent. They were not looking at me. I dared to look at their faces. They were all huddled on one side of the cell, looking down at the other side. I followed their gaze, and as my eyes adjusted to the poor light, I discovered a heap of battered bodies bleeding onto the bare concrete floor.

Just like the rest of my cellmates, a fearful silence entered my spirit. The bodies on the ground, writhing with pain, looked broken – blood, mixed with sweat, covered them in a sickening slime. Fresh bullet wounds on limbs, necks, and torsos were still flowing red.

I felt like I was going to be sick again. Then a noisy party arrived at our cell. It was Hot-Temper with his brothers-in-arms and a woman who looked thoroughly roughed-up and in bare feet. The policeman who'd locked me up was frantically working to unlock the door, hurried on by Hot-Temper.

'We have arrested a lot of criminals today,' Hot-Temper said, stepping into the cell.

We all retreated, squeezing into each other. The rest of his party followed him in. They did not pay us any attention, thank God. They had come to show off what remained of the Iron Benders gang.

'Which one of them robbed you?' he said and waved at the dying bodies.

The woman placed her palms one on top of the other to cover her nose and mouth. Her bulging eyes showed she was petrified. She took one look at the bodies and turned away. Poor woman.

'Madam, is it this one?' He stooped down by the wounded men and held their heads up one after the other for her to see. She shook her head each time.

He stood up, and with his foot, pushed the barely breathing criminals apart. He reached down and scooped up the head of a dead man.

'Abi na this one?'

The woman turned away. Tears rolled down the fingers covering her face.

'You mean, out of all these criminals we have arrested tonight you cannot identify the crooks that robbed you of your car?'

The woman shook her head.

'You must be a criminal yourself. You have come to waste police time. Oya, join them. I will lock you up with them now-now.'

He swung his assault rifle round and held it in a battle stance, waving the nozzle at her to join the other detainees in the cell. His face had transformed into an uncompromising violent glare.

One of his comrades patted his shoulder. 'Let her take another look,' the man said. He turned to the women. 'Madam, are you sure you can't identify the boys who snatched your car? These boys here are very notorious; they have snatched many cars this night before we caught them. Take another look.'

She shook her head at the officer. Her eyes, now flowing with tears, pleaded with him.

'She is a criminal. Let her join them,' Hot-Temper said. His weapon, held at waist level, was pointed at her belly.

'Give her some time. Madam, please, identify the boys who hijacked your car.'

Tears kept rolling from the woman's eyes. She trembled as if she was going into a fit but she managed to take one hand away from her mouth and without looking, point at one of the gang members on the ground.

In a swift motion, Hot-Temper swung his gun up to point at the ceiling, cocked it in a flash, brought it down to his waist, and fired a single deafening shot into the head of the fingered man.

The smell of gunpowder filled the air. The woman let out a scream and collapsed. Someone shouted 'Jesus.' My cellmates moved closer to the wall. I stood, open-mouthed, unable to believe what I'd just witnessed. I think I shouted 'fuck' over and over again, but I couldn't hear a thing; I was temporarily deaf from the bang. Hot-Temper was holding his gun aimed at his victim and quivering with laughter as if he had just played a practical joke. But it was no joke. The fellow's head was splattered all over the cell floor: brain, blood and bits of skull.

'What was that?' Amaka said. She was crouched by Ibrahim's desk. He was on the floor on his side. He stood up with his pistol in his hand.

'Stay here,' he said. Amaka followed him. Other officers were moving towards the sound of the shot, guns pointing the way. He entered the cell behind a bare-chested officer holding an AK-47 in a shooting pose.

'What the fuck happened here?' Inspector Ibrahim said, looking at Hot-Temper, the obvious culprit.

Hot-Temper, still sniggering, lost in his own delirium, said, 'This boy is the one that robbed this woman today.'

'And you shot him? Here? Why?' He aimed at Hot-Temper's head.

Hot-Temper stood grinning. Ibrahim kept the pistol pointed at his head, and with his other hand, he took the sergeant's weapon.

'Take him away.'

Amaka made her move. 'I think Mr Collins should come with me now.'

Overwhelmed, he said, 'OK.'

14

The woman took my hand. 'Please, come with me.'

Who was she? Why was she was talking to me?

'Mr Collins, I was sent to get you. We have to leave now.' She tugged at my hand.

'Stop,' a voice commanded.

I walked even faster.

'Stop.'

She stopped. The men in the corridor parted as he walked up to us, taking his time. Her grip tightened. The inspector came close until our eyes locked in contest: the hunter and the hunted, suddenly on the precipice. I would give in to the rage that had replaced my fear, at this moment. I would punch him, and Hot-Temper would use his gun on me. If I hit him hard enough, on the neck like my mate Roger had shown me in school, it would be worth it.

He placed his head beside mine. 'This is not over,' he said, just loud enough for only me to hear. 'Try to mind your own business and perhaps we won't have to meet again. Understand?'

Amaka shook my hand and shook it again. She placed her hand on my shoulder and pulled me away from his face. I relaxed the fist I'd formed and I left with her.

As we stepped out of the station, police officers watching us, the interior of a black Volkswagen Jetta lit up and its tail lights flashed. She hurried to the car, opened the door for me, got into the driver's seat, fired up the engine, and did a two point turn faster than I'd ever seen one done. Then she charged at the uneven ground and turned onto Ahmadu Bello without checking that the road was clear. The engine wailed. I didn't realise we'd been driving up the wrong way until at the turning by the infamous glass building she pulled across onto the other side. She looked in the rear-view mirror as if she expected us to be followed.

Nothing made sense. Was I a free man now? I studied her side profile. She was concentrating on our getaway. Who was she? Who sent her to get me? Where was she taking me?

'Did Ade send you?' Maybe my absentee minder had tried to contact me at the hotel, found that I was missing, and launched a manhunt that somehow led to Inspector Ibrahim's police station.

'Yes.'

She answered too quickly.

'Ade from the British High Commission?'

'Yes.'

A chill crept over my skin.

'Stop the car.' I got ready to open the door and jump out.

'What?'

'You heard me. Stop the fucking car.' I undid my seat belt and turned to her in a provocative manner. I would wrestle her for whatever weapon she had hidden under her skirt.

'Why?'

'You are not from Ade. He didn't send you. Stop the fucking car or else.' She was working with Inspector Ibrahim. They were kidnapping me after all.

'Or else what? You want to go back there? You just witnessed a policeman murder a detainee. You really want to go back there?'

She was right. But, who the hell was she? 'Stop the car or tell me who you are.' I felt slightly ashamed that I was ready to pounce and fight her if I had to.

'My name is Amaka. I work for a charity that works with prostitutes. One of the girls I work with told me that a foreign journalist was arrested outside Ronnie's. I came to get you out.'

It sounded rehearsed. 'Why?'

'I'll explain everything later. First, we have to get to your hotel and check you into another room.'

'Why?'

'I lied to Ibrahim to get you out. He'll soon figure out that I tricked him and he'll come looking for you.'

I wasn't convinced but she was driving towards Eko Hotel. Once there, I would call the British High Commission and be on the next flight out of Nigeria.

15

A black Toyota Land Cruiser rolled down Falomo Bridge and turned at the roundabout onto Awolowo Road. Knockout – a five-foot tall man whose dark leathery skin was stretched by his prominent chin and cheekbones – was driving. He had not found the controls to adjust the seat so he perched on the edge, his toes just grazing the pedals, and he watched out for police checkpoints.

Go-Slow, who at seven-foot tall dwarfed his companion, was kneeling backwards in the passenger seat. His feet, crossed, touched the windscreen and his back pressed into the ceiling. He was cleaning blood off the rear seats and the windows and the headrest. It was everywhere. He found a box of tissues on the dashboard and spread blood over the beige leather upholstery until the perfumed sheets broke into useless red clumps. He looked at the blood gathered under his nails and cursed. The night before, his wife had spent an hour giving him a manicure while he watched Arsenal being thrashed. She was right about Knockout: he would get them into trouble one day.

'How far?' Knockout said.

'Just drive.'

Maybe he should strangle the fool himself and set the car on fire with his little body in it. He wanted them to ditch the car but the moron wouldn't listen. They had killed before, but what they just did was wrong and it was all because of that conversation they'd had a week ago with Catch-Fire.

When they learned that the bus stop pickpocket was spending dollar bills at beer parlours on Lagos Island, they remembered the money he owed them. They found his new home and he settled his debt in hundred dollar bills. He boasted of his new business that involved juju and human sacrifice and said he'd graduated beyond their ranks. Knockout spent a week ranting about Catch-Fire.

They'd met earlier that day at CMS and walked to Dolphin Estate where Knockout stood at the foot of a bridge, holding up a strip of mobile phone recharge cards, while Go-Slow hid with their guns in a nearby bush. A woman in a Land Cruiser stopped to buy recharge cards and Go-Slow got into the seat next to her. They threw her shoes into the bush, searched her handbag for her address, and said they would come for her if she went to the police.

They changed the number plates and drove to Sanusi Fafunwa because Knockout wanted to take a girl home. Before they parked, a woman was walking towards them, adjusting her red miniskirt, and rearranging her breasts inside her tight bra. She leaned into the window to haggle.

'Two K,' Knockout said.

'Five,' she said.

'Three.'

'Is it both of you?'

'No. Just me.'

'OK.'

She got into the back, shut the door, and pulled out a rusty revolver from her clutch bag.

'Bastards. Drive.'

Her gang were waiting round the corner by the Law School. She waved the gun from one hoodlum to the other, wondering why they just stared at her. Then she gently placed the revolver on the seat and slowly raised her hands, unable to dodge this way or that way from the barrels of both their guns pointed at her belly.

Knockout jumped over his seat and started hitting her on the head with her own weapon. She shouted for help and Go-Slow put his big palm over her face, wrapped his other hand around her neck, and twisted.

Cars drove by and girls walked past but the tinted glass hid what was going on inside. Go-Slow unfolded his arms and her body slumped onto the seat.

Her shirt had torn and her breasts were exposed. Knockout's face lit up. He pulled out a jack-knife from his knee-length boot and flicked the blade out in a move he had been practicing in front of his mirror. He tore off the rest of the girl's shirt and brought his dagger down on her chest in a massive blow that punctured through flesh and bone. He wriggled the blade free and went at it again. Go-Slow, with the unblinking interest of someone stoned, watched, thinking that his partner might have snorted too much cocaine before they met. When Knockout held the girl's warm heart in his hand, he expected him to take a bite from it but instead he said, 'Let's go and find that morafucker, Catch-Fire.'

The light of an electric torch flickered ahead. Knockout tapped his partner's leg and shifted his foot from the accelerator to the brake. Go-Slow turned and saw the checkpoint. He sat back in his seat and cleaned his hands with the last tissue from the box.

It was no use. He wiped them on the bottom of his trousers then rolled up his sleeves and checked for spots of blood on his shirt.

The police had stopped a yellow Hummer ahead. A hand with a clenched fist reached out of the car's window. A policeman took whatever was in it, put it into his own pocket and waved the Hummer on.

Knockout inched forward. He stopped between two worn tyres set on both sides of the road. The kerosene lamps that balanced on them had run out of fuel. He looked at Go-Slow's shirt. He had taken off his own and noted with relief that blood had not seeped into the black vest underneath. He pulled the vest over the pistol in his belt then he pressed the button to roll down the tinted window.

An albino officer with transparent bristles on his cheeks peered into the car through the little gap Knockout had made. He pointed his torch at the driver's face and Knockout held up his hand.

'Ol' boy, don't shine that thing in my face,' Knockout said.

The policeman withdrew his torch. The car was new and it was big, so the occupants could be men who would make trouble for him. He wanted to take a closer look at the driver's face. He knew what big men look like and the man who had told him to take his torch away did not look like a big man. But in Ikoyi, anybody could be somebody. He placed his palm on the driver's door and turned to search for his boss.

The higher-ranking officer was standing on the sidewalk, leaning on a Kalashnikov he used as a walking stick, watching his men work. The Hummer had yielded only fifty naira so he had sworn at the young constable who spoke to the driver, called him the 'bastard son of a prostitute witch,' and commanded his officers to make sure the jeep dropped 'something big'. He told them: 'Make sure you check their fire extinguisher and blow it. If it is liquid type, it is illegal. Check their c-caution if the face don scratch. Check their spare tyre – poke it, if it is too soft. If they have laptop, ask for the receipt. If you find any file or any documents inside the car, ask them for release note wey dem take carry am commot office.'

The boss looked at the driver of the four-by-four.

'What is the problem?' Knockout said.

The policeman was waiting for his superior officer to nod or shake his head. 'Oga, no problem, just take am easy.'

'Are you mad? You are telling me to take it easy? You must be a fool.'

The officer took his hand from the car and stood almost at attention. He cast a glance back at his boss, who looked away.

'Sorry sir,' he said and waved them on.

When the checkpoint was out of sight, Go-Slow used the sides of his palms to scrape blood off the rear seats – it was everywhere. They had been lucky this time but there would be more checkpoints on the mainland and the police there wouldn't be afraid of drivers with big cars. His eyes fell on Knockout's discarded shirt in the rear footwell and he reached for it.

16

All Chief Ebenezer Amadi could see were the nipples and the brown breasts that ballooned out of focus behind them. The girl on top of him dug her fingers into his fat hairy chest, ground her groin against his, and asked him to say her name. He tried to remember what it was but another pair of breasts appeared over his head, dangling close to his lips, and he forgot the name all over again.

The second girl took his earlobes between her fingers and rolled them the way his mother used to, and then she placed her lip-gloss-wet lips on his ear and whispered, 'Say my name.' He tried to remember but his phone was ringing and he had to answer it. He feared that if he didn't say their names, the one would stop playing with his ears and the other would cross her leg over his belly and roll away.

The ringing phone was vibrating on the mahogany bedside table, making a knocking noise that made it impossible to think. Soon, it would rattle its way to the edge, fall off, and break into pieces on the marble floor, and the person calling, whose call he had to take, would get upset.

He woke to the phone still ringing. He sighed, reached for it on the table, felt a body, and remembered the two girls he had met at Bacchus, whose names he did not know, who now lay on either side of him, and who had inspired the interrupted dream. He folded back the duvet from his naked body and began to shiver. The phone continued to ring as he considered where exactly he'd left the remote control for the air-conditioner.

He leaned over the girl on his left side and enjoyed the warmth of her body. Once the call was over, he would play out the dream with both of them, then, after a glass of Hennessy and a Viagra, he would do it all over again until they had to leave at five a.m.

He didn't check the caller display – it could only be one person; a man whose voice he knew but whose face he had never seen. The Voice would probably ask him if everything was OK and he would say yes and that would be it. After the call, he would wake the girls who had spanked each other, called him Daddy, and sniffed cocaine from his belly-button.

'Hello.' His spare hand found a breast and started fondling it. The girl stirred and searched for the duvet.

'We have a problem.'

The Voice always went straight to the point, just like the first time they spoke many years ago when the Chief was not yet a chief and had a different name.

'What kind of problem?' His hand found its way down to the girl's thighs. He tried to push her legs apart.

'Are you alone?'

'Yes.'

'The man we used the last time, the one who calls himself Catch-Fire, he's been talking.'

He took his hand away from the girl and climbed over her to get out of bed. His toes curled as his feet landed on the cold marble tiles. He walked into the adjoining room, fat deposits wobbling under the folds of his skin with every step.

'Is he talking to the police?'

'No, not the police, but they'll soon hear something. He's a risk. You need to take care of him.'

'OK.'

He first spoke with The Voice during Christmas in 1989. He'd been a tenant of Kirikiri Maximum Security Prison back then, awaiting trial over a robbery. His gang, the police alleged, conspired to rob one Emanuel Ofoeze of Onipanu, Lagos. The victim was in possession of a large sum of money he had withdrawn from the bank earlier in the day. The cash was for the payment of salaries at Omo-Boy Sawmill Ltd. in Maryland where he was chief supervisor. When the gang broke into his house at around midnight, the late Mr. Ofoeze refused, under pain of gratuitous torture, to reveal where he had hidden the money. The gang proceeded to axe off each of the victim's fingers. After his toes, they gouged out his eyes, and sliced off his ears. His tongue was the last to go, before he died, the police said in their report.

A tip-off led to a member of the gang and subsequently to the mastermind of the operation who had inflicted the devilish wounds observed on the victim – one Okafor Bright Chikezie, an apprentice sawmill operator where the dead man worked.

The other suspects confessed in return for life sentences, but the boy they called Bright insisted on his innocence, telling the police a counter story of how some boys approached him to take part in robbing the site supervisor. When he refused, the conspirators threatened his life. He spoke to his pastor and together they went to meet the supervisor to warn him and to pray. The man didn't take enough precautions and the criminals, now convinced that it was Bright who had exposed them, were determined to rope him in. Bright provided an address for the pastor and the man confirmed his story.

The case of Okafor Bright Chikezie lingered in the classification of 'awaiting-trial,' a concept used by the Nigerian police when they don't want to let a suspect go to court or go free. It was while he was in a cell shared with twenty-four other inmates, that the chief jailer had him brought to his office, fed him rice and stew with meat for the first time in the three years, and given him the green phone on his table to talk to 'someone who could help him.'

How The Voice got all his information was still a mystery, but he was told from the first day not to ask questions. He was already thinking of the best way to make Catch-Fire disappear. A plan began to form; it involved a prostitute and a bottle of chloroform he kept in a drawer in his room.

'Tonight,' The Voice said.

'Tonight?'

He looked at his wrist and remembered he had left his watch on the bedside table. He made a mental note to slip the Rolex back on before falling asleep again next to the girls. It was too early in the morning to make arrangements with the girl he had in mind. He would have to do it himself.

'It's almost morning.'

'It has to be done immediately. It may already be too late.'

'Consider it done.'

'Call me when it's over.'

'OK.'

The Voice ended the call. Amadi walked to the window and drew the curtains. Moonlight threw shadows behind him. He looked out onto his compound. The heart-shaped swimming pool shimmered in the moon's glow.

He had built his mansion in just three months. When you have money, you can throw a picture in front of an architect and say, 'Build me this house, I want to move in when I get back from America,' and it will be done. You can buy the latest Mercedes every year, then send your family on holidays to Switzerland to hide your money in safe accounts and give you space to do the things with pretty young girls that you could only dream of doing when you were a struggling hustler on the streets of Lagos.

When he first came to the city as a boy, he spent afternoons under the sun, peddling handkerchiefs in traffic jams, and in the nights he dug up the potholes that caused the traffic jams – him and many like him living day to day like scavenging animals. No matter how much money he made, or how many chieftaincy titles he bought, he still saw his old self in the street-kids that surrounded his car in traffic jams. Beggars and pedlars who pushed their wares and begging hands in front of his windscreen, left dirty palm prints on his window, and wouldn't give up until the traffic started moving. He used to be one of them, but now he was on the other side of the rolled-up window, and in the owner's seat of a big car. He would do anything to remain on this side of the divide.

He pictured Catch-Fire nodding as he gave instructions the same way The Voice ordered him. This was not the first time he had to do something about someone who threatened to send him back to hell. Nor was it the first time a promising new recruit would screw up and become a risk.

He glanced into his room and sighed. The things he planned to do with the girls would have to wait. There was business to attend to. Catch-Fire had to die, and anyone who the stupid boy had spoken to had to die as well, God willing, before dawn.

17

He went back to his room and picked up his neatly folded clothes from the seat of an armchair. He dressed in the darkness, then he looked at the girls sleeping with their backs to each other. He opened a chest of drawers and found a Bible under rows of folded socks. Within its pages was an envelope that contained fine white powder. As he left, he quietly closed the door and turned the key to lock it.

Eremobor jogged up to his boss. Anytime the Chief had female guests, he stayed awake to take them home.

'We are taking the Pajero,' Amadi said. He got into the back of the SUV. 'We are going to Ojuelegba.'

Eremobor's hand froze above the ignition. He looked at his boss. 'Ojuelegba, sir?'

'Yes. I'll find the address on my phone before we get there.'

Eremobor first knew Ojuelegba from a Fela Kuti song. Years later, when he was a bus conductor, he witnessed ordinary people turning into killers for the sake of a pickpocket there. They had chased the boy to the Ojuelegba overhead roundabout. The boy, still in school uniform, was too exhausted to defend himself against the sticks, stones, planks and cement blocks they used on him. They threw two discarded tyres over his head and doused him in petrol that they'd siphoned from cars stuck in the jam. Eremobor had never forgotten the smell of burning human flesh. Ojuelegba was a dangerous place during the day and much worse at night.

They parked in front of a house, on a road that undulated with caked-over mud hills. The neighbourhood was in darkness from a power failure but a generator powered the house. It sputtered black fumes to the rhythm of its diesel engine, causing stray dogs to howl in unison.

By the light of a gas lamp set on the ground, Area boys were playing football on the road. They stopped to watch at the sound of a car navigating the bumps. Amadi opened his door himself, stepped out onto the dusty road, and walked towards the house with loud music pouring from it. Eremobor locked the doors and kept the darkened windows rolled up.

Amadi walked down a corridor, past couples cuddling on worn sofas, to a room bathed in red light. He parted a curtain of glass beads that hung over the doorway and stepped in. A large plasma TV on the wall still had the manufacturer's sticker on the corner of the screen. Six men and a dozen women sat on sofas and armchairs staring at a Premier League game.

The men watched the match while the girls stroked chests underneath unbuttoned shirts, or used their phones. Directly opposite the big screen, Catch-Fire was on a sofa, topless, bottles of beer on a stool in front of him and two girls on either side, one caressing his sweaty chest, the other jerking him off under his boxer shorts.

18

Knockout pulled up behind Chief Amadi's car. 'Look, the morafucker has bought a jeep.'

Staring at his rear-view mirror, Eremobor waited for the headlights of the car to go off. Perhaps he would recognise a business partner of his boss, and a driver who he had made friends with on the kind of nights when servants bonded outside while the masters congregated inside.

Go-Slow inspected his shirt for blood while Knockout walked over to the car in front. Eremobor did not recognise the midget in the side mirror, or the giant standing behind him. He went for a dagger he kept under his seat.

Knockout circled the car, peering through the darkened windows. He kicked the front tyre then walked round to join Go-Slow.

A girl in black micro shorts and a studded bra was the first to notice Amadi. She looked at his shoes and at his watch and then got to her feet before any of the other girls saw him.

Catch-Fire looked up. In the red light, it took a moment to recognise his new business partner. His erection poked out from the slit of the Tommy Hilfiger boxers. He tucked himself back in, brushed aside a girl's arm, and stepped over the stool in front of him, knocking over a bottle of beer.

'My Chief, I wasn't expecting you, sir. I hope nothing is wrong. Please come, sit down. What will you drink? I have cold beer, I have brandy, I have girls.'

Catch-Fire bowed as he shook his hand. The men and the girls watched.

'I was at a party in Surulere. I remembered you lived here, so I said I should stop by to say hello.'

'My Chief, I am so honoured. Please, let them get you something to eat. I have fish pepper soup.'

'Don't worry. I didn't know you were having a party. I'll come another time.'

'Oh, Chief, you cannot come to my house and leave like that. Let me entertain you. Please, sit down. Should they bring brandy?'

'OK, brandy would be good. But I'm only staying for one drink.'

Amadi sat on the sofa where Catch-Fire had been. The girls stood to make space for him. They lingered.

'Bring Rémy Martin for my oga.' He gingerly sat on the edge of the sofa next to Amadi. 'Chief, I cannot tell you how happy I am that you have come to visit me in my house. You are sure there is no problem?'

'No, no problem. So, when does your party end?'

'Ah, Chief, it is not a party. These people, they stay here with me.'

'All of them?'

'No, sir. Only the girls.'

'I see.'

'Chief, I am very happy that you came to visit me. Me, Catch-Fire. Chief, I must entertain you.'

He jumped to his feet and had to adjust his boxers again.

'Everybody, clear out.'

The party moved lethargically towards the door.

'All the girls, stay.'

The men gave him unsavoury looks. He darted to a stack of new electronic equipment that sat on a wooden stool with thin legs tapering to even thinner points. He fumbled with the controls, temporarily plunged the room into silence, then found the track he was searching for. Makossa music played from deceptively slim speakers at the corners of the room. The girls started dancing. Catch-Fire took a moment to admire them then he turned to his guest.

'My Chief, these girls are from Cotonou. They dance Makossa very well and they fuck like dogs. Please, take your pick.'

The girls undressed. They had colourful beads around their waists, bouncing as they danced in their thongs. Some of them had not been wearing underwear. A girl with nipple piercings poured Amadi's brandy and pulled his hand to come to the dance floor. He smiled and remained on the sofa.

'Chief, please, pick anyone you like.'

'Another time, my friend. I have to leave now. Come and see me before seven a.m. We have work to do.'

Go-Slow held the beaded curtain for Knockout and bent his head to pass through the doorway. He stopped when he saw the girls. Knockout grabbed a girl and pulled her to himself, gripped her bum, and pressed his open mouth onto her breast. She pushed him away and slapped him.

The other girls covered their breasts with their palms and gathered round their friend. Go-Slow stepped in front of Knockout and spread his arms. 'Calm down, please.'

Knockout tried to get past Go-Slow. 'What is wrong with her?' he said, eyeing the girl. 'Aren't you a prostitute? Aren't you all prostitutes? Why are you covering your breasts?'

One of the girls spoke: 'Oga, you cannot just be treating her anyhow. After all, you are not the one who brought her here.'

'Oh, really? And what are you going to do about it?' His hand went under his T-shirt.

Go-Slow knew he was going for his weapon. He turned and wrapped his arms around Knockout before he could draw the pistol.

Catch-Fire pushed his way through the girls. 'What are you boys doing here?' he said.

'We bring you business,' Knockout said. He shook himself free from Go-Slow's embrace.

'Please, I do not do business at this time. Why didn't you call me first before coming here?'

'So we now have to call to make appointments?'

'Look, my friend, I don't have any business with you. I have paid you guys what I owe you. If you think you can just come to my house and start harassing my friends you are mistaken.'

'What do you mean?' Knockout's hand found the handle of his pistol.

Go-Slow tapped him on the shoulder and nodded sideways. Knockout looked and saw a buxom girl pointing a revolver at his head. Another was handing out pistols from a rucksack.

'What is this bullshit? We brought you business and you allow your prostitutes to draw guns?' Knockout said.

'I don't have any business with you anymore. Get out of my house. And if I ever see you on my street again I will feed your testicles to the rabid dogs of Surulere.'

Go-Slow stepped forward. 'We have made a terrible mistake,' he said. 'We will leave now and you don't have to worry about us.' He began to back out of the room, tugging Knockout's arm.

Knockout stayed in the same spot staring into Catch-Fire's eyes; the corners of his lips formed into a scornful smile and his fingers twitched with intent on the butt of his pistol.

'Kanayo, let us go,' Go-Slow said, raising his voice. All the girls now had guns which were pointed at them.

'Why are you saying my name?'

'Let's go.'

Knockout looked past Catch-Fire and locked eyes with Amadi.

'Kanayo.'

He shook Go-Slow's hand off his shoulder. His hand remained on his undrawn weapon, his nose twitching from his snarl.

'I am leaving,' Go-Slow said.

Knockout began to back away, escorted out of the room by Catch-Fire and the girls.

When the last girl had left the room, Amadi, who had been watching in silence, searched the stool for a glass and found none. He checked the beer bottles and found one that wasn't empty. He looked at the beaded curtains still dangling, took out the folded white envelope from his pocket and straightened it. He checked the curtain again, cupped his hand over the bottle to form a funnel and tipped the contents of the envelope into the beer. The alcohol foamed. He returned the empty envelope to his pocket and dusted his hands off each other and off his lap. He held the bottle by its neck and gently shook it then he relaxed back into his seat and picked up his glass of brandy from the floor.

19

Knockout and Go-Slow walked backwards down the corridor and into the night. Catch-Fire and the girls spilled out onto the road after them. The boys that were playing football stopped to watch. Eremobor saw the girls were holding guns and he sank down below the window and contemplated speeding off without his boss.

Go-Slow got into the driver's seat of their car. He drove slowly at first, looking into the rear-view mirror, then he floored the throttle and the car bounced on the uneven road.

'Fuuuuuuuck!' Knockout said, banging his fists on the dashboard. 'Fuck, fuck, fuck, fuck, fuck. Fucking Shit. Bastard. Me? Knockout? Fuuuuuuuck.'

'Cool down,' Go-Slow said. He strained the engine, charging at potholes as if they weren't there.

'Fuck. Catch-Fire is dead. He is a dead man.'

'Cool down.'

'Fuck. Let's go back.'

'And do what?'

'Fuuuuuuuck.'

'Let it go.'

At the Ojuelegba flyover, Go-Slow finally eased off the throttle and slowed to a crawl. He drove round the roundabout twice then he pulled up on the kerb. He got out and crossed the road to reach the overgrown enclosure under the bridge. He unzipped his trouser and began whistling as he peed.

A disabled man on a wooden board with squeaky metal wheels rolled out from beneath a shelter of cardboard and wooden planks. Go-Slow ignored the man and looked around. He pulled out three pistols from his belt: his, Knockout's, and the one they had seized from the girl who tried to rob them. Without speaking, he handed the guns to the man who then rolled himself back into his shelter, propelled by callused palms that pulled against the rough ground. When he got back into the car, Knockout was silent. He drove to Matori, the motor vehicle spare parts centre of Lagos, and stopped in front of a dilapidated colonial era building with rows of second-hand motorcycles chained together in front. A fading sign said: CHUCKS AUTO DEALERS AND AGENT. DEALERS IN ORIGINAL SPARE PARTS, GENERATORS AND TOKUNBO MOTORCYCLES.

Across the road, on the flat roof of the adjacent building, a man lying on his belly, with a twelve gauge pump-action shotgun by his side, watched them through a pair of military issue binoculars.

They walked up to the building and Go-Slow knocked on the wooden door behind a second entry-way of iron bars which were in turn secured by heavy-duty padlocks at four different points. They waited for an answer. He knocked again – still no response. Knockout banged on the door with the side of his fist.

'Who is that?'

'We are looking for Chucks,' Knockout said. 'We have a delivery for him.'

'He has travelled.'

'Travelled? When?'

'I don't know. Go away.'

The man on the roof adjusted his binoculars. He fetched his phone and made a call.

A boy in worn khaki shorts and an oversized singlet dotted with holes laboured with the locks, making clanking sounds, then stepped out to meet them.

'Oga said I should bring you,' he said. He looked like he had been woken from sleep.

'Where is he?' Knockout said.

'I'll take you to him. Is that the car you brought?' He pointed at the stolen SUV and started walking towards it.

'What is going on here? I thought you said he had travelled?'

'Yes. He's back. I'll take you to him. Let's go.' The boy opened the back door, pulled himself onto the seat, and closed his eyes.

The criminals exchanged looks. Go-Slow shrugged. They got into the car and Go-Slow started the engine. 'Where are we going?' he asked the boy.

Head slumped back and eyes shut, the boy pointed the way: 'Go like this. Take the next turn left, then turn left again and drive to the front of the Glo kiosk.'

They exchanged looks again. Go-Slow shrugged. They followed the boy's directions and ended up on the next street, behind a row of closed shops.

By now the boy was snoring. Knockout reached back and shook him. 'Hey. Where is he?'

'He will soon come.' He shifted and continued sleeping with his mouth open.

A tap on the window jolted the crooks. Knockout went for his gun and remembered they had 'deposited' their weapons.

Chucks stood by the window holding the pump-action in

one hand and a phone in the other. A pair of binoculars hung from his neck.

'What are you boys doing here?' He drew his fingers over the door where he thought he saw a dent, then he leaned back to look at the tyres.

'Bros, what's going on?' Knockout said.

'This is a very bad night. Those foolish Iron Bender boys were supposed to deliver twelve cars tonight but they have all been arrested.'

'They did not settle the police?'

'I don't know for them. Maybe the bribe was not enough. Maybe the officers they bribed were not the ones out on patrol tonight. Maybe their ashewo girlfriends cursed them, I don't know. But the information I have is that they have all been arrested, and once the police start to torture them they might give me away.'

'Damn. Well, it serves you right; those boys are not professionals at all. I warned you.'

'Look, if I have a big order, those boys can deliver twenty cars in one night. What can you do? You bring me one car in two months. You expect me to wait for you when I have customers waiting for me?'

'All I'm saying is that those boys are amateurs. They are not clean. We, we do neat jobs; no police problem at all.'

'Whatever. So what have you come to see me for?'

'We came to deliver this jeep.'

Chucks was still inspecting the car. 'I don't think I can take it,' he said. 'Town is too hot right now. Those boys will soon start talking. I can't handle any delivery today.'

'So, what do you want us to do with this car?'

'You can return it to the owner. If I were you, I would lay low till things settle.'

Go-Slow had been watching him and had seen the way he looked at the car. 'What is the best price you can give us?' he said.

'Well, I really don't want to do any business today, but because it is you boys, I will use this one for spare parts. It is too dangerous to drive it out of town tonight.'

'How much?'

'Well, one hundred thousand.'

Knockout spread his fingers at him. 'Fuck you. This car is worth at least two million.'

'OK, go and sell it yourself.'

'Two hundred thousand,' Go-Slow said.

Chucks hissed. 'OK. But please, no more business till I contact you. Town is very hot right now.'

'And a motorcycle.'

Go-Slow and Knockout puttered along Third Mainland Bridge on a second-hand scooter. Go-Slow was driving. Knockout held him tight from behind.

'It's because of that man that Catch-Fire embarrassed us like that,' Knockout shouted over the passing flow of air. 'He didn't want us to talk in front of his new oga.'

'Let it go,' Go-Slow shouted back.

'He must be the one that brought that car. Did you notice how Catch-Fire tried to block him? He didn't want us to see him.'

'I didn't notice anything.'

'What's that kind of big man doing with a common thief like Catch-Fire? He must be the one he's doing the business with.'

'Let it go.'

'He is the one we should be talking to.'

'Kanayo, let it go.'

The boys who had been playing football raised their fists, chanting 'Baba Catch-Fire.' The girls did not cover their bodies and the boys did not stare. Catch-Fire did a little dance to a song the boys sang for him then he waved at them and waved his girls back into the house.

Amadi was sipping brandy and watching the game on mute. The sound system had stopped playing.

'My Chief, sir, I am very sorry about that embarrassment,' Catch-Fire said.

'Who are those boys?'

'Just some stupid thugs like that. No need to worry about them, sir.'

'What was the business they brought?'

'Nothing, Chief. Not our business.'

'I did not ask you if it was our business.' Amadi realised he had to take care of the two clowns as well.

'They look like reckless guys.'

'Very reckless,' Catch-Fire said.

'I might have a job for them.'

'Those boys? They cannot be trusted, Chief. See how they came here and caused trouble for no reason? We cannot be doing business with people like them. They will just be causing problems up and down. No, Chief. They are not good for business. They are too reckless.'

'Yes. The job I need them for is very dangerous, they might not survive it. I've been looking for someone to use for the job. Not our business. Something else. You understand?'

Catch-Fire knew that Knockout, at least, would retaliate. 'They would be very good for that kind of job,' he said.

'Write their numbers down for me. What are their names?'

'The big one is Go-Slow; I don't know his real name. The midget, they call him Knockout but his real name is Kanayo.'

He had just learned that tonight. He planned to make an anonymous call to the police to give them this tip.

Amadi folded the sheet of paper on which Catch-Fire wrote down the names and numbers. He slipped the paper into his pocket then he lifted his brandy.

'To more money.'

'More money,' Catch-Fire said. He searched the stool for his beer and raised the bottle to touch Chief Amadi's glass. He took a sip from his bottle.

'Chief, please, take one of these girls home. Any one.'

'Another time, my friend. Another time.'

'Or two, sir. Take two. I'm telling you, they are very good. And clean. No HIV. Take three.'

'You tested them yourself?'

'No, sir, 'is not like that. I am not sleeping with all of them. Only one is my girlfriend and she is not even here. Any one you want, I promise you, only you will have her.'

'You are not drinking your beer.'

'It is warm. I will get another bottle. Please, sir, have more brandy.'

'No, no, no, no. It is late. I really have to be going.'

'Ah, Chief, you are angry with me because of those boys.'

'Angry? Why? Finish your beer and see me off.' Amadi stood up.

'OK, sir.' He downed the rest of the beer in one gulp.

20

The dark sky was just beginning to break into patches of grey when Go-Slow stopped in front of a bungalow on King George V Road in the heart of Lagos Island. Knockout got off the scooter and the criminals shook hands, agreeing to meet at Tarzan Jetty later that night.

Knockout held his share of the spoils in a nylon bag that also contained, in wraps of paper and cellophane, the heart of the girl he had butchered. He watched his partner turn round on the whining machine before leaving the way they had come, then he turned to his house.

He had inherited the building from his father who had inherited it from his own father, and so on for four generations. He had once shared it with two other brothers who had since secured the necessary forged papers to fool immigration in Nigeria and in Germany. He liked to think that most of the big families in Lagos still had family homes close to his in the shanties of Lagos Island – even if the once proud homes were now divided into rooms rented to the people the city didn't care about.

He walked down the side to the backyard where a wire fence stretched from his wall to the wall of the adjacent bungalow, five feet away. He undid the latch lock on the tiny gate and stepped into his back garden.

'Whisky, Gaddafi.'

Two pure-bred Dobermans ran up to him from their open cage and jostled for his fingers to rub through their black coats. Unlike many such breeds, they still had their tails. He was shocked when he discovered Dobermans aren't born with stumps; he couldn't understand how anyone could chop off a puppy's tail shortly after birth. What kind of person would do that to a dog?

Knockout unwrapped the parcel and tossed the meat at his dogs. He had been excited since the thought first occurred to him to feed his dogs a human heart. He watched the beasts nervously sniff at their meal, nudge it with their wet noses, look up at him unsure, then sniff again. The thrill built in him; he couldn't wait to watch them feed on it. One dog snatched the meat and growled, clenching it in its jaws. The other fought for it and Knockout chuckled. Then his eyelids retracted as a thought landed in his head. Shit. Why didn't he think of that before?

He had to get the meat from the dogs. He dived into the tussle and quickly learned that dogs, in the end, would always be dogs.

21

The sky was brightening and cocks were crowing in the slum beyond the station, but Ibrahim was at his desk, waiting for the police commissioner's next call, wondering what he would give as an update, and fighting the urge to send an officer to buy a packet of cigarettes.

If he hadn't called the commissioner in the first place, to boast about capturing the Iron Benders gang, the man would probably have continued sleeping and missed that damn report on CNN. The commissioner had also asked how it happened. Ibrahim started to explain how his boys had been out on patrol but the commissioner cut in with 'How did you let this get on the news?' As if Ibrahim could arrest every journalist in Lagos.

A local report would have been bad enough. Pompous reporters would have asked rude questions, used long words, and blamed everything in the country on police corruption. Their real gripe would have been where the crime happened: Victoria Island, one of the few enclaves of relative safety in the city – an illusion that those who lived on the Island, and those who aspired to, guarded religiously.

But it had gone international, and no doubt, the same way Nigerians are always ready to take issue with any foreigner who dares to insult their country, everyone who had a platform from which they could make noise would be fuming and raging at CNN's 'unfair' portrayal of Nigeria. And he, Ibrahim, would be the grass under which two elephants battle; not because a murder was committed on his watch, but because he was the policeman meant to make sure that such things, when they do occur, do not tarnish the precious image of the island of the rich.

There was also the body in the cell. Taking care of the carjacked woman was easy. She thanked him when he told her that all she had to do was sign a statement that he had written for her. In few words it said she was carjacked near CMS, she walked to the station to report the crime, she recognised one of her assailants in the cell and the suspect became violent and tried to escape. The woman signed the statement and he tore up the one she had originally written. A police car took her home.

Amaka, on the other hand, would not be so easy to gag – if that was even possible. Ibrahim's predecessor briefed him on her: 'Be careful with that one. She'll give you a lot of problems.' He called her a 'frustrated lesbian' and the charity organisation she worked for, 'a club for prostitutes.'

When she first turned up at the station and said that a girl was raped while in detention there, Ibrahim called his predecessor and asked what to do. The man laughed and told him to find a lawyer.

She walked into his office as if she was his boss. She introduced herself as the girl's lawyer. He wanted to warn her that he knew all about her, but when she shook his hand and beamed that beautiful smile, he forgot she was the enemy.

She was not the man-hating witch he'd expected. She appeared to be intelligent and she acted politely. She didn't want to take the police to court; she just wanted the officer in question to pay the girl he had arrested in front of Y-Not. She agreed that it could hardly be called rape, as the woman offered sex for her freedom. But, she argued, since the girl shouldn't have been arrested in the first place – for soliciting, which couldn't be proved – she shouldn't have had to bribe anyone to regain that freedom. The way she saw it, the officer owed her client for services rendered, or the Nigerian police had to answer a case of forced imprisonment and rape.

She impressed him with the way she made her case, though he tried not to show it. She was blackmailing him to make a police officer pay a prostitute – too many crimes to list. But she was dangling before him a court case that made her offer seem gracious.

Unlike his predecessor, he understood her. Here was a woman who used her knowledge, her charm, and anything at her disposal, to look after other women. She was like Mother Theresa to those girls.

Several times, he asked for her number but she always turned him down. It had become a friendly game they played each time they met. If he were single, she would be the perfect wife for him. But why would such a sophisticated girl want to marry a common policeman? They would never have met, and even if they had, they would never have been friends. Yet, her line of work made her a constant visitor to his station and they were now friends, even if not close.

Why did she have to come that night? Why didn't she stay in his office when he told her too? She'd taken the British journalist to the Minister of Information. What happened in the cell would probably be discussed. What was she doing with the bloody minister, anyway? Maybe powerful men were her thing? Perhaps for all her charity work and seeking justice for all womankind, she was just like every other female. Maybe that was why she had never allowed them to talk seriously about seeing each other outside the station. Maybe he just wasn't rich enough. Either that or she really was a lesbian.

He picked up the phone: 'Musa, come here.'

'This is not Musa, sir. This is Oyebanji.'

'Where is Musa?'

'He has handed over to me, sir.'

'Call him now. Tell him to come back.' He slammed the receiver down. If he couldn't go home, nobody could. He thought for a moment then he picked up the phone again. 'Tell Musa to go to the Sheraton. The Minister of Information is staying there. I want to know when he leaves and who is with him when he does.'

Five minutes later, Oyebanji called back. 'Sir, Musa is not answering his phone, sir.'

'What? OK. Ask Femi and… whoever is there, to come to my office now.'

In a room at the back of the station, four shirtless officers, sweating and exhausted, fists sore, were interrogating a member of the Iron Benders gang.

Hot-Temper stepped in front of the body of the boy who was hanging head-down from a broken ceiling fan to which his feet were tied using a watering hose.

'Ol' boy, you want to die for nothing?'

The boy's body swayed, dripping sweat and blood into a pool on the ground.

'We already have information that one of the cars you snatched was the same one that you and your boys used to dump the girl that you killed. The madam you snatched the car from has come to report in this station tonight. Just tell us who sent you and we'll let you go.'

The boy did not respond. Hot-Temper sucker-punched his belly. He coughed blood and saliva.

'Bring the ring boiler.'

An officer who had been leaning against the wall unplugged the apparatus in his hand. It had a plastic handle with a power cord on one end, and the two ends of a thin metallic tube on the other. The tube, which was about the thickness of a pen, extended five inches from the handle and looped four times to form a coil at its furthest point. Through swollen eyes, the boy saw the glowing red coils dangling before his face. His body twisted like a snake held up by its tail.

'Remove his trousers,' Hot-Temper commanded.

The policemen gripped the boy. With the tips of his thumb and index finger, Hot-Temper held the boy's penis and inserted it into the hot coil. The boy's scream reverberated through the building and the smell of burning flesh wafted through the room. He howled and writhed like a snared animal until his energy was spent and then he whimpered like a dog.

Hot-Temper yanked the coil away, and with it, sizzling, seared skin.

'Look at what you are making me do to you for nothing. I don't want to punish a young boy like you. I know that other people sent you. Just tell me their names and all this will end. If you don't tell me what I want to know, I will put your blucos back into this thing and plug it until you fry like suya.'

The boy recalled the blood oath he swore when he joined the gang. He remembered the walk through a bush path. He smelt the wet soil. He felt the tickle of tall blades of grass brushing against his arms, leaving dew on his skin. All around him there was nothing but beautiful, open green land. He was standing in a clearing before the oiled wooden figures and bloody plucked feathers of the shrine. He tasted the dry blandness of his own blood mixed with the blood of the others as he sipped from the clay pot that sucked his tongue. He remembered the witch doctor's warning: 'You have vowed to keep each other's secrets secret. Whoever breaks the promise made upon this ground shall be swallowed by the ground.' He saw the decaying bodies of those who had sworn at the same shrine and went on to break their promises. They were left to rot unburied, scattered like refuse around the shrine, playthings of the gods. If he spoke now and broke the oath, he would die and he would become one of those shameful corpses whose souls would roam this earth as ghosts unable to find their way home. He would die.

Hot-Temper opened Inspector Ibrahim's door without knocking.

'Sir, we have a name, sir.'

'Really?'

'Yes, sir, Chucks.'

'Chucks? The same Chucks?'

'Yes, sir.'

Ibrahim leaned back in his chair. He had seen it happen all too often; a small-time crook gets ambitious and forces the police to come after him in spite of the bribes he has paid in the past. Chucks had been a reliable snitch who told on any criminal encroaching upon his operation. His scam was selling impounded motorcycles that he bought illegally from officers of the state's traffic task force and passed on as imported second-hand goods. So, he had graduated to stolen vehicles?

'Oga, let me take some boys and go and bring him, bulldog style.'

Ibrahim thought about it. It was almost five in the morning. Matori, where Chucks lived, would have long woken up. If they tried to grab him bulldog style like Hot-Temper suggested, without a warrant, they could provoke a riot. It had happened before. Officers sent to get someone were barricaded by spare parts traders and Area boys. They didn't allow the men to leave until they gave up on the armed robbery suspect they had gone to fetch. Besides, he could update the police commissioner with news of a suspect, and have another update later when they had the man. Why waste the two good updates on one? There was only one thing to do: wait until night when Matori would be quiet.

'Who else knows?'

'Knows what, sir?'

'About Chucks?'

'Just me and the officers interrogating the boy.'

'Good. Don't mention it to anyone. I want to see all of you now.'

In a notepad on his desk he wrote 'Operation Bulldog.' He drew two lines under the words and added 'The siege on Matori.'

22

Only a hunted spy sprinting through the gates of a friendly embassy would understand how I felt when we drove into Eko Hotel.

I pointed out empty spaces but Amaka continued driving and pulled up far from the entrance. Her phone rang again. Who kept calling her? She had promised to explain everything once we got to the hotel. What could she possibly have to say? If she wasn't working with the inspector then who was she? Why had she come to get me? What exactly did her charity do? Why did she lie about being sent by Ade?

She answered her phone as she stepped out of the car. I couldn't tell if she was speaking English. She walked with quick strides and was soon ahead of me, deep in conversation. Did it have something to do with me?

In the early morning light I got a better look. She was tall: maybe five ten. She had a well-toned, yet feminine body. She worked out. She stood straight and walked in a no-nonsense manner that made her even sexier. Who was she?

Climbing the steps leading to Eko Hotel's open-plan lobby she put the phone down. Someone was on hold.

'I'm sorry. I had to take that call,' she said.

'It's all right,' I said. I was embarrassed that she might have caught me looking at her bum. 'You have to check out of your room now. I'll get another room in my name for you to move into, for the moment.'

'Wait a minute. You still haven't told me what all this is about.'

'I'll explain everything in the room. Please, we have to hurry up and get you into another room.'

I saw her point. At her urging, we walked in separately. She met me at my room and together we packed my bags then I went downstairs to check out, leaving my suitcase behind. I made a show of walking out of the hotel with my laptop bag and a backpack. Then when I was sure nobody was watching, I walked back in from the other side and took the elevator up to her floor. I knocked, half expecting her to be gone with all my belongings but she smiled as if she was happy to see me. Maybe she had also been afraid I wouldn't return.

She had taken off her shoes.

'Did you tip the man at the desk?'

'Yes. Five thousand naira like you told me to.'

'Good. He'll remember you.'

'You've done this before haven't you?'

'It may come as a surprise to you but I generally don't spend my nights rescuing white boys from the police.'

'OK, how long are you going to play that card?'

She smiled again. She took my laptop bag from me and placed it on the table.

'OK, let me explain.'

As she spoke, she sat on the bed and lifted her legs onto the covers. She pulled a pillow under her arm and lay on it on her side, facing me.

'Like I said, I work for a charity. We work with prostitutes. We give them counselling, financial support, shelter if they need it, medical aid, that sort of thing. Prostitution is illegal in Nigeria so nobody watches out for these girls. They are molested, extorted, short-changed, raped, killed, you name it. You saw something tonight, outside Ronnie's bar?'

I nodded. The terrible scene replayed itself in my mind. I pulled a chair up to the bed and sat facing her.

'What you saw, it has happened before. Not like that, not so openly, but at its worst that's exactly what we try to prevent. Many of the girls have my mobile number. Someone, one of them, called to tell me what happened. I went there and luckily for you, people saw you getting yourself arrested. That's how I got to know about you. I knew you would need help so I came to find you.'

'Well, thanks for that. I guess I owe you one. But why come for me?'

'You work with the BBC, that's what you told the police. You went out there for a reason. You sensed a story, didn't you? I came to get you because you're a journalist. What happened at Ronnie's will happen again and nobody will do anything. You know why? Because the girls are prostitutes and the killers are powerful men. The media won't get involved because they're afraid of these men. The police won't investigate this murder, or those girls who disappear daily. Why? Because they too are afraid of the big men who pay them to keep the peace and the so-called black magic they use the girls for. When I heard that a foreign journalist had witnessed it all, I had an epiphany.'

I wanted to tell her that she was right; I had gone out there because I sensed a story, but I did not work for the BBC. She wasn't done, and it seemed a frivolous little detail, so I let her continue.

'You witnessed something terrible. You can do something about it. You can tell the world what you saw.'

'I have to tell you something. I'm trained as a lawyer. This journalist thing, I'm not really that good at it.'

'You're a lawyer?'

'Yes. I mean I used to be. I still am, I guess, but I always wanted to be a journalist, so now I am. But I am not John Pilger or John Simpson. I wish I were, but I'm no investigative journalist.'

'I'm a lawyer too.'

'Really?'

'Yes.' She looked at me as if she'd recognised a friend, and I swear her face softened, changed, almost like she saw me in a different light. 'I'm not asking you to do anything dangerous. All you have to do is write. I have information that I'll give you. Names and facts. You will treat me as a source, of course. Nobody can know about me. I can give the information to any other journalist, but you've seen what happens with your own eyes. This is your story to tell.'

'All I have to do is write?'

'Yes. All you have to do is write.'

I got that feeling you get when you still have time to back away, to make a different choice, but you can't stop yourself making the wrong one.

'And you think it'll make a difference?' I said.

'I hope it will. It's a start. The alternative is to do nothing. I won't do that, and I don't think you want to either. Someone has to tell this story. You were there, at Ronnie's, for a reason. You went outside to see the girl, for a reason. Who better to tell this story?'

'You said you have information. What kind of information?'

She rolled her legs off the bed and sat on the edge. Barely a foot separated us.

'What I'm going to tell you now, I have never told anyone. You'll understand why, in a moment.'

She reached for her bag on the bed then changed her mind and turned to face me.

'I keep a record of men who use prostitutes in Lagos. I have their names, their addresses, their phone numbers. I know where they work, what they like, how much they pay. I know the ones who are rough, the ones who are married, the ones who beat the girls, the ones who take two girls at a time, the ones who don't use condoms. I have their licence plate numbers, their pictures, videos of them. I know where they take the girls – you name it. I even know the ones who know each other.

'I record it all to keep the girls safe. When a man wants to pick up a girl, she sends me his licence plate number. I check my records and tell her what to expect, how much she can charge him, stuff like that. I've been keeping the records for over two years now and the database keeps growing. There are some names I have that I tell the girls not to go with.'

'The violent ones?'

'Yes.'

'What do they do to the girls?'

'What men do. What do you expect? They beat them up, refuse to pay them, rape them, make them sleep with their dogs. I don't get it, how a man, given birth to by a woman, can be so cruel to other women. But, never mind about the beaters and the rapists; I'm taking care of that. The names I'll give you are the names of the men who girls have gone with and then vanished.'

'Those who did that to the girl tonight?'

'Yes, the people who do such things. I must warn you, they are powerful men. They are well connected, rich, and influential. I see them on TV accepting awards and making speeches and I wonder what people would do if they knew what I know about them.'

'Exactly what do you know?'

'I know that girls have gone with some men then simply dropped off the face of the planet. A man picks up a girl, she's never seen again, doesn't answer her phone, doesn't call her parents, doesn't touch her bank account, what do you think happened to her?'

I remembered the girl in the gutter; had she simply gone with the wrong person?

'How did you come to be involved with all this?'

I had imagined that her charity simply tried to get girls off the street, but now it was obvious that her operation was a lot more complex than that. She didn't judge these women, challenge their way of life or try to change them. She only wanted to them to be safe. Was she was once one of them herself?

'You mean why do I work with prostitutes? I guess it was bound to happen.'

She got off the bed, eased out of her jacket, straightened her blouse and pushed her feet into her shoes.

'Where are you going?' I didn't want to be left alone right then but more than that, I knew that something big had just dropped onto my lap. This wasn't going to be a simple column or a random blog post. This was not just a scoop – it could be a detailed, thoroughly researched book. The kind that's talked about on breakfast news. It was perhaps more than I could pull off, I mean, writing a book is not something you just wake up and do, but thinking of the possibilities filled me with excitement. I could do something big here, something important, something that could change my life and other people's lives. Perhaps coming to Nigeria wasn't such a mistake after all. I thought of Mel. What would she be doing right now? Probably on her way to work, or to the gym; I forget which days are her gym days.

'Are you OK?' Amaka said.

'What? Oh. Yeah. I'm good.'

'I need to take care of something. Go to sleep. You need to rest. I'll be back soon, and in the morning there are some people I want you to meet.'

23

A band was dismantling their equipment by the poolside, watched by a red-haired woman cradling a large wine glass, and sprawled on a lounger. A tanned greying couple were hunched over a table, seemingly sharing secrets. At the far side of the pool, a black man and a white woman held hands over a burnt out candle. The only other guest was a girl in a sparkling, black evening gown. She was alone. Her clutch bag was next to an unopened bottle of water. She looked tired. Amaka did not recognise her.

The waiter at the bar was biting the end of his pen, staring at a calculator and a notebook. Amaka walked up and asked if the bar was still open.

'We're open 24 hours ma,' he said.

She stepped away, out of earshot and called Chief Ojo. They had been exchanging text messages: her, assuring him that she would come and him asking her where she was. She told him that a girlfriend had hit someone's car so she had to go to the police station to bail her out. He offered to call whoever was in charge at the station. She thanked him but said she had it under control.

He answered on the first ring.

'Iyabo, where are…'

'Are you in your room?'

'Yes. Where are you?'

She ended the call.

She asked the barman how much a bottle of Rémy Martin XO cost. She didn't have enough cash for it and she didn't want to pay with her MasterCard so she asked for a bottle of VSOP and a glass. He started filling the glass with ice and stopped mid-scoop when he looked up at her.

'I'm sorry ma. I thought you asked for ice.'

'It's OK. Can I have another glass, please? I don't like to pollute my poison.'

While he fetched a dry cup she opened the bottle. She took a long swig and their eyes met.

'I'm really thirsty.'

He nodded. She left him the change.

The doors of the lift closed and she poured brandy into the glass and placed it on the floor then she reached into her bra and pulled out a small sealed plastic bag. In it was a generic form of Rohypnol. She had researched the drug. It was odourless, tasteless, and unlike the original medicine which had a blue dye and dissolved slower when liquid was added, it was undetectable. She poured it into the bottle.

Getting it was simple; she had kept some of the evidence from a case in which a girl woke up bleeding in a boy's hostel. The girl had no memory of what happened: anterograde amnesia – a side effect of the drug. The rapists, however, had made a video and sent it to their friends who sent it to their friends. When Amaka and the girl went to the dorm room with the police they discovered the rest of the supply. The medical students bragged that nothing would happen to them. A particularly ugly one asked: 'Do you know who I am?' Amaka didn't, but she found out: his father was an ex-governor. She spent her own money convincing every journalist she could trust to run the story. The boy ended up disowned by the father who also used the media to set the record straight that the boy was not biologically his. The young men got life sentences: the maximum penalty for rape in Nigeria.

Her phone, tucked into the back of her skirt, vibrated. She held the bottle up to check that the drug really wasn't detectable.

She undid a couple of buttons on her blouse, pulled her skirt up, and pushed her breasts together before she knocked. The door to the presidential suite opened as if he'd been waiting behind it. He was fully dressed, smiling like he was grateful. She sniffed and looked into the lobby. She stepped past him and walked into the lounge. It was large, like someone's living room. There was a round dining table with six chairs next to a bar area, and there were three large sofas arranged around a large TV on a wall. She walked further. There was a separate dining area with a long dining table and ten chairs but there was no one there. She sniffed. The bedroom door was open. Inside, cigarette smoke was suspended in a slowly morphing cloud. She knew he didn't smoke. She walked inside and found the culprit: a gaunt man in a white dashiki similar to his, in an armchair, a fat long cigar between his fingers and a bottle of Star in his other hand. Shit.

If the stranger was his friend, Mr Malik, it could be a setup. She'd been trying to find the man called Malik, but no one seemed to have his number, or know where he stayed, or the places he visited. Apart from the girls who had told her about him, no one she had spoken to had ever heard of him, or of the secret sex club he ran.

She had already stepped into the room and the man had seen her. It was too late. He smiled. She thought she smelt a hint of marijuana. She looked into his ashtray, in the middle of the bottles of Star and Guinness. They had been drinking for a while. The girls had told her that Malik neither drinks nor smokes. They also said he was light-skinned and had a beard; this man was dark and clean-shaven. Her initial panic abated, but was immediately replaced with disappointment. She had been looking for Malik for weeks and she was beginning to suspect that Malik was either a fake name, or he knew he was being tracked, and was hiding in the shadows, watching the hunter.

Chief Ojo grabbed her by the waist and she jumped. He laughed and tried to kiss her on the lips. The smell of alcohol was strong on his breath. 'Iyabo, meet my friend, retired navy commodore Shehu Yaya. Shehu, this is my babe, Iyabo.'

'The one who has been keeping you waiting?' The retired navy commodore stood up. He was at least a foot taller than the Chief and her. He grinned and held out his hand in slow motion. Amaka pulled her hand away when she felt the tip of his index finger rubbing the inside of her palm. She shot him a look. He winked. She pulled Chief Ojo to the door.

'I told you nobody could know about this.'

'Shehu is my good friend. We were meant to be at an important function together but it didn't hold. He has been keeping me company till you come. Shehu, you have spooked my babe.'

He could have just said sorry. Why did he have a ready explanation? She looked at the man. She could say she was going to get something from her car.

Shehu pulled his cigar from his lips.

'Darling, it's OK. I'm sorry to crash in on your little soiree like this. The old boy told me he was lonely waiting for a pretty bird and I just had to see for myself who the chick was that could keep a whole chief waiting. You are right, 'ol boy, she is absolutely stunning.'

Chief Ojo put his arms around her.

'Off-limits.'

They both laughed.

Or, she could tell him she had to return to the police station.

'I have to go. This was a bad idea.'

'Oh no, please don't go. Shehu is leaving soon. Shehu, you are leaving soon, aren't you?'

'I'll be on my way once I finish my Star.' He returned to his chair and sat down. 'I never waste a good drink. Darling, you look scared. I don't bite. Come and sit.' He patted his lap.

She tried to smile but only managed to stretch her lips over tightly clenched teeth. She didn't recognise him; that was good. It meant he didn't recognise her either, and as far as she knew, Chief Ojo wasn't into threesomes that involved other men.

'You brought a bottle.' Chief Ojo moved to take the brandy from her. She held both the bottle and her glass away. He took the bottle anyway, and downed a large gulp.

'Shehu, brandy?'

Shehu searched the stool for an empty glass before shaking his head.

'No thanks. At our age it's not a good idea to mix drinks. Iyabo, come and sit.'

Chief Ojo held her hand and led her to the bed. It had not been slept in. She climbed in and sat against the headboard. The two men carried on with their conversation. She picked the TV remote and listened while flicking channels. Shehu kept trying to make eye contact. She watched Chief Ojo. He was drinking from the bottle.

The men were talking about a friend's undeclared-but-well-known intention to run for governor of the state. Amaka knew the man they were talking about – not personally – but she didn't know he had any ambitions for political office. She also knew that he liked young girls: eighteen was too old for him. Chief Ojo's eyelids closed. Amaka pressed her foot into his side. He stirred and looked at her.

'Don't sleep.'

He smiled and squeezed her thigh.

'Shehu, let's call it a day.' She thought he sounded drowsy.

Shehu didn't seem to have heard him. He was watching the smouldering glow on the end of his cigar, as if the burning tobacco revealed something profound. He blew a jet of smoke at it. The glow brightened.

'OK.'

He stumped his cigar and stood up.

'Are you seeing me off or what?'

Chief Ojo groaned. He looked at Amaka. She rolled her eyes.

'I'll see you off to the lift.'

He stood up and spread his arms to stop himself from stumbling. Amaka watched. She suspected his friend was watching too.

'I need to use the toilet first. Give me a minute.'

'Just how many bottles have you had tonight?' she said as he stumbled towards the bathroom.

Shehu waited for the door to shut then he turned to her.

'Darling, I like you. Can I see you when you are done with this old man? My house is here on the island. He doesn't need to know.'

That he was so direct did not offend her as much as the fact that it didn't bother him to have sex with her just after she had had sex with his friend. How about sparing a thought for the girl? He might as well have asked to join them in bed. She didn't know what to say. He waited. She had to get rid of him, but what did he know about her?

'So, he showed you my…' She waited for him to finish the sentence for her.

'Your what?'

She raised her eyebrows at him.

'Your picture?'

'No. Never mind.'

'Can I see you later?'

'Don't tell him.'

'No problem. What's your number?' He was holding his phone.

She looked at the closed bathroom door. She took the phone from him and punched in her number. It was the same number she had given his friend. He was saving it when the door opened. Chief Ojo eyed them suspiciously. She shifted on the bed and concentrated on her fingernails.

'Can I take a picture of your girlfriend?' Shehu said. He pointed the lens of the phone's camera at her face.

She picked up a pillow and hid behind it.

'Please, don't. I don't look good in 2D.'

'Old Navy, you haven't changed,' Chief Ojo said. 'What do you want my babe's picture for?'

He led his friend to the door and held it open for him.

'Goodnight, old friend. My girlfriend and I need some privacy now.'

They shook and winked at each other. He shut the door and secured the latch then he turned and saw Amaka unbuttoning her blouse.

'Why did you show him my panties?'

He fixed his eyes on her red bra, not wanting to miss the moment it came off.

'I did not...'

He blinked. She was out of focus. He wiped his face but she remained a blur. He took a step and felt himself falling.

24

As Chief Ojo dropped to his knees, he rubbed his face and shook his head. He reached for Amaka and fell forward. With his head by her feet, she slipped out of her skirt, knelt, and shook his shoulder.

'Chief Ojo,' she said, pinching his neck.

'Chief.'

She slapped his cheek and he moaned. Slapping and kicking, she made him crawl along the wooden floor of lobby, across the lounge, into the bedroom and then onto the bed. She pulled off his clothes then she took the bottle of brandy to the bathroom and poured it down the sink. She saw her reflection in the mirror, naked and sweating. She yanked the light switch. She turned the tap and cleaned the enamel bowl, finishing just as the water turned hot.

His phone was on the stool between bottles and cups. The battery was low. She searched the stored contacts for Malik, then for all entries that started with M, then she went through the entire address book. She recognised politicians and businessmen. She dialled the number of the girl who had helped set him up. It showed up as 'Mr Ali.' She selected all contacts and pressed delete.

She scrolled through pictures of his family, of him, of him next to politicians, then opened his movie folder. She clicked the first file and heard the monotone voice of a girl played through the phone's tiny speaker as the picture panned from white sheets to the girl standing on the bed.

The girl could have been as young as fifteen. She was naked save for a string of purple beads round her waist. Her hands were on her hips, her legs apart, and she was talking to someone, asking them what they wanted her to do with it. His voice said 'Put it inside.' The girl bent to pick something up, then hunching, with one hand reaching between her legs from behind and the other in front, she brought a bottle of Rémy Martin to her vagina.

Amaka stopped the video. She saved all the recordings to the memory card and removed it, then she tossed the phone to the ground.

She tugged at the sheets under him, ruffled the pillows and scattered them, then she got in next to him. She placed his hand across her breasts and held her phone up to take a picture, making sure her face didn't show.

She got dressed, put the memory card into her bra and dialled the only other number saved on her phone.

'Hello?'

'Does your phone receive MMS?'

'Who is this?'

'Does your phone receive picture messages?'

'Yes, who is this?'

She ended the call, selected the picture she had taken and sent it to the woman's phone. Next, she sent the name of the hotel and the room number. Then she removed the SIM card, broke it in two and left the pieces in the ashtray.

She retrieved her panties bundled up inside his trousers, then went to the bathroom where she held them over the basin and put her lighter underneath. The fabric burned slowly, curling away from the flame. It smelt of burning hair.

Then she walked out of the suite, closed the door behind her, looked down both sides of the corridor, took a deep breath and exhaled slowly.

If his marriage wasn't ruined, she would send his wife the videos from his phone. If she learned that he was still picking up young girls and beating them up, she would send the videos to every blogger she knew. This was only the first punishment. He was still going to pay more - him and the man they call Malik - when she found him.

25

Someone knocked. I knew it was Amaka but I checked all the same. She had been gone for about an hour and I was beginning to think that she had left me at the hotel. She walked in before I could make way for her, her shoulder brushing against my arm.

'I'll take a quick shower,' she said. 'Promise not to fall asleep before I'm done.'

'Promise.'

She returned dressed and smelling of soap.

'How much do I owe you for the room?' I said.

'It's on the house,' she said, sitting on the chair.

'No, really, I've got to pay you for it.'

'Pay me by writing the story. What are you doing in Nigeria, anyway?'

And with that we started talking. Conversation flowed easily, meandering without pause into unrelated things. Soon I was telling her about the sports injury that ended my rugby playing and she was telling me where to get good coffee beans in Lagos.

'Are you married?' she asked.

I can't remember what led to that, or if anything did: by now we were talking like old friends. I showed her the bare fingers of my left hand.

'That doesn't mean anything,' she said. 'I don't know one

married man in Lagos who wears his wedding ring.'

'I'm not married.'

'Girlfriend?'

'No. What about you, are you married?'

She showed me her left hand.

'Touché. No boyfriend?'

'Several.'

'Several?'

'Yes, I can't seem to decide what I want, so I keep many just in case one of them is the one.'

'Me too. I've got loads of girlfriends back home.'

'OK, I was joking. But you, let's examine that.'

I wanted to tell her about Mel and about my connection to Nigeria. If I'd had a picture of her on my phone, maybe I'd have shown her, but like Jen she might have concluded that I wasn't over her. 'How old are you?' she asked.

'Thirty-six. Why?' I knew better than to ask her age. I guessed she was also in her thirties.

'Thirty-six, handsome, single. Why are you single? What's wrong with you?'

'Work,' I lied. Mel wanted out. She returned my CDs a week after our 'break.' She also went on a date with someone. She mentioned it casually when I called to ask if I could drop by. She didn't have to tell me she was going on a date, and I didn't ask her who with.

'There was someone, but we broke up recently.'

'Who broke it up?'

'She did. She said she wanted a break.'

'Is she a lawyer too?'

'No. She studied history but she's a financial analyst. Why?'

'We lawyers tend to end up with lawyers. You should know that. Do you want her back?'

'No, it's over.'

'Shame.'

'What?'

'What's her name?'

'Mel. Melissa.'

'It's a lovely name. OK, time to sleep. We have a lot to do in the morning.

Can I borrow a pair of boxers?'

'Oh. Yeah.'

I went to get a pair from my bag. When we started dating, Mel used to sleep over in my T-shirt and boxer shorts.

'Clean ones,' Amaka said.

I looked at her and we both smiled at the joke. I fetched a pair of boxers from my bag and turned to hand them to her. She was unbuttoning her blouse. I looked away, but not before I saw her lacy red bra.

'I hope you don't mind that I'm staying?' she said.

'No, it's cool.'

She stepped into the boxers and drew them up under her skirt, which she then pulled down, and she climbed under the duvet. I considered the floor: it was going to be uncomfortable even if I got them to bring up extra covers.

'And I hope you don't mind that I'm sharing your bed?'

'It's cool.'

I got in on the other side.

'Sweet dreams,' she said.

I switched off the lights and stared into darkness. What did she mean when she said 'Shame'?

The din of a ringing phone woke me up. I shifted and realised that I was still fully clothed. I checked the time: the luminous dials on my wristwatch showed just past noon. A second later I remembered where I was and everything that had happened: Ronnie's, the police station, and that Amaka was in bed next to me. I checked to make sure. She was fast asleep and facing me, her lips slightly parted.

That I slept at all surprised me. I had gone over everything we'd said, enjoying the conversation all over again. And I'd spent God knows how long wondering if she was turned on too, under the same duvet as me, barely an arm's length separating us.

She stirred and I closed my eyes till I heard her going for her phone. It had stopped ringing. I looked and in the glow of the screen I saw that she was puzzled.

I was dying for a smoke so I faked a yawn that became real, stretched, and got out of the bed.

Her eyes darted towards me. I didn't know how long she'd been aware that I was awake watching her.

'Where are you going?' she said.

'Hey. Good morning. I'm going to have a smoke outside.'

I hoped she would tell me it was OK to smoke in the room, but she nodded and answered the phone that had started to ring in her hand. I stepped into the corridor, shut the door and realised that I hadn't taken the key card. She would have to open the door for me when I returned. I would see her in her bra again.

I planned to go to the poolside and get coffee to go with my cigarettes but I remembered a newspaper stand down by the car park, at a stretch of huts where foreigners haggled over souvenirs and got thoroughly screwed. If CNN had reported the events of the night before, the local media would have caught on to the story as well.

The sun felt good on the back of my neck. The air-conditioned room had felt like winter. At the huts, a man in a long white robe behind a table of stacked newspapers handed one to me. I was standing shoulder to shoulder with Nigerian men who were also flipping through papers they had not yet paid for or were just renting. I was standing with them as if I were one of them and I had done this morning ritual with them many times before.

In time I was done with the paper. It was the Vanguard and there was nothing about Ronnie's Bar in it. I went through it again just to be sure. I scanned the papers on display, then paid for a copy of This Day, which I only bought because it felt wrong not to buy something.

I flipped through the pages until a headline screamed at me: 'Mutilated Body Dumped in Victoria Island, Foreigner Arrested.' I read the article quickly, searching for my name. Surely, I was the foreigner. I knew the story but there were a few additions, some background, some embellishments, and a few inaccuracies. 'The police commissioner was unavailable for comment. Early reports indicate that the police were quick to arrive on the scene where they arrested several suspects including a journalist with the British Broadcasting Corporation, BBC, who witnessed the crime.' At that, the entire world seemed to suddenly run towards me from all directions. I was a suspect? I had witnessed the crime?

I almost dropped the paper. I saw Inspector Ibrahim's face morphing into a dangerous frown as he read the same paper. I saw Sergeant Hot-Temper cocking his AK-47 and laughing as he emptied the gun's magazine into my belly. It was no longer such a good idea to be out in the open, outside the room, away from Amaka. I started walking back to the hotel, quickly, taking my death warrant to show her. She would understand why I had to get on a flight back home to London as soon as possible.

I had walked a few steps into the lobby before I recognised the blue and black uniform, but I was already committed to the next step – what felt like the loudest footfall in the world. Inspector Ibrahim was at the front desk with his back to me, his elbow resting on the marble top, talking with my friend Magnanimous the concierge. I froze.

Magnanimous looked at me. I stood fused to the ground. His eyes shifted and he said something to the inspector. They both focused on an open book on the front desk. I willed myself to move but my feet weren't listening.

I took two steps backwards before turning. It took all the willpower in me not to break into a full run. With each step, I expected to hear my name called or to feel the no-nonsense hands of a police officer grabbing me by the collar. My heart felt like it would explode through my sweat-soaked shirt. I went back to the huts. I wanted to keep walking but my white face stood out. I needed to hide. I sat on the ground, on a patch of grass, and watched the hotel from behind a hedge of hibiscus flowers. Inspector Ibrahim stepped out of the lobby area and pulled a pair of sunglasses on to his face. He looked my way. I bent lower. He spoke into his radio.

'Oga, any problem?'

I looked up and saw a dozen men looking down at me. It was the vendor who had spoken. He was standing in front of the group of bewildered people, bemused by the mad foreigner on the ground.

'I'm OK,' I said, but he didn't look convinced. I opened up the paper and pretended to read.

'Oga, you need help to enter the hotel?' Maybe he thought I was drunk.

'No, no.'

I peeked over the top of the newspaper. A blue, battered looking police car pulled up to the entrance. An officer got out and the inspector handed him the radio.

'Oga…'

'I'm fine. I just need to rest my legs for a while.'

He shrugged and said something in his language that made the other men laugh. Crazy white man, I guessed.

The inspector got into the back of the car. The officer waiting on him closed the door then got back into his own seat. No sooner had the aide shut the door than the car began to move with some speed. I ducked. The car revved past my hiding place. I waited till it merged with the Lagos traffic that had built up outside the hotel, then I ran.

Amaka looked at the caller display suspiciously. The number was withheld. The only people who had that number were the girls who relied on her for the information she gave them and they knew better than to withhold their number when calling her. She answered anyway.

'Hello?' she said, ready to chastise the person on the other end.

'Hello ma.'

'Who is this?' She usually received calls on the number between nine p.m. and one a.m. when men went out looking for girls to pick up.

'It is Rosemary, ma.'

'Why is your number blocked?'

'I'm sorry, ma.'

'What can I do for you?' Her tone was bland. She did a mental search. She wasn't sure which Rosemary it was, but if the caller had the number she must need her.

'Please ma, I have a man's number that I want you to check for me.' The girl sounded nervous.

Amaka tried to place the voice. 'The man wants to pick you at this time?'

'No ma. I'm looking for my friend, ma. Yesterday night she followed a man. I took the car number like you told us to do. She had not returned by the time I went home. When I woke this morning and she still hadn't returned I decided to call you.'

She got up from the bed. All night she had struggled to suppress involuntary thoughts of who the murdered girl could be. She had sent text messages to all the girls whose numbers were on her phone, asking them to text her back with their locations. Some of the girls had still not replied. The girl who called to alert her had since switched off her phone – she'd probably gone into hiding.

'Have you tried calling her phone?' Amaka said.

'Yes ma. It is saying the caller is not available.'

'What is her name?'

'Janet, ma.'

'Her real name.'

The girl paused. 'Ekaite, ma. Ekaite Okoro.'

'Why didn't she contact me before following the man?'

'She is a new girl, ma. She just came from the village.'

'So, why didn't you tell her what to do?'

Hers was a frustrating job; it demanded superhuman patience. How was she to look after these girls if they didn't look after themselves? Each day, with each call she took, each girl she tried to keep safe, she felt a bit of herself slipping into their world and into the dark cracks in which they lived, where sex and perversion mixed freely with violence and death. Each day, a bit of her was erased to make space for the fear and concern she carried for each and every one of them.

'What is the licence plate number?'

She was already booting up the notebook computer that she carried in her handbag all the time. There was no way to know for sure that the information she provided was keeping the girls safe, but the fact that she had not lost one girl must mean something. Her constant fear was the day a girl would turn up dead because she didn't warn her not to go with someone. For the past few hours, she had been constantly tortured with the possibility that this day had finally come. Some days she wished she could just make all of them stop working altogether, but it was a fleeting fantasy that she never allowed herself to dwell upon. What would they do? Starve? Become house girls and be raped by their bosses? Beg on the streets and be raped by the Area boys? She knew these girls, these women. She understood their world. For them, prostitution was not a choice; it was a lack of choice.

Knockout wrote down the name and the address Abigail, his on-off prostitute girlfriend, got from Amaka, and gave her the five thousand naira he had promised her. She had once boasted of a secret number she could call to get information on any big man in Lagos. Lucky for him he remembered her careless bragging when he was watching his dogs feed on the heart he had hacked out of the girl with his jack-knife.

Abigail took the money and counted it before tucking it away in her handbag – a habit of her trade.

'So, what happened to your hand?' she asked again, referring to his crudely bandaged right arm.

'Forget that one.' He got up to leave her rented room.

'So, you won't tell me why you are looking for the man?'

'It is none of your business.'

'He picked up one of your girlfriends?'

'I said it's none of your business.'

'OK, if you say so. But are you going to just leave like that? Won't you take care of me?'

She spread her legs on the bed to let him see that she wasn't wearing anything under her pink chiffon slip.

He took one look at what was being offered. He knew he would have to pay extra for it, but it was not the expense that made him turn her down. He was just more excited about getting into the human ritual killing business with Chief Amadi.

26

The lift felt like it was taking forever. I couldn't wait. I charged up the stairs, two steps a leap. At the second floor I stopped to catch my breath. Panting, my brain went into overdrive and connections formed: Amaka, her charity, the list of names, the story she wanted me to write. Could she have something to do with the article in This Day? All those calls she made. And where did she disappear to when we got to the hotel? Was I being played like a pawn in some deadly, righteous game of hers? Was she upping the stakes for the benefit of her story?

Anger slowly built till it encouraged me up the remaining two flights of stairs.

Magnanimous was in front of the room poised to knock on the door when he saw me.

'Ah, Mr Collins. Good morning.' His face brightened.

'Good morning.' What was he doing at the door? I was now suspicious of everyone. I tried not to take deep breaths but he could see that I was sweating.

'Why were you hiding from the police?'

He had played along in the lobby so I guessed I owed him the truth.

'Something terrible happened at Ronnie's Bar yesterday. The police came and took me with them.' I gave him the abbreviated version. Despite his smile, he seemed to have a knowing look when I mentioned Ronnie's bar, swiftly replaced by a concerned grimace.

'Yes, yes. I heard,' he said. And then: 'Terrible thing. Terrible thing.'

And just like that it was gone. The next instant, his face had fluidly changed into a blankness that a poker player would have envied.

'The policeman came to return your phone. You left it at the station.'

'He did? Where is it?' I held out my hand.

'Oh, I am sorry. When I saw you, I told him you checked out in the morning.'

So, Inspector Ibrahim had only come to return my phone and not to cart me away for more lessons on how not to cross the Nigerian police. I felt like a coward. It was a feeling I was fast getting used to.

'How did you know I was in this room?'

'A member of the night duty staff told me you had moved into a different room with a girl.'

So much for not being seen. He really did have a gift for facial expressions: he looked alarmed and concerned at the same time, then lowering his voice and nodding towards the door to the room I shared with Amaka, he said: 'Are your things safe?'

'Yes,' I said. 'I moved everything over this morning.'

'No. I mean, things like your passport, money, valuable things.'

'Oh no. She's not that kind of girl.'

It registered with me how quickly I defended her, and with that I became ashamed that I'd already made up my mind to forget her story and flee to London – to abandon the woman who had saved me from Cell B. Then again, there was the piece in the newspaper and many questions. I waited to see him get into the lift before I knocked. Amaka opened the door quicker than I expected. She had a towel wrapped around her body. I held the page with the article up to her face even before I stepped in.

'What do you know about this?' I said. I was surprised to hear the forcefulness in my own voice. Surely I wasn't angry with her. How could I be? But for once, I felt like I was thinking clearly, and good sense demanded that I not be soft.

She took the paper and walked back into the room, reading where my finger had pointed. I watched her butt cheeks gliding against each other under the towel.

She tossed the paper onto the bed as if it was of no consequence.

'I had nothing to do with it,' she said. Without turning to look at me, she unravelled the towel, held it out in both hands and rewrapped it around her then crossed her hands across her chest.

I believed her but I couldn't just back down after charging in accusing her.

'Your friend was just here looking for me,' I said, as if it was her fault.

'Who?'

'The bloke in charge at the station.'

'Inspector Ibrahim?'

'Yeah, him.'

'He's not my friend.'

'But you know him.'

'In my line of business I meet many people, police officers included.'

'Well, he was just here. I almost bumped into him.'

'Did he see you?'

'No.'

'Is he still here?'

'No. He left. They told him I'd checked out.'

'Good. If he really wants to find you he'll search every room in every hotel in Lagos but he'll not come back to this one.'

She was right. Now it made sense that she had not simply checked us into another hotel.

'You want to back out now?'

'Look, I don't really know who you are,' I said. 'I don't know anything about you. Who are you? What is this charity you work for? What's it called? What exactly do you do and why do you do it? I'm getting myself mixed up in this thing and it appears there's so much I don't know. I've been arrested, I've watched a man's head blown to pieces, and I'm being hunted. It's all a bit too much. I've got a feeling there's a lot you're not telling me. If we're going to do this thing together you've got to tell me everything – full disclosure. I'm one minute away from getting back on a plane home.'

She turned and I saw that she had been crying. My shoulders dropped.

'Hey, what's wrong?'

'Nothing. Nothing is wrong. Street Samaritans.'

'What?'

'Street Samaritans. That's the name of the organisation I work for. I'm the fundraiser – officially. What I do for the girls, what I told you about, that's my own thing. No one else knows about it and I want to keep it that way. What else do you want to know?'

I wanted to wrap my arms around her and tell her everything was going to be OK.

'It's OK,' I said.

'No. You want to know, so I'm telling you. What next?'

I stood, silent.

'Ask me.'

I had to say something. 'What did you do before this?'

'This is the only job I've ever had.'

'Really, Amaka, it's…'

'Next.'

'Does the job pay well?'

'No. Money isn't everything.'

'Why this? Why this job?'

'Why not?'

'No. Earlier, when I asked you why you do this, you said it was bound to happen. What did you mean by that?'

She took a long look at me with her wet, unblinking eyes. I felt like hiding. She walked over without releasing me from her gaze and she pushed her hand into my trouser pocket. I felt her fingers wriggling against my leg. She got my cigarettes and lighter. With her thumb she flicked the lid of the pack of Benson & Hedges and with her front teeth she pulled out a stick. She lit it, took a short drag and pulled a chair over.

'Sit,' she said.

I pulled the chair from the dressing table and sat opposite.

'You saw that girl? You saw what they did to her?'

I nodded.

'Have you ever seen anything like that before?'

I shook my head.

'I have. And it was someone I knew.'

She took a long drag and released the smoke slowly.

'I was brought up by house girls, maids. When I was young my parents were away a lot. My father was a diplomat. My mother didn't want me to keep changing schools so I stayed in Nigeria but she always went with him wherever he was posted. So, the nannies raised me. I hated her for leaving me alone like that but now I understand she didn't trust her husband to be alone.

'I had a particular nanny, my favourite, Aunty Baby. She was Ghanaian. In those days a lot of Togolese and Ghanaian people were in Nigeria. Economic refugees. They thought they would find a better life in Nigeria, but most of them, especially the girls, ended up becoming servants, housemaids. They were the lucky ones. The rest became prostitutes, to survive. These were people who came from middle class families, whose parents were university professors and doctors, but when they came here we would only trust them to clean our homes, cook our food, clean up after our children.

'Aunty Baby was a special person. She loved me. She talked a lot. She told me about her life in Ghana – about the boyfriend she'd left back home, about her journey to Nigeria, about the sixty-year-old gateman down the road from ours who wanted to marry her. She was twenty-one. She'd been studying to be a nurse back in Ghana, but in our house she was the nanny and even then only by name. In truth, she was my servant – my own personal slave at my beck and call. But she was also my friend. She was the perfect big sister I didn't have. I'm an only child.

'We had other servants in the house, many. A lot of them were boys. I developed early. The house boys were the first to start touching me, then the drivers, then the gatemen. I was only ten and it was open season on me. They would take me into a room and make me do things to them.

'One day, I don't know how, Aunty Baby found out about me and one particular boy, Sunday. My father was posted to South Africa, then. When they came back, Aunty Baby told mum what had happened; she was furious. She called for Sunday and me. She asked him what he'd been doing to me. He lied that it was he who had caught Aunty Baby interfering with me and that he had threatened to report her. Mum asked me if this was true. I said it was. I don't know why, but I lied. I said Sunday was telling the truth.

'I remember the look on Aunty Baby's face that day. She kept calling my name, 'Amaka? Amaka?' Mum slapped her. Beat her. It was horrible. That evening, my parents sent her away. She didn't have a place to go but they had the soldiers march her out. They sacked everyone in the house. They got me a new nanny. A Nigerian girl. Iyabo.'

She stopped to take a drag.

'Several years later, when I was in university, I saw Aunty Baby again. It was at the hairdressers. She was the one who recognised me. She came to me and lifted the dryer off my head. She shouted 'Amaka' and embraced me. This woman, who I had betrayed, embraced me. I thought she worked there but she had only come to do her hair. She took me to her house. She had a nice flat. She told me all that had happened to her since she left our house. She lived rough on the streets for some time, doing odd jobs, then in '83 when immigrants were being expelled from Nigeria, she married the old gateman so she could stay.

'The man died and his sons drove her from the house he left behind. She was back on the streets. She started selling her body to feed herself. At first, she had boyfriends. She had five or six at a time, all young, decent civil servants. She told me about each one of them: the one with a small dick, the one with a bent dick, the one who was miserly, the one who snored like the wind if he didn't have sex before he slept, the one who wanted to marry her.

She joked about the shit she had gone through because of me.

'We laughed together at her stories. She and I, we always had laughter. I visited her often at her flat. I met her prostitute friends. We all became friends. They also told me their stories. They had all been forced into that life when they ran out of choices. They were not loose women; they had dreamt different lives for themselves but survival forced them onto the streets. She never once brought up my betrayal.'

She took another drag and looked around for where to flick the ash building up on the tip of her cigarette. I got the glass ashtray from the dressing table and held it out for her. She took it from me and uncrossed her legs to rest it on her lap.

'One day, I gathered the courage to ask for her forgiveness. She told me I didn't have to. She said I was a child then; what did I know? But I knew I'd forced her into this life – I had made a prostitute out of her. I begged her to let me do something, anything, to make it up. I would give her money, I would confess to my parents – anything.

'She told me about the people who looked after her at her worst time. She never wanted to sell her body like that. She never blended in. It was killing her. She heard about some foreigners talking about getting people like her off the streets and she went to look for them. That's how I came to know about the Street Samaritans.

'The charity was in trouble and they needed money. She told me that if I felt like doing something, maybe I could get my parents to donate money to them. She told me that every month a portion of her income still went to the Street Samaritans. I decided to work for the charity instead.'

'You were raped as a child.'

'No. It never went that far.'

'So, when did you lose your virginity?'

I heard myself and realised it had not come out as intended. Thoughts of her getting violated as a child had caused me to ask such a foolish, insensitive question.

'I did not lose it,' she said. 'I got rid of it.'

She stubbed out the cigarette.

'Ever since I was young, men have always wanted to sleep with me. I was curious and my virginity was in the way. One day, I picked the right boy and I let him do it. For me.'

'What about Aunty Baby. What happened to her?' I knew she was going to tell me she was murdered, like that girl in the gutter.

'We are going to see her tonight.'

'But I thought…'

'It wasn't her. It was Iyabo, her replacement. When the girl came to live with us my dad told me she was a distant relative. Anytime my parents were away she would sneak out of the house and not come back till the next day. One day she didn't come back. The soldiers – we had soldiers guarding the house – called my parents. Iyabo had been gone for two days when mum flew in from Togo. I went with the driver and a soldier to pick her up. We were staying on the mainland then, Ikeja GRA, not far from the airport. We had sirens. The driver was going so fast that it was too late by the time he saw the body.'

She stopped to light another cigarette.

'We drove over her. She'd been on the road, three blocks from the house, all the time. The soldier told the driver to stop. I watched from the backseat. He went to the body and covered his nose. We all knew it was her. She was still wearing the red jeans mum gave her.'

She offered me her cigarette. I took it. The tip was wet. I wanted to hold her against my chest.

27

'Maybe he was using a different name?' Ibrahim said.

The plain clothes police officers standing in front of his desk looked at each other and were somehow able to communicate who should take the question.

'I don't think so sir,' said the man who had drawn the short straw.

'Why? Why don't you think so?'

'Sir, after we checked the hotel register we also spoke to the night manager and he assured us that the minister has never lodged at the hotel before.'

'He said that?'

'Yes, sir.'

'But that doesn't mean the minister wasn't there. Maybe it wasn't official. Maybe he sneaked in and sneaked out. He didn't want anyone to know he was there. He used another name and he didn't come with his official car. He used her car. She took him there. No one would have recognised them.'

Ibrahim was talking to himself and his subordinates were dutifully standing at attention until he started making sense again. He pulled out a pen from his breast pocket, held it in a fist, brought it close to his forehead above his right eye and rubbed his thumb up and down its lid while looking at the ceiling.

'Do you know what the minister looks like?' Ibrahim asked.

The officer hesitated before shaking his head.

'What about you?' he asked the other.

'No, sir.'

Ibrahim nodded like his point had just been proven.

'So, you see? They were together. They were at the hotel. Together.'

'Sir,' the first man said. His body shrunk in subservience. 'Who, sir?'

'Who?'

'You said they were together, sir?'

'Yes. They were.'

'Who, sir?'

'What?'

'Nothing, sir.'

'I know what to do.'

A knock broke the awkwardness. They all turned to look. An older policeman walked in.

'Sir, the car is ready,' the man said.

'Car?'

'Yes, sir. You said I should go and wash the car; that we are going to Victoria Island.'

'Oh, yes.'

Ibrahim ran his palm over his stubble and ended by scratching under his chin where it had begun to itch. He was going to a mansion in Victoria Island to meet with people he didn't like, but who could cost him his job, if they so decided.

His predecessor had advised him that when the crimes of the mainland spill over into the island, the island folk panic. They form associations, they plan, they plot, they influence legislation and they get police commissioners sacked and replacements installed. They do whatever it takes to keep their beloved island safe, including ordering a senior police officer to come to waste valuable police time pandering to their self-importance. The man blamed them for his redeployment to Jigawa.

It was getting close to the next hour. The police commissioner would call for another update. The man had stayed up through the night as well, perhaps also taking calls. During one of the tense, short phone conversations, he told Ibrahim to attend the Victoria Island Neighbourhood Association meeting in the afternoon. That call made Ibrahim sick to his belly.

The association was probably one of the most powerful organisations in Nigeria. He knew about it before his predecessor warned him not to offend any of its members; it brought together oil company chief executives, senators, retired generals, important politicians, old money, new money and government money. Rival CEOs sat together on its board, united by their determination to protect the sacred image of their island. The attendance register of meetings read like a Who's Who of the most powerful people in Nigeria. He knew a few enterprising businessmen who rented apartments on the island just to become members of the association.

It was, he concluded, his bad luck that it was having its monthly meeting that day, and an ominous sign that they had specifically asked for him.

The landlords and landladies would have questions for him. They had heard about the ritual murder, some of them had even seen it on television. Now they wanted the man in charge of Bar Beach Police Station to come and explain to them how such a thing could have happened on their island, close to their homes and offices. They would demand assurances that this was a one-off, and that he would never let it happen again. He had to convince them he could deliver on this. If they were not convinced, they would find another police inspector and he would be posted to Kontagora. If he was lucky. 'Compulsory retirement' was how they got rid of the man before his predecessor.

The meeting was at the home of a retired Supreme Court judge. He made his driver use the siren, so that they would arrive early and find a place to park in the vast compound.

Chauffeured bulletproof cars brought the other attendees. He didn't have a bulletproof car and here they were, arriving in theirs to ask him why the police were not chasing down more armed robbery gangs.

A servant showed him to his place: a dining table chair at the end of a large parlour where sofas and armchairs had been arranged in rows all facing the same direction. He sat quietly adjusting his uniform while waiting to be summoned.

The meeting started with prayers, then they worried over a new nightclub that had opened on one of the quieter streets of the island. A man with a grey Afro, dressed like he was on his way to play golf, said he would look into it. Ibrahim recognised him. He was the State's Commissioner for Works and Housing. Next, they were concerned with a proposal by a son of a wealthy northern industrialist to build a commercial helipad on the island. The boy's family did not live there. The Commissioner for Works and Housing told the meeting he would see what he could do.

Waiters in white uniforms rolled in platters of hors d'oeuvres on silver trolleys. It would be unprofessional to eat, so in agonising silence he suffered the smell of food while others snacked. The meeting continued with talk of funerals and parties and he began to hope they might have forgotten about him. His mind wandered to Amaka and the minister. What was she doing with him so late, and at his hotel? Surely she was sleeping with the man. He got out his pen and rolled it in his palm.

'Where is the policeman?'

The host was standing in front of his guests, his weight supported on a walking stick.

Ibrahim felt them watching him as he walked to the front. Hardly had he composed himself when the salvo of questions began to fly.

'Who is the girl?'

'Have you caught the people who did it?'

'How did CNN hear about it?'

'Is it really a ritual killing?'

He answered their questions, making sure to include at every opportunity the actions he had taken to keep the island and its inhabitants safe. He was mostly making it up as he went along.

'What exactly are we going to do about this?' an old, Greek lady said. She was the matriarch of a successful shipping family.

'We have doubled patrols around the Island, ma. From tonight, checkpoints will be deployed at every route into V.I. We are working on a lead that should help us recover the vehicle used in the crime. I assure you that I am dedicating all my resources to getting to the bottom of this. We will solve this crime. In the meantime, increased visibility of officers will make sure that this does not happen again.'

He considered it, but decided not to tell them about the operation planned for later that night when his men would lay siege on Matori and hopefully capture Chucks and the dregs of the Iron Benders gang.

A young man who had been listening with the intense look

of someone really paying attention raised his hand. He was MD of a new bank that was doing very well on the stock exchange.

'How many ritual murders have the police solved in the past?' the MD said.

'To my knowledge, not many, sir.'

'Give me an estimate. Would you say, fifty, forty per cent?'

'I do not have the statistics to answer that question, sir.'

'Give me a ballpark.'

'Sir?'

'Hazard a guess.'

'Maybe 10 per cent, sir.'

'Or five, or one?'

'Maybe.'

'It seems to me that if the police are so inept at solving such crimes, it would be a criminal waste of your resources to try to solve this one. It seems to me that concentrating your resources on policing Victoria Island would be more efficient.'

Ibrahim understood what he was saying. He had spoken the minds of the rest of his neighbours. They didn't care what had happened to the girl – she wasn't one of them. They only cared that it had happened on their island. They would rather have him keep the island safe than solve this crime and get justice for the girl. He avoided looking straight at the MD. Who was this small boy telling a police inspector how to do his job?

'Yes, sir,' he said, and hoped that was the end of that.

Saying sir to someone younger than him never made him happy.

The son of a former governor spoke next.

'What is this thing in the papers about a BBC reporter who was arrested at the scene?'

'We arrested no such person.'

'Good. We don't need that kind of exposure here. I'm sure you understand?'

The boy co-owned a wine bar on the island. His customers were mostly expats. The others agreed by exchanging murmurs with each other.

'But if you didn't arrest any Briton, why are the papers reporting that you did?' said an elderly lady whose family owned one of the biggest five-star hotels. Like the young man and the rest of them, she didn't want to lose her foreign clients. She had a hotel while others had luxury flats that they rented out to expats for yearly sums that could buy whole buildings in other parts of the state. VI attracted foreigners and their deep pockets because it was a relatively safe place to live; a place where crime was low and the police did not disturb them.

'I don't know where they got the story from,' Ibrahim said.

'But they cannot just make up something like that. Did you arrest someone then later release him or what? Were there foreigners at the club when the thing happened?'

'Yes, ma.'

The governor's son wanted clarification. 'Yes, there were foreigners at the scene, or yes, you arrested someone and later released them?'

'There were foreigners at the scene and we took their statements.'

'But you arrested suspects at the scene?'

'Yes.'

'Real suspects or just people you found there?'

'We took some people back to the station for questioning. Naturally, by the time we got there the perpetrators had fled, so there was no one to arrest. We took some statements at the scene and we took some people back to the station for proper interrogation. There were no suspects, just people who may have seen something. We needed to get as much information out of them as possible. That is the only reason we took some of them back to the station. We didn't arrest anybody.'

Ibrahim didn't like where the questions were leading. The people arrested at the crime scene were not criminals and everyone knew it. But it would have looked bad in his report if he didn't make any arrests, even if he later released all the 'suspects' on the same day. It would also not have gone down well with his boys if they had not 'arrested' some suspects who would later pay 'bail' to regain their freedom.

'I'm just wondering where they got the story from,' the lady said, turning expectantly to the woman seated next to her and resting back into her chair.

From the back of the room someone else spoke.

'I think we need to increase the monthly allowance to the police. We need to pay for extra officers on patrol and get more patrol cars. I move that we increase the allowance to ten million.'

A soft murmur travelled round the room. They all agreed and Ibrahim had to bite his lip to hide a smile.

It was not an official obligation to honour their invitations but these were the people who subsidised the paltry budget the Federal Government provided. Their generosity propped up his officers' meagre salaries and at least kept some of them from temptation. Being posted to the station at Bar Beach was the miracle his pastor had seen in a vision. His children were in good schools, his wife was back in school to finish her master's, and he now drove a reliable second-hand Honda Accord with air-conditioning and an automatic gearbox. The monthly allowance they gave him paid for it all. The poor girl's murder had just doubled that allowance. He had no doubts he could keep their island safe, or at least appear to. The only thing that threatened it all was the situation with the British journalist. And Amaka. He had to find her and find Mr Guy Collins of the BBC.

The meeting ended and the rich folk gathered into groups. The man who had suggested increasing the monthly allowance caught up with Ibrahim.

'Good afternoon, sir,' Ibrahim said and bowed slightly as he greeted Chief Ebenezer Amadi. Amadi asked after each of his five children by name.

'They were a bit tough on you in there, Ibrahim,' Amadi said.

'Sir, it's not easy.'

'Don't mind them. Here, use this for the weekend.'

Ibrahim slipped the brown envelope into his pocket and they bade each other farewell. He got into the back seat of his car and looked inside the envelope. It contained fifty-dollar bills, one inch thick. He looked at the rear-view mirror, at the driver and the officer in front. He put the envelope back into his pocket and smiled as he left the mansion.

28

The two officers sent to spy on the minister were waiting on a bench outside the station when Ibrahim returned. They marched to his car.

'Sir, we have double-checked at the Sheraton and they are 100 per cent sure that the minster did not lodge there last night,' said the officer who had the initiative to return to the hotel to check again. 'We also enquired with the ministry. They said that for the past week the minister has been on official duty in Norway. He isn't due back for another week.'

'You called the ministry?' Ibrahim said, eyeing him suspiciously.

'Yes, sir.'

'What did you tell them?'

'I asked for his aide-de-camp. They told me he was with the minister and I asked where I could reach him. That's when they told me they are in Norway, sir.'

'They didn't ask why you were looking for the ADC?'

'No, sir.'

'Good. And you're sure they are in Norway?'

The two answered as one: 'Yes, sir.'

Ibrahim went to his office and shut the door. He searched his desk for the card Amaka had given him and found it under a file. He sat down and held it up, scrutinising it as if somewhere on the printed ink and the scribbled note he would find the answer to this new puzzle.

On the one hand, she wasn't sleeping with the minister or at least she hadn't done so last night. On the other, she had tricked him into releasing the British journalist. That was a serious crime. But why had she done it? She didn't know the man: she had said that, and the man didn't seem to recognise her. So why did she come looking for him?

Ibrahim had been warned to be careful when dealing with her, but now Amaka had committed an offence and it was she who now had to be careful with him. She had hindered an investigation, aided a suspect in absconding – he was sure he could think of many more laws she had broken. All he had to do was find her, and find the man she took from him, particularly now she didn't have any Minister of Information to protect her.

He stood up from his desk, pulled out his pen and began to pace his office. He had her. He didn't know where to find her but he had more than enough resources at his disposal. Before any of that, he had a press briefing to attend to. In a few hours he would parade the captured members of the Iron Benders gang to the media. An opportunity like that, to show the nation that the police were doing their job, was too juicy to miss. He also had to set things in motion to deliver all he had promised to do, or lied that he had done, at the Victoria Island Neighbourhood Association meeting. Then had to revise the plan for Operation Bulldog: the siege on Matori. After that he would hunt Amaka down.

Guy's phone was still in his pocket. He switched it on and found the address book. There was only one number stored on it. He copied it down onto a notepad. Next he checked the media folder but there were no pictures. There was, however, a voice recording.

As he listened, he realised it was from the night before, outside Ronnie's bar. The sound was not perfect but he could make out clear voices mixed in with the noise of cars passing or starting, then he recognised his own voice talking to the British journalist. He listened to the entire recording – it was long. He played it again then he sent an officer to find a charger.

He set the phone down on his desk, leaned back in his chair and clasped his fingers behind his head. So, the man had planned to do some reporting, after all.

Ibrahim's phone rang. It was the police commissioner again. He knew he was also under a lot of pressure. Once news about the body got out, he'd have received a lot of phone calls from residents of Victoria Island, some of them able to terminate his appointment at the slightest irritation. He would have been dealing with their panic and subtle threats. He answered the phone, sitting to attention in his chair.

'Ibrahim, I just received a call from the British High Commission. Do you have a British citizen in detention?'

Ibrahim bit his lips. 'No, sir.'

'Did you have any British citizen in detention?'

'No, sir.'

'So, where did they hear that?'

Ibrahim shut his eyes as he prepared to lie to his boss.

'There were many white men at the scene of the incident last night, sir. We questioned some of them. Someone must have seen us talking to them and assumed we were making arrests.'

'So, I can tell the High Commissioner that there is no British citizen in detention at your police station?'

'Yes, sir.'

'OK. Make sure your story doesn't change. Do you understand?'

He kept the phone to his ear long after the call had ended. Finding Amaka and the Briton had just moved to the top of his priority list.

And then Guy's phone rang.

'Can you hear me? It's Ade. I'm back from Abuja. I am at the hotel. They said you have checked out. Guy? Are you there?'

He pressed the end button, paused to think, then composed a text message. 'Can't hear you. Wait for me in the lobby.'

29

Bent over, dripping with sweat, holding his stomach in both hands, Catch-Fire left the toilet and closed the door. His bowels made a sound like water rushing through a pipe. Pain radiated up to his throat as he reached for the handle. He grabbed his belly and leaned forward. Alcohol, mashed-up food and blood gushed out of his mouth with the force of a firefighter's hose.

The girls in the corridor backed away as vomit ricocheted off linoleum. Another wave passed through him, forcing tears from his eyes as he threw up again. He placed his hands on the wall.

'It is Chief Amadi. He has poisoned me,' he said, his head down, debris and saliva dangling from his chin. 'He wants to kill me.'

The worst of the spasms shot through his body and forced him onto his hands and knees in his own vomit. He threw up blood.

'My phone,' he said.

Chief Amadi was eating lunch at the twenty-two chair dining table he had shipped from France. He checked to see who was calling, then he checked the time.

Catch-Fire looked up at the girls.

'Chief has killed me,' he said. 'He has poisoned me. Catch-Fire must not die. Go and call Doctor. Catch-Fire must not die.'

Doctor raced ahead of the girls who had come to fetch him from his one-bedroom home and clinic where he diagnosed his neighbours with unpronounceable ailments and charged them whatever they could afford for his treatments.

He arrived in the corridor to find Catch-Fire, surrounded by worried onlookers, in a foetal position. He recognised the smell that greeted him.

'Doctor, help me.'

Doctor bent close to the ground and sniffed to be sure, then turned and sprinted out the way he had come.

'Ah, even Doctor has run away,' one of the girls said.

Catch-Fire watched the man leave and he began to cry.

'I am dead. Catch-Fire don die. Chief Amadi has killed me.'

Outside, Doctor searched for two weeds that grow side by side wherever there is vegetation. He found them and plucked a handful of each. He ran back to Catch-Fire's side and began to rub the plants together in his palms, chanting incantations as he did, and spitting into the paste after each dose of spells.

Catch-Fire clenched his teeth as the paste was brought to his face. The girls and the men gripped him and forced his mouth open and Doctor put the medicine in his mouth.

'Bring me water,' Doctor said.

Catch-Fire struggled with the hands holding him down. The doctor pinched his nostrils closed and poured water down his mouth and Catch-Fire gagged.

'Leave him.'

Catch-Fire, regaining his freedom, spat and spat again.

'Don't vomit it,' Doctor said.

Catch-Fire looked at him and spat again.

Chief Amadi finished his meal. The last call from Catch-Fire had been over an hour ago. Maybe it was all over by now. Then the phone rang again. The caller withheld their number. He decided to answer it. If it was Catch-Fire, still alive, he would tell him he had been in the bathroom and he would invite him to a drink at his house.

'Chief Amadi? Is this Chief Amadi?'

Amadi did not recognise the voice.

'How may I help you?'

'Chief, you do not know me but I know you.'

Strange introduction, he thought. It was likely someone about to beg for a loan that wouldn't be repaid.

'Who are you?'

'My name is Kanayo, they call me Knockout. I am the gentleman that your boy, Catch-Fire, used guns to chase out of his house yesterday.'

Amadi shifted the phone to his better ear.

'Yes?'

'I brought business for the boy, but because his girls are making his head swell he chased me out like that.'

'Yes? So, what can I do for you?'

'Sir, I want to do business with you.'

'What kind of business would that be?'

'The kind of business you do with that boy, sir.'

'I do not know what you are talking about, Kanayo. I think you have mistaken me for someone else.'

'No, sir, no mistake at all. Please, call me Knockout – that is what my friends call me. I understand that you don't want to talk on the phone but I assure you, I am very professional, unlike that pickpocket they call Catch-Fire.'

'I don't know what you are talking about, but perhaps if we meet in person, you can explain yourself to me better.'

'I am near your house, sir.'

'Near my house?' Amadi walked to a window and parted the curtain. 'How do you know where I live? How did you get this number?'

'Don't be afraid, sir, like I told you, I am very professional. I can get anybody's number that I want to get in this Lagos.'

'Is that so? You say you are near my house?'

'Yes, sir. I am calling you from outside.'

'Come to the gate.'

A short man approached the compound alone, holding a phone to his ear. It was the man from Catch-Fire's house. Amadi rang the gatehouse and asked the guard to let his visitor in. He met Knockout outside in the compound.

'What did Catch-Fire tell you?'

'Sir, he told me everything. I came with a fresh heart that I took out myself but he did not want you to know. That is why he used his prostitutes to disgrace me in front of you like that. You should not be doing business with that kind of person, he is not professional. You and me, we can do better business together. Clean business.'

Amadi could have struck him with a blow to the head, confident that his guards would then finish him off. That would take care of one loose end.

'And you are sure you have the stomach for my kind of business?'

'I can do anything, sir.'

'Do you know what I do?'

'Rituals.'

'Do you know what kind of rituals?'

'Money rituals.'

'Do you know what we use for the rituals?'

'Human beings.'

'And you can do this?'

'Yes. I brought one heart for you yesterday. Anything you want me to do, I will do, Chief. Tell me to bring ten hearts right now and I will go and come back with twenty.'

'No, no. That is not how we do it. You don't just kill people anyhow. The gods must choose their own meal. There is a lot you still have to learn.'

'Teach me, sir.'

'And you are sure you will not be like your friend, Catch-Fire? He has failed me several times. I've been trying to replace him.'

'Never, sir, I am very professional, and that cockroach is not my friend.'

'Can you keep a secret that even the maggots feeding on your dead body would never hear?'

'For sure, sir.'

'OK. But first you must do one thing for me. To prove yourself.'

'Tell me, sir.'

'You must eliminate Catch-Fire.'

'Eliminate him?'

'Yes.'

'As in, kill him?'

'Yes.'

'Is that all?'

'Today.'

'Today, today?'

'Is that a problem? You can't do it?'

'I can do it, sir. No problem at all.'

'So, what are you waiting for? Kill him then call me and I will tell you where to meet me. And remember, if like Catch-Fire you fail me too, you will also be eliminated.'

'There will be no need for that, sir. I will never fail you. Consider the boy eliminated.'

In his air-conditioned room, two of his girls took turns fanning him with a newspaper folded in two, while Catch-Fire sat exhausted and sweating, spitting each time he remembered Doctor's saliva.

'Let's go and burn down the bastard's house,' one of his girls said. The others nodded.

'If you go there, he will kill all of you, and then he will come back here and kill me too.'

'Let us go to the police.'

'And tell them what? They'll arrest me and even report to him that I came to report him. He is a powerful man. The police are working for him.'

'We cannot just let him go like that. What if he had killed you?'

'But I am alive. Ordinary poison cannot kill Catch-Fire.' He spat. 'He will try to kill me again.'

'Why does he want to kill you?'

'That is what I don't understand. Maybe the spirits that he worships have told him to kill me.'

'We have to kill him before he kills you.'

'Yes. Yes. Bring me my phone.'

He had been thinking about it and the two people he knew who could do the job were Go-Slow and Knockout. He would offer the one million naira under his bed to Go-Slow, the one he could trust.

He called Go-Slow and explained his predicament. He swore by the womb of his mother that it was not a trap. He begged Go-Slow to come to his house immediately, and he begged him not to tell Knockout.

30

Amaka lit another cigarette, stood up and walked to the curtains. I walked up to her, stopped behind her, our bodies inches apart, the tip of my nose almost touching her braids. She didn't move. I raised my palms to the sides of her shoulders and they just floated there. I dropped my hands back to my sides. I wanted to say something but couldn't come up with the words. I held my breath, tucked my hands under hers and wrapped them around her body. I was ready to let go at the slightest objection. Her fingertips touched my forearms. She gripped and pulled them tighter round her. She held my arms in place with one hand while holding her cigarette with the other.

I buried my head into her neck, drew in the faint smell of her perfume, and said 'Everything is going to be OK' as she stroked my arm.

'I got a weird call this morning,' she said, 'A girl. Her friend followed a man last night and by morning she had not returned.'

She pulled my arms apart, gently, went to get the ashtray and sat back in the chair. I sat opposite.

'She had the man's plate number.'

'Was he on your list?'

'Yes. Chief Amadi. He has a huge house here on the island.'

'Is he one of the bad guys?'

'I'm not sure. He pays well. He treats them well. He usually takes them to his house. Two at a time. Always. He's only been on my list for a few months. None of the girls have complained about him, but a girl once said she recognised him. She said that about five years ago, on the mainland, he and his friends picked up six girls and none returned. Apparently, it was a big thing then. It happened before I started keeping the records. The girl said she wasn't a 100 per cent sure it was him, and no one else seems to have heard the story. But all the same, anytime a girl calls about him, I tell them not to go, just to be safe. I hear some girls still go with him but he tends to stick to the same girls.'

'Could he be the one we are looking for?'

'Looking for?' She looked bemused.

'Yes. The one who murdered that girl? Is that what you are thinking?'

'Look who has suddenly become the detective.'

'If you think it might be him, we have to do something about it.'

'Slow down, cowboy. I didn't say I think it's him, just that the call was strange.'

'How so?'

'Well, for one, the girl sounded scared.'

'We need to talk to her again.'

'That's the thing; she called with a hidden number.'

'Do you know her?'

'I'm not sure. She told me her name. Rosemary. I've called every Rosemary on my phone. It's none of them. I should have asked for her number. There are so many of them. The girls, I mean. The way it works is they never meet me. It's safer for me and for them that way. They don't know who I am. They don't even know my name. Someone tells them about me and they call. First time they call, I save their number and I tell them what to do when they get to a man's house. They take pictures if they can, copy down the licence plates of the cars in the compound, the address, anything at all that can be used to identify the person. They send everything to my phone and when they get back they call to tell me what he was like. I usually recognise the voices but this girl's voice escapes me, maybe because she was scared. Nervous. I should have asked for her number.'

'We must find her, Amaka.'

She looked into my eyes and smiled. 'That's why we are going to see Aunty Baby. If anyone can find someone in Lagos, it's her.'

The way she looked at me seemed odd, but she was smiling.

'What?' I asked, smiling back.

'You just called me by my name for the first time. And you pronounced it correctly.'

My smile turned to a blush.

Her eyes focused intently on mine, perhaps waiting for me to say something. Those eyes of hers: she could stare at me with them till I shrunk and backed down. She could smile with them without moving another muscle on her face. Now she was doing something I'd not seen yet. Her eyes were speaking to me, saying what she wanted me to know, what was OK for me to do. I saw myself lean towards her, put my arms around her and kiss her. That is what I should have done, but instead I said the first string of words that popped into my mind: 'Are you hungry?'

Her body shifted slightly – as if she was surprised. She held my eyes for a moment longer then stood up so swiftly that the towel, now loose, simply stayed back on the chair. She stood in front of me, perfectly and beautifully naked, just inches away. We both went for the towel and our hands touched. Something flowed from her fingers into mine, raced up through my body and gathered at my groin. I let her have the towel. She wrapped it round her body, went to the bathroom, and the lock clicked.

Inspector Ibrahim's car pulled up in front of the Eko Hotel lobby. He had changed into a pair of blue jeans and a black T-shirt that he kept at the station. He picked a spot close to the elevators where he could see people coming and going. He scanned the faces around him. Sooner or later, Ade, the man who had called Guy's phone, would walk into his trap and eventually lead him to the journalist.

The muffled sound of the shower running behind the locked door convinced me that it was pointless to check if she was OK. Anyway, we were going to have lunch. The lock clicked and she peeped through the gap in the door. She smiled shyly.

'Can you please pass my clothes?' she said and stretched out a wet hand.

I gathered her stuff and handed it to her. She locked herself back into the bathroom. I didn't know what to make of the fact that she felt she needed to lock the door. I was still processing my thoughts when she stepped out, smiling, dressed, and looking smart in the clothes she had worn the night before.

I got clean clothes from my bag and went into the bathroom. It was steamy. The mirror was misted up. I stepped into the shower cubicle conscious of the fact that she had just been there, naked.

'Shall we?' she said when I stepped back into the room. She didn't look at me.

'Sure.'

Why didn't I kiss her when I had the chance? Was it because of Mel? Was it cowardice? Did she want me to kiss her? Had she dropped the towel intentionally?

We didn't speak as we waited for the elevator. Inside, she gave me that polite smile again and looked away. I couldn't take it anymore.

'Amaka.'

'Yes?'

She turned to look into my eyes. I had not thought of what to say so I pulled her to me and kissed her.

Ibrahim was standing with his back to the elevator when it opened. A porter behind him picked up two Louis Vuitton bags at his feet and stopped. The woman standing next to the porter lowered her large shades and said 'Oh my.' The man in the lift, eyes closed and still kissing the woman whose arms were around his neck, found a button without looking and the doors began to slide together.

Ibrahim turned to see what the fuss was about. He caught the last two seconds of the metal doors closing and he turned back to searching for Ade.

I expected her to push me away but she put her arms round my neck and drew me closer. Our lips did not part as we fumbled to our door and I tried to open it.

At the foot of the bed I pushed my hand under her shirt, pretended to just want to rub her back, then I began to work my way up to her bra fasteners. She took her arms away from my neck and forced them between us. I thought I'd blown it and

I let her go, ready to apologise, then I realised she was undoing the bra herself. I went to kiss her again and our heads bumped. We laughed. As we kissed she unzipped her skirt and I pulled back to yank off my shirt. By the time I was done, her skirt was on the floor and she was standing in front of me naked.

She began to undo my belt. I went to kiss her again but she had started to bend at her knees as she pulled my trousers down. If she took me in her mouth, I just knew I would come, so I pulled her up and began to move us onto the bed.

We climbed in. I lay her on her back and with my lips I found each breast. Her fingers ran through my hair. I placed one leg between hers. She moved her other leg away from under me so I was fully between her. Then she curled her legs round my waist and pulled my lips to hers. We were still kissing when she suddenly pushed me till I rolled on my back and she climbed on top of me. She took my arms and placed them on her breasts, then she lifted herself off slightly and with one hand she found my erection and slid it into her.

Ibrahim studied all the faces lingering around the lobby. He found Ade's number on Guy's phone, pressed the call button, and put the phone into his pocket.

A man with his back to him, in blue jeans and a sleeveless khaki jacket, pulled a phone from his pocket. Ibrahim already suspected he was his man. He smiled and walked towards him.

31

We stayed in bed kissing, touching, talking. Amaka told me funny stories from her childhood. She seemed to have been everywhere in the world, just like Mel. She asked about my life in London. She guessed right that I was a public school boy. I went to St. Paul's. She wanted to know why I gave up law to become a journalist. If I liked what I did. If, like her, I had come to realise that one lifetime is just not enough to be all you want to be. I cheesily asked who she got her button nose and pink lips from: her mum or her dad. Did she miss not having siblings? How many children did she want? We lay in bed, her head on my chest, my fingers curling her braids.

Between kisses, she made calls to try to track down the girl who had called her that morning. With each call, she spoke differently, switching between the way she talked to me, to pidgin, to a local language. She spoke quickly at times, almost as if she was upset with the person on the line; at other times she took time to ask how the person was. She soon became so engrossed that I had to let go of her.

I lay beside her, watching. She was about the same age as Mel, I guessed, but while Mel had a great job as an analyst in the City and a nice flat in Maida Vale to show for it, Amaka's job meant more. The increasing worry on her face as she ended each call and dialled the next, was not angst over a half a million pound mortgage, or an increasing waistline. Watching her propped against the headboard, just doing what she does, I could not imagine her having enough spare time for things like exhibitions in Cairo, or retrospectives at the Barbican, or boyfriends.

I shimmied over to her, put my arms around her shoulders and buried my head in her neck. She shrugged away and, without looking up from the message she was typing said, 'What are you doing?'

'Nothing,' I said, moving strands of braids from her neck.

She looked at me as she continued typing. 'Not now,' she said. 'Why don't you start working on the story?'

'How?'

'Google Otokoto Hotel,' she said, then she spelled it out.

The first page I opened had a picture of four shirtless men sitting on the ground in front of what looked like a decaying head set upon an upturned plastic bucket. I leaned away from the screen. Could that really be a human head? Who were the men? How on earth could a website publish that picture? I turned to look at Amaka. She was waiting for someone to answer her call. I continued reading, trying not to look at the picture.

A syndicate of ritual killers was exposed in 1996 when the Nigerian police arrested a man named Innocent Ekeanyanwu, in Owerri, in south-eastern Nigeria. He had a parcel on him. The severed head of a young boy, Ikechukwu Okonkwo, was in it. The police found the torso buried on the grounds of Otokoto Hotel, owned by a certain Chief Duru, a respected wealthy local businessman, and his gang was uncovered. Their business was the sale of human parts. Violent protests, looting and burning of properties belonging to the ritual killers followed, then a trial, and in February of 2003, the suspects were sentenced to death by hanging.

How many more such syndicates had managed to avoid arrest? Dreading what I'd find, I searched for ritual murders. The first five results on the search engine mentioned Nigeria. There was a piece on the BBC website about something that happened in London in 2001. I remembered the story. The police recovered a headless body floating in the Thames, near Tower Bridge, not far from where I work. They named the unknown boy Adam. They believed he was victim of a ritual killing. Forensics led detectives to south-west Nigeria. The case was never solved.

There were other stories about ritual killing syndicates in the country and in Tanzania, Liberia and Malawi. Body parts – heads, eyes, tongues, breasts – sold to witch doctors for up to ten thousand dollars apiece; tempting money in a continent with serious poverty. Apparently, witch doctors use the organs in rituals at the behest of their clients, to ward off misfortune, cure diseases, grant good luck and defeat enemies.

The more I read, the more I grew worried and the more I appreciated the vulnerability of the women Amaka looked out for and why it was so important to her to do something about this. How such a dark practice had survived into the twenty-first century perplexed me.

She crept up behind me and leaned over my shoulder to see what I was doing.

'Do Nigerians really believe in magic?' I asked.

She sat next to me on the edge of the bed.

'Everywhere you look in Lagos, there's a church,' she said. 'New churches appear every day. The people are poor, they are desperate. They turn to God for help, and when that doesn't work, they turn to crime. The young boys become fraudsters, armed robbers. The girls become prostitutes. Some turn to black magic. Just like they believe in God, they also believe in the devil. God asks them to be patient but the devil says, 'I will give you what you want; you only have to do one thing in return.' '

'What is the government doing about it? Can't they outlaw black magic, ban witch doctors, make arrests?'

'What can they do? The police don't have forensic labs like CSI, and even if they did, people don't talk to the police. Most victims are never identified and the witch doctors do not exactly go about announcing that they use human body parts in their rituals. What can the police do?'

'It just doesn't make sense,' I said.

'A lot of things here don't make sense. You know, it's not just the people who kill that bother me. One of the girls I work with, let's call her Florentine. She was picked up on the Lagos-Ibadan Expressway walking naked like a zombie. She had been beaten so badly, it was a miracle she was alive. The people who found her took her to a hospital but the doctors wouldn't admit her. They wouldn't even give her first aid. They asked for a police report. They said she was either an armed robber or something of the sort for her to have been beaten like that.

'Luckily for her, one of the nurses knew about Street Samaritans and told them to take her to our office. When I saw this girl, I cried. And I don't cry that often. Anyway, we took her in. We took her to a hospital that doesn't ask questions and we paid for her treatment. All through, this girl refused to tell anyone who she was, why she was on that road, or why she had been beaten like that. The gossip around the hospital was that she had escaped from a mental institution.

'I needed to know what I was dealing with so I told her that since she was getting better, the police would be coming to take over her case. I didn't have the intention of doing any such thing, but it worked. She opened up. According to her, she was a 'guest' in a place known as the Harem, a mansion deep, deep in the forest somewhere outside Lagos. What she told me about that place still scares me till today. The Harem is a sex club run by some guy they call Mr Malik. It's a secret affair. The girls are taken to the house in the middle of the night, blindfolded, and they stay there for months without any contact with the outside world. Big men, members of the club, go there every weekend to have their pick of a dozen or so girls.

'Apparently, this Mr Malik pays them well. Some of them, when they eventually leave the Harem, leave as millionaires. But I can only imagine what they must have gone through to make all that money.

'In Florentine's case, she had a regular customer who decided to beat her up one day. He beat her till she was unconscious then Mr Malik helped him dump her body on the Lagos-Ibadan Expressway. They thought she was dead. So many bodies turn up naked on that road and people assume it has to do with rituals but sometimes it's just a sadistic bastard who likes to beat up young girls.'

'This Mr Malik, do you know him?'

'Nope. I'm still trying to find him, and when I do he's going to pay for what he did to that girl. I've already found his friend.'

'The one who beat up the girl?'

'Yes. I took care of him last night.'

'How do you mean?' I remembered she had been away during the night.

'Don't worry about it. It's a long story. Maybe I'll tell you about it someday.'

Talking about ritual killings and brutal men filled the room with a heaviness. She had insisted that we could not see Aunty Baby till very late at night – I didn't ask her why; I somehow already knew I would trust her with my life. She asked if I wanted to get something to eat. It was about seven p.m. and we had skipped both breakfast and lunch. I didn't realise how hungry I was until she asked.

'Yes. Should we get some room service?' I turned to find the phone by the bed.

'Nah. I'm taking you somewhere nice. You'll love it. Then afterwards I'll take you to a decent bar. Not like Ronnie's.'

She winked when she mentioned the pickup joint. I managed a smile, but truth be told, I would have preferred to stay in the safety of the room rather than tempt fate in another Lagos night. But I could see she was excited by her idea, and when I thought about it, I still wanted to see the Lagos I'd heard so much about.

Amaka had sent her clothes down to the hotel laundry and they had been returned. She rolled up her blouse sleeves and left the top three buttons undone.

I chose a pair of blue denims and a white short-sleeved linen shirt but couldn't help feeling that no matter what I wore, I would still look second-rate next to her. The last time I felt this way was back in school when, by some anomaly in the order of things, I found myself dating Betty Stewart, the daughter of a millionaire MP and also the most beautiful girl in our year. It lasted two weeks – before Timothy Spencer-Rye started telling everyone my father was originally Polish and Collins was really my mother's surname.

We drove to a boutique hotel in Ikoyi called Bogobiri. In the small bar area of the hotel a light-skinned man walked up to us. Amaka was busy with the waiter and the food menu and didn't notice him.

'Hi,' he said, holding out his hand. Close up I realised he was mixed race. His dark curly hair had streaks of grey but his clean-shaven face didn't look that old.

'Gabriel,' he said with a wide smile. He had a strong grip.

'Guy.'

Amaka looked up from the menu.

'Gabriel.' She practically jumped into his arms. He lifted her off the ground and rocked her body from side-to-side. From their excited talk I gathered that he had just returned from a trip to London, someone had told her he was doing something in Ghana, and they hadn't seen each other in almost three months. Three months didn't seem to me long enough to miss someone so much. I took a closer look at him.

32

The night was hot, humid, and dark. Inspector Ibrahim gathered the men of Fire-for-Fire into a sweltering room in the back of his police station to brief them on Operation Bulldog: the siege on Matori. First, he had a senior officer inspect their eyes; anyone high on drugs would be excluded from the operation.

It was to be a textbook raid and so hardly needed instructions beyond an address and a target. But Matori was a place deep in the dark heart of the slums where hoodlums and miscreants owned the streets. Ibrahim didn't expect their target to be ready with his own little army but he didn't want to spark a riot among police-hating neighbours keen to rush to the aid of one of their own.

'We're going to go in quietly,' he said. 'First, we secure the perimeter; two men to every house on the road. No torch lights. If anyone confronts you, tell the baga to go back into their house. If they don't, do not arrest them. The offensive will begin exactly five minutes after everyone is in place, so no need to worry about any bloody civilians. I don't want a single shot fired unless it is absolutely necessary: we don't want to attract any attention. We just go in, fetch him, and we get out. Remember, he must be delivered alive. I repeat: Chucks must be delivered alive. Hot-Temper is the commanding officer; nobody farts unless he authorises it. Boys, let's go and do our job.'

Outside the station, on Ahmadu Bello Road, officers stopped danfo buses and told the passengers to get out. The braver commuters who had paid their fares demanded an explanation. 'Police business' was all they were told.

The commandeered vehicles were directed to park in front of the station where members of Operation Fire-for-Fire waited. The bus drivers were given bulletproof vests to wear under their shirts. It was too much for a lanky young boy. Shaking with fear, he lost control of his bladder and tears fell from his face. A desk officer was nominated to drive the bus in his place.

The men piled into the vehicles. At five-minute intervals they set out into the night.

Ibrahim and three officers, each of them in plain clothes, got into Ibrahim's car. He was off to deal with another matter that required delicate handling. His men would keep him informed over the two-way radio tucked into his belt, next to his semi-automatic pistol.

33

Amaka took Gabriel's hand and introduced us all over again – out of courtesy, I assumed, because she immediately turned her attention back to him. She did not bother to explain who I was but she did say I was a journalist. 'Gabriel owns an estate agency,' she said. 'He sells properties all over Europe to rich Nigerians. Anybody worth knowing is his client.'

'What is this, Gabriel? No glasses? Have you finally started wearing contacts?' she asked him.

'Ah. There's a story there,' he said, pushing away the menu and the salt and pepper shakers as if he needed space to talk. 'On the flight, just as we were on our final approach into Lagos, a hostess announced that she had a pair of glasses that someone had left in the bathroom. I wasn't wearing mine so I couldn't see what she was holding up. I placed my hand on my breast pocket and felt my glasses case and went back to sleep.'

'You fool. They were yours.'

'Yup. I took them off to enjoy crapping over the Atlantic and I left them there. Or I was subconsciously trying to get rid of them.'

Next, he was talking about baggage handling.

'You know that sorry looking battered old bag that keeps going round the carousel unclaimed? I don't think it caught the wrong flight. I think the owner is just too ashamed to claim it while people are watching.'

Amaka laughed, I only smiled, even though I thought the little anecdote was clever. Then he turned squarely at Amaka.

'Your goddaughter is just like you,' he said. 'I'm starting to suspect foul play. Honestly, if you were a bloke, I'd check her DNA. The other day, she was coming down the stairs…' He turned to me momentarily, 'She's five. Madam said she could dress herself; they were going to party or something. Anyway, she's coming down the stairs. She's got on every new thing she has: dress, jacket, belt, sunglasses, socks. She even had her little pink handbag. So, she's coming down the stairs and she's taking her time like 'look at me', and Madam says: 'Yemisi, you have your shoes on the wrong legs.' You know what she says? I swear, she's just like you. She stops there, one hand up on the banister like that, the other hand on her hip; she looks at her mum and calmly says, 'Mum, how can they be the wrong legs? I only have two legs.' '

Amaka laughed, I laughed, a couple on a table next to us laughed. He wasn't so bad.

We ordered omelettes and fried plantains with goat meat stew – Gabriel's suggestion. I had never eaten either. When the food came, on trays balanced on one hand by waiters, I could smell the scale-busting hotness of the fiery stew which had massive chunks of meat still with skin on in it. Gabriel shovelled through his meal while I had to douse each peppery mouthful with a gulp of water. Amaka was totally tuned in to his constant, rapid delivery of stories and oblivious to the plight of my English palate. I knew my face was going through all shades of red.

He turned to me and I was sure he was about to make a joke.

'So, Bob, where are you staying?'

I started to correct him but Amaka chuckled and placed an arm on mine.

'He calls every man Bob,' she said.

'No, not every man, just your men.'

'Yes. That's how he refers to every man he sees with me. It's a private joke.' She looked at him and they both chuckled. 'Not that I've ever understood it. But don't worry, he soon grows tired of it or he forgets to do it and he'll call you by your real name.'

He let Amaka finish then he turned to me.

'So, where are you staying?'

'We're at the Eko Hotel,' I said.

'Oh. You are staying together?' He raised an eyebrow at Amaka.

I was afraid to look at her.

'It's a long story,' she said. 'And wipe that look off your face, you dirty old man. It's not what you think.'

'Dirty, yes. But I have to object to old. So, how come you two are staying together?'

'He has a girlfriend. Her name is Melissa. So, stop digging.'

Why ever did I tell her about Mel?

She went on to tell him about the events of the previous night. She wasn't completely honest with her narrative. She told him a friend had asked her to help spring me from the police station, and she entirely left out the part about the service she provided to the girls. It made me feel good that I knew something about her that he didn't know.

'You, my friend, are the easy motion tourist,' Gabriel said, looking at me after Amaka finished her abridged version of the story.

'What?' She looked bemused, as if she was expecting one of his jokes to follow.

'Easy Motion Tourist. It's an old song by Fatai Rolling Dollar's old band. Bob, did you ever listen to Highlife music?'

I shook my head.

'Shame. Really good music. So, Easy Motion Tourist, it's an old Highlife number from the seventies, or sixties, by the Harbours band. The inspiration for the number came after a night out jamming. The group returned late from a gig and one of the band members couldn't get into his house. The chap had been locked out of his own home. They wrote a song about it the next day – or something like that. In the end it's a song about nocturnal misadventure. That's what you've had, and that's why you, my friend, are the easy motion tourist.'

He raised his glass of water to me in a toast. I raised mine. 'Come to think of it, they were all young Nigerian musicians playing their music in Nigeria. Not one foreigner amongst them. Makes you wonder where they got 'tourist' from. I want some of whatever they'd been drinking that night.'

We talked a lot. Gabriel kept asking random questions that I felt were intended to trip me up – to let slip the true nature of my relationship with Amaka. It made me feel good to think that he thought there was something between me and her.

At eight p.m. Amaka told him we had to leave. He was reluctant to let us go and he only relented when Amaka promised to have lunch with his family the next weekend.

'Do you guys have anything planned for tonight?' he said.

'No, not really,' Amaka said. 'I thought I'd show Guy a little bit of Lagos then we were going to see an old friend. Do you have anything in mind?'

'You know that my madam's MD is cousin to the Attorney General?'

'Yes,' she said. She turned to me, somehow realising I was lost. 'His wife's boss.'

'Well, it appears they've found a suitable governor's son to be her husband – the Attorney General's cousin, that is, not my madam. The engagement party is tonight. We have been invited to the owambe at the Yoruba Tennis Club.' He turned to me. 'Have you been to an owambe party yet?'

'No. What is an owambe party?' I tried but I'm sure I got the pronunciation wrong.

'Ah, you are in for a treat.' He turned to Amaka, 'You haven't taken young Bob here to an owambe? Haba. How is he going to get to know Lagos?' He turned to me. 'An owambe party is a spectacle. I don't know how to describe it; you just have to attend one to understand. Promise me you'll come. Amaka, promise to bring Bob to the party.'

'I don't know, Gabriel, you know society parties are not my thing.'

'Maybe not, but it would be criminal to deprive Bob of a chance to get to see the movers and shakers of the country in their element. Besides, you keep telling me you want to raise money for your charity; this is a perfect opportunity to meet some of the deepest pockets in the city. And I'll introduce you.'

'Come to think of it, there are a couple of people I'd like to meet. A certain Chief Amadi, he stays here on the island. And a man they call Mr Malik. Know them? Perhaps they will be there?'

'Ebenezer Amadi?'

'Yes, I think.'

'Why do you want to meet him?'

'It's business, Gabriel. Why do you suddenly look so serious?'

'Do I? Anyway, come to the party and bring Bob. I'll introduce you to some of my clients.'

'Do you know him personally?'

I paid attention. He glanced at me and caught me studying his face.

'Yes. He's a client,' he said with finality, as if he meant to end the conversation.

'So you can introduce us?'

'Yes.'

'What about Malik? Do you know him too?'

'Do you know how many Maliks are in Lagos?'

'Which ones do you know?'

'I don't know any.'

He was abrupt.

'Gabriel?' she said, in a way that reminded me of my mum calling my name when she knew I was deliberately trying to miss the point that she had just made.

'What if I know the Malik you are looking for?' he said. 'Then what? Are you going to tell me why you're looking for him?'

'You don't need to know. It's nothing.'

'If it's nothing, why can't you tell me?' He turned to me. 'I know her too well. She's up to something, and if I'm right it's something dangerous.'

'Dude, there you go doing your big brother thing again. How many times do I have to tell you I can look after myself? Do you know the guy or not?'

'I said I don't know any Malik. At least not any you should know.' He turned to me again. 'She once asked me to introduce her to a senior civil servant, only for the guy to later give me a ten million naira cheque made out to her charity and tell me to warn her never to get in touch with him again. I lost a lot of business from the guy.'

'He was sleeping with the youth corpers posted to his ministry.'

'And how you knew that, I still don't know. You blackmailed the guy, and you used me. Not good.'

'He had it coming. He deserved worse.'

'And you are not the police. Look, there are lots of really nasty people out there that you don't want to be messing with the way you messed with that commissioner. You were lucky; the guy could have come after you, you know?'

'What can he do? If he tries anything he'll regret it. He knows it.'

'See? Talking like that, that's the reason I'm afraid to introduce you to people.'

'Is Malik your client too?'

'You think this is about me being afraid to lose a client? I'm afraid for you, sis. You think you're superwoman or something and I keep telling you, this is Nigeria. You can't go about waging your own personal war on corruption and filth.'

'I'll find him, with or without your help.'

He shook his head at her. 'Come to the party tonight. And bring Guy. If Amadi is there I'll introduce you. And if you tell me why you're looking for Malik, if it's the Malik I know, we'll talk.'

34

Near Matori, on a street on Palm Avenue, beside stagnant black water in an open gutter, people sat on metal chairs, drinking beer and eating fish pepper soup. They were shouting to be heard over loud Fuji music playing from a speaker hung over the front door of the beer parlour.

Chucks, on his sixth bottle of Guinness, looked around, took another look at a light-skinned woman with large hips, a full back, and breasts that stretched the words STARING WON'T MAKE THEM BIGGER across the front of her T-shirt, and pointed at her.

She had been waiting for his eyes to sweep back to her. She picked her handbag, went and sat next to him and fixed her attention on men at other tables, those sitting alone and still drinking up the appetite for sex.

'Let me see you properly,' Chucks said.

'You want me to stand up?'

'No. Just uncross your hands.'

He read the words on her shirt.

'How much?'

'Ten k.'

'Five.'

'Seven.'

'Five.' He looked around and spotted a large woman getting off a motorcycle taxi.

'Won't you even buy me a drink?'

'What do you want?' He would deduct the cost of the drink from the five thousand.

'Malt.'

He raised his hand for a waiter and felt his phone vibrate. It was Sergeant Saliu calling. When he had learned that the Iron Benders had been arrested, he called Saliu and asked if the boys had mentioned his name. Saliu didn't know. He told Saliu that, if the gang members died in detention without mentioning his name he would pay two hundred thousand naira for such good news.

The girl placed her hand on his thigh. He put his hand on her crotch and tried to dig through her skirt. She took his hand away and he laughed.

'Let me talk to my friend,' he said.

He stood up and had to steady himself. He pulled out a wad of one thousand naira notes and plucked one off, tossing the money onto the metal table.

'Buy whatever you want.'

He walked away from the noise.

'Hello, Saliu, how you dey? Any better?'

'Where are you?'

'Why are you whispering?'

'Where are you?'

'I'm at Palm Avenue. Wetin dey happen?'

'Please, delete my number from your phone.'

'What?'

'Delete my number from your phone. From all your phones.'

'Saliu, what is wrong?'

'Those Iron Bender boys have sold you out. They have told the police everything. They are coming to get you now. They know where you live. They know all your hideouts.'

He stopped walking. This was not a call to warn him. Saliu was calling to protect himself.

'You say they're coming for me now? Why didn't you warn me earlier?'

'I just got the information now.'

'Saliu, what will I do now? Where will I go?'

'I don't know, but please, delete my number from your phones.'

'Saliu, if I go down you go down with me.'

'What do you mean? Am I the one that said they should come and arrest you? There is nothing I can do, I can only advise you to leave Lagos today-today.'

'Saliu, I'm warning you, get me out of this mess or else I'll tell them everything that you have been doing for me.'

'Why? Why would you do that? Am I not warning you now?'

'You are warning me when they are already on their way. What kind of warning is that? What do you want me to do? Where do you want me to go? You said they know all my hideouts.'

'Look, what else can I do? This is a very serious matter and they are determined to catch you tonight. Just get out of town immediately.'

'Saliu, I will not delete your number from my phone. You must help me get out of this mess.'

'What do you want me to do?'

'Saliu, you have to help me or we both go down together.'

'What kind of talk is that? What do you want me to do?'

'Where do you want me to go and hide now? You have to help me.'

'Fine. Go to my house. You know the window by the door? Put your hand in the hole in the mosquito net. My key is at the bottom. When I finish my duty I'll come and meet you. Do not let anybody see you.'

'I should go to your house?'

'Yes. Now. And don't warn your boys. If they reach your shop and they don't find anybody there to arrest they'll know you received information. Go to my house and do not call anybody. And delete my number.'

'OK.'

'Do not call anybody.'

'OK.'

Chucks turned to look at the girl. She was wrapping her lips round the neck of a bottle of Maltina. She must have bad luck and she had infected him with it. He turned and began to walk away – slowly at first, then he picked up his pace, till out of sight of the beer parlour he broke into a sprint.

Each bus took a different route towards Chucks's shop that was also his home, and parked in side streets. As usual, a power failure had the neighbourhood in silent darkness. Hot-Temper told a swollen-eyed member of the Iron Benders gang that it was time.

The cleaned-up, battered criminal limped alone on the road. Silent shadows followed him, finding hiding places in his wake. He stopped in front of Chucks's house and called out for his receiver of stolen goods.

'Chucks, come out.'

'Who is that?'

'I want to see Chucks. Tell him to come out.'

'Chucks has travelled.'

'Pascal, is that you? It is me, Rotimi. Pascal, where is Chucks? Tell him to come out and meet me.'

'Rotimi? They released you?'

'Tell Chucks to come out and meet me.'

The boy unlocked the door, stepped out of the frame and caught someone moving out of the corner of his eye. He raised his pistol at the crouching policeman. A shot shattered the silence and found its mark between the man's eyes. Shots cracked from the building, illuminating the previously dark windows.

The policemen returned fire. The Iron Bender's body wriggled as bullets flew through him from both directions.

'Hold yah fire, hold yah fire,' Hot-Temper said.

By the last shot, plaster had been peeled off the walls, the glass had vanished where louvres had been, and the house was silenced.

'You bastards,' Hot-Temper said. 'You have killed everybody.'

Chucks paced around Saliu's studio apartment, opening drawers and looking behind seats. He lifted the cover off a pot left on a kerosene stove and sniffed at the stew inside. He squeezed his face, turned away, and replaced the lid. He wanted to call his home. Had the police come for him? He sat on the thin mattress on a narrow bed covered in a sheet that smelt of sweat. How could the Iron Benders sell him out like that, after the blood oath they had sworn? He held his phone. At least, he should warn Pascal, the son of his eldest brother. A knock on the door made him jump.

'Saliu, is that you?'

'Come and open the door.'

He switched on the light to undo the lock. Saliu walked in, followed by three men Chucks did not recognise.

'What is happening? Saliu, who are these people?'

Saliu grinned, mischief in his eyes. 'Chucks, meet my oga, Inspector Ibrahim.'

Ibrahim shook hands with Chucks. When he didn't let go, Chucks looked up at him. Ibrahim kept a tight grip as an officer slapped a handcuff onto the criminal's wrist. Chucks did not struggle as his other hand was pulled behind his back and secured with the rusty manacles.

'Saliu, what is happening?'

'You're under arrest,' Inspector Ibrahim said.

'Saliu is working for me. He has been giving me information. He takes money from me.'

'And we are very grateful for the money.'

The policemen laughed. Chucks wobbled and the men held him up. Inspector Ibrahim's radio crackled.

'Whisky Bravo, Whisky Bravo.' It was Hot-Temper's voice over the static-laden line.

'Talk to me,' Ibrahim said, putting the device to his ear.

'We have recovered the car, sir. It even has blood inside it.'

'Good. Take it back to the station.' He returned his gaze to Chucks and smiled. 'Now, you will tell me what you've been up to.'

35

We left Gabriel with a couple who had come to meet him in the hotel bar. He was telling them about an Arab sheikh and his Nigerian mistress when Amaka took the opportunity to say goodbye.

She took me to News Café at the Palms Shopping Mall in Lekki. The car park in front of the complex was crammed with Mercedes and BMWs. I counted six Range Rovers in the row we parked in. There was a Ferrari between a Bentley Continental and a Porsche 911. I was still looking at it when a white Rolls Royce Phantom pulled into a parking space. I had never seen so many luxury cars in one place at the same time.

The bar was on the ground floor of the mall. The front was all glass, overlooking the car park. Tables and chairs were set out in front. There, white folk mixed with the local crowd, holding champagne flutes and having animated conversations. Nigerians, I find, are very expressive when they talk. Somehow, it reminded me of standing outside my favourite bar in London, Abacus, in the City overlooking the pillars of The Royal Exchange, being locked in intense conversation with a mate over a cigarette before going back inside to join the group.

The doorman recognised Amaka and smiled. It was packed inside and the music so loud you could feel it pounding through your chest. Amaka took my hand and led me through the crowd. People stopped her to say hello. She introduced me each time by telling them my name and I in turn shook their hands and strained to hear the names they shouted back into my ear.

Without warning, Amaka started to dance and I remembered Mel. It was at a mate's bachelor party that we met, Mel and I. At Carbon Bar. I was out with the lads and she – she confessed weeks later – was on the bride's spy team. She came up to me and asked to dance. The track ended and we went out for a smoke. Out in the winters' cold she admitted that it was my dancing that made her want to talk to me. We spent the rest of the night outside, talking, lending our lighters to strangers, and eventually, exchanging numbers. But I was dancing with Amaka now.

She wasn't a bad dancer, Amaka. She turned and did a bump and grind against me, then she pressed her back into my chest and raised a hand up and round my neck. I took her hand and spun her round, then I palmed her butt, drew her into me, and went to kiss her but she dodged it. She stepped back from me, pulled me towards her and shouted in my ear: 'Let's go.'

'What?'

'Let's go. We are going to see Aunty Baby.'

She pushed past me and didn't look to see if I was following. I caught up with her at the car, by which time she was already seated and had started the engine.

'I'm sorry about that,' I said.

'What?'

'Back there, when I tried to kiss you.'

'Oh, is that what you were trying to do?'

'I got carried away.'

'We all make mistakes.'

She didn't look at me as she said it. It wasn't a conversation. Had what happened at the hotel ended at the hotel?

36

Knockout took a motorcycle taxi to Obalende, an area bordering Ikoyi, where the wealth stops and the slums begin. The okada galloped down a street where different genres of music blasted from loudspeakers in front of beer parlours, short-stay motels, and outright brothels. Teenage prostitutes lined both sides of the road, waving at cars. Behind them, sloshed men sat on rickety plastic chairs and tables that took up all of the pavement. It was a neighbourhood of cramped, decaying houses that provided the island with drivers, house girls, messengers, and handymen. Criminals, who preferred to live close to easy pickings, also lived there.

The motorbike drove through a series of alleys. Knockout tapped the rider to stop in front of a long narrow bungalow between two dilapidated apartment blocks. He waited for the driver to leave then he whistled three times and waited.

Someone whistled back, three times, from the building and Knockout whistled again.

A young man opened the door, stepped aside for Knockout to enter, and scanned the street before closing the door and locking it. A corridor ran the length of the bungalow to a door at the back. The walls and doors had been fashioned out of plywood to create six separate rooms; three on either side.

'Kekere, long time? I've come to see your brothers.'

Kekere went from room to room, knocking on the doors and calling his brothers: 'Brother One-Nation, brother One-Love, brother Oscar, brother Romeo.'

Muscular thugs emerged from each room, shirtless. Their scarred, tattooed bodies glistened with sweat. They were once a family of amateur boxers, following in the footsteps of their late father who had been a boxing trainer in the sixties. Their mother died of pneumonia long before their father passed on from not being able to afford the drugs to treat his high blood pressure. They grew up as orphans, putting their training to good use as bouncers until a local politician asked them to be his bodyguards. Over several elections, they chose their street names and amassed an arsenal of weapons provided by the campaign trail. It was because of this cache of arms that Knockout had come to see them. Catch-Fire and his girls had embarrassed him with their guns; when he returned, he wanted to impress them with his.

'A boy messed with me today and I want to teach him a lesson,' he said.

The brothers did not ask what the person had done or who he was. Knockout told them about the situation at Catch-Fire's house and the thugs found it amusing that prostitutes were now being used as bodyguards. A price was agreed and Knockout didn't even have to fetch the extra money he had hidden under his shirt.

'When do you want the job done?' One-Nation asked. He and his twin, One-Love, were the eldest of the brothers.

'Today. Now.'

The man shrugged. 'No problem. And how do we find this Catch-Fire?'

'I will take you there. I dey come with you.'

A king-size bed in the middle of Catch-Fire's bedroom was draped with a glossy sheet printed with large Armani logos and above it a chandelier had a clearance of four feet. From wall to wall stretched a rug with flowers in all the primary colours – the source of the new-fabric smell in the room. Electronic appliances were stacked on a shelf against the wall connected to an extension box by a mess of entwined wires. A midsize refrigerator was constantly humming and changing tone.

Catch-Fire was in a large armchair opposite Go-Slow who sat on a stool. He was still recovering from the poison but Doctor had assured him that death had missed him and he just had to continue taking plenty of water and avoid alcohol.

'My Brother,' he said, 'I'm sorry about what happened here last night. It is the fault of that boy, Knockout. He cannot just come to my house like that and start talking carelessly. I had to do what I did. It was for you people's protection. I hope you understand?'

Go-Slow nodded.

'That man that was here with me, he is the one I am doing the spare parts business with. His name is Amadi. Chief Amadi. We have been doing the business without any problem for some time, but now he suddenly wants to kill me. Thank God that my parents are not just sleeping in Heaven but watching out for me. He did not know that ordinary poison cannot kill Catch-Fire.' He spat into a bowl by his side. 'As he has tried and failed, he will surely come back for me. I don't know when, but what I know is that he cannot rest until I am dead. I know too much about his business. Right now he will be afraid that I will leak information to the police.

'I have to eliminate him before he eliminates me. If not for this poison he has used on me that has made me weak, I would have gone to find him and finish him myself. But I am too weak. That is why I have called you here.'

Go-Slow doubted that, poisoned or not, Catch-Fire had it in him to pull a trigger in the face of another man, but he let it slide. He had come to see him for two reasons: first, he needed the money, and second, he did not need an enemy, even in the person of such a low life as Catch-Fire.

Catch-Fire continued with a rambling speech meant to convince Go-Slow to do the job, then he got up and walked to his bed, knelt down beside it and pushed the mattress up. Through a space between the wooden planks he fetched a Ghana-must-go bag and emptied the contents onto the floor at Go-Slow's feet.

'That is one million naira,' Catch-Fire said. He emphasised the million as though Go-Slow might doubt it, then returned to his chair. 'Will you do this favour for me, my brother? It must be done as soon as possible. I will give you his address but I don't think it would be safe to do it at his house. He has a button that he can press to summon the police immediately. There is another place that would be easier.

'We drug the people we use for the rituals then we take them to a house off Lekki Expressway, on the way to Epe. The house is very far from the road. It is the only building in the area, inside a big forest. Me, myself, I do not go inside. I just deliver the people and when he finishes, we drive back to town and he pays me. He kills them himself and does his juju with them inside the house. I am the only one that drives him to the place. Even when I don't have anybody for him, he phones me to take him there every Sunday night around ten p.m. I think he has to do the rituals at that time. We always go there alone. I am sure he will go there again this Sunday even if he has to drive himself. That is the best place to waylay him.

'You cannot take a car there. You have to go during the day and hide until he comes. He is a very wicked man but he never carries any weapon; he only relies on his juju, so it should be easy. I have made this charm to protect myself.' From his pocket he got a small object wrapped in white cloth and bound with red thread. He handed it to Go-Slow. 'Take it with you; you will need it.'

Knockout followed the thugs to their backyard. Romeo, whose Mohican had begun to grow out of shape, opened the wooden lid on a well. He reached in, and with both hands pulled the rope till he had the large bag tied to its end. He placed the bag on the ground and unzipped it. Knockout beamed at the guns and ammunition inside.

The thugs took turns reaching in to select weapons. They had AK-47s, Uzis, pump-action shotguns, and automatic pistols to choose from. They inspected their arsenal and cleaned them, concluding their preparation by tying strings of amulets around their waists, wrists, and biceps.

Knockout stared longingly. He began to formulate a plan to get his hands on their guns once the night's job was done.

'Do you have transportation?' One-Nation said.

'No.'

'That will cost you extra.'

'No problem.'

He thought of Go-Slow and dialled his number but cancelled the call before it rang. He was moving up. No more carjacking for him. He was now one of the big boys. He was going to be bigger than Go-Slow.

37

We were on the Third Mainland Bridge. Darkness spread out on either side of us, behind us, and before us beyond the reach of the headlamps' beam where the bridge continued it's ambitious stretch over deep water. I remembered the driver who picked me up from the airport told me the bridge would soon collapse from lack of maintenance. He told me this while we were stuck in an endless traffic jam and as I was looking down at the lagoon below.

Amaka overtook a white bus and I did a double-take. A child appeared to be driving. Behind him, stony-faced men and two frightful dogs stared back at me.

Aunty Baby's place was a large two-floored building that looked like an office block. An old man in a brown khaki uniform hopped off his stool by the front door and his wrinkles stretched into a smile.

'My daughter,' he said, and embraced Amaka.

They then spoke in pidgin. I was lost.

'This is my friend from overseas,' she said, taking my hand.

He embraced me too. He smelt of VapoRub.

We walked down a wide corridor lit by a single bulb, to a flight of stairs that ascended into darkness. On the first floor landing, we came upon girls in various stages of undress, all waiting their turn to hug Amaka.

She would explain later that Aunty Baby and her husband Flavio bought the rundown hotel years ago, intending to fix it up and make a business out of it, but Amaka convinced them to turn it into a safe house for the girls. Here they got free medical care, training in different vocations – all paid for by the Street Samaritans. The couple charged five thousand a month for a room shared with other lodgers; it was a fraction of what they could make running it as a regular hotel.

The girls were at different stages of leaving the streets. Aunty Baby didn't mind – so long as they didn't bring men to the hostel. When they found husbands, or learned trades and got jobs, they would have no excuse to continue hustling, but in the meantime they had to feed. Amaka did the maths for me: if a girl has four 'boyfriends,' and each time she visits a boyfriend he gives her five grand, if she sees each boyfriend once a week, in a month she would have made eighty grand. That was a lot more than some bankers earned, she claimed. It was with this money that the girls – some of them – were able to buy hair dryers, rent small shops and open salons, or pay their siblings' school fees. Some were paying off family debts. Not one of them was spending the money on frivolous things like high fashion or holidays. They were selling their bodies for a good reason, as disturbing as that sounds.

Flavio turned out to be a middle-aged, seriously tanned, Italian ex-sailor. Amaka had not mentioned this. He was on a sofa, in a pair of white shorts, in a room that looked like an office. His short-sleeved shirt was unbuttoned, showing off his hairy chest, and he was eating peanuts that he prised from their shells while watching the news on TV. He jumped to his feet on seeing Amaka.

'Amaka, my second wife,' he said with arms outstretched. 'Why do you do this to me? Why don't you come and see me during the day when your aunty is away?'

I swear, he sounded Nigerian.

'And who is this young man? Is he trying to steal you from me?'

'His name is Guy. He's a journalist from Britain. He's doing a story about the Street Samaritans.'

'Guy, welcome. Come and sit with me. Drink?'

Aunty Baby entered through another door. Looking at her I could tell she had a kind heart, just like Amaka said. I guess character moulds the face.

'My daughter, you just show up unannounced any time. I don't like the way you drive around this our Lagos at night,' Aunty Baby said.

'This is Amaka's new boyfriend,' her husband said.

'Really? You are welcome. You must be David. No, no. It's Andrew. Is it Andrew? Oh no, wait, I remember, Antonio.'

I got the joke. Amaka introduced me once again as a journalist writing about the charity. The three of them sat together on the sofa and chatted. They looked like a family. Her family. I suddenly felt out of place.

'Aunty, I'm looking for a girl,' Amaka said. 'And we have to talk.'

Aunty Baby looked at me and smiled. 'Yes, we have to talk,' she said. 'Come.'

The women left the room, leaving me alone with Flavio.

'So, you like her, ehn?' he said with a wink. I liked his Nigerian accent.

'On no, it's not like that.' I was ready to repeat the story Amaka had already told about me doing a story about the charity.

'We are warm blooded men, my boy. I saw the way you looked at her. You like her.'

I smiled, or blushed, but thankfully, in the heat no one could tell the difference.

'She is a great girl,' he said. 'I've known her for a long time. You know, my wife is like her mother. If Baby says she likes you, the game is won. Amaka listens to Baby and Baby listens to me. But since you say you don't like her…'

He shrugged.

'She is a nice girl,' I said. I wanted to talk about her.

'Oh, she is the best. And you know what? I can tell you how to get her.'

'How?'

'Ha-ha.' He slapped his palms together. 'I knew it. You like her.'

He was laughing at my expense but I didn't mind. He was right. He recovered and launched into tales of the exploits of his youth: how he became a sailor in Livorno, how he moved up to captain his own vessel, how he ended up in Nigeria, and his many conquests along the way. He all but claimed to be an emeritus professor on matters concerning the workings of a woman's heart, and he was willing to teach me what I needed to know.

'Do you have a talent?' he said.

'A talent?'

'Yes. Girls like a man who has a talent. What is your talent?'

Not that I took him seriously, but he made me think. I'd never considered what my talent was – if I had any at all. I'd briefly captained the first fifteen rugby team in school, but that didn't seem to qualify.

'I don't have a talent,' I said. It was more of a realisation.

He looked at me as if I was his son and I had just come home with all Fs on my report card.

'You must have a talent, or have money, or something special.'

And in one breath, he condemned my chances with Amaka.

The boy in me wanted to tell him what she and I had been up to earlier at the hotel.

'What is your talent?' I asked him.

'I am Italian,' he said, his palms outstretched.

Amaka and Aunty Baby returned while he was still laughing at his own joke. Aunty Baby sat next to him.

'My daughter tells me you are writing about Street Samaritans. This girl is a special girl. When Flavio and I bought this hotel, she came to me and said 'Aunty Baby, let's use this place to help the girls.' Her father was an ambassador, you know?'

She had not told me this.

'She can have any job she wants, she doesn't even have to work, but instead she took over the charity to help these girls. She said 'Aunty Baby, these girls need a safe place. Let us start a hostel for them. They will pay and we will be able to keep an eye on them and make sure they are OK. They will have somewhere to come to where they feel safe.' I called my husband and I said, 'Flavio, this is what Amaka is asking me to do, what do you think?' He said 'why not?'

'That is how we started this hostel. At least five hundred girls have passed through this place and moved on to better things. They have cleaned up, they have found good jobs. A lot of them are married now with children. They have decent lives, all because of Amaka. But she cannot do it all alone. She needs money. She needs donations. Please, tell your readers about the good job she is doing. Tell them to donate money to her charity. Tell them she is the only hope for so many desperate girls here in Nigeria. If not for her, a lot of them would still be on the road.

'I'm telling you, Chiamaka is the only hope for these girls. Will you write that in your paper? Will you tell them?'

'I will.'

'What would you like to know? Do you want to talk to some of the girls?'

I looked at Amaka for help. Was she blushing under her flawless black skin? The more I saw and understood of Amaka's world, the more intensely drawn to her I felt and yet the more inadequate about myself and my part in it.

Aunty Baby picked up the intercom phone from her table: 'Tell Agnes to come to my office now.'

Agnes opened the door and pulled her unbuttoned shirt close at the sight of me. She was curvy, with the face of a child. She did her buttons, then her face brightened when she saw Amaka.

'Agnes, this man has come from Britain to learn about Street Samaritans,' Aunty Baby said. 'Please, tell him how you came here to this hostel.'

Agnes stayed at the door, twiddling the hem of her shirt. Flavio and Aunty Baby made space for her to sit between them. She looked at me, then at Amaka, then back to me. She seemed uncomfortable.

'Tell him how Amaka found you.'

'I was working at Bar Beach,' she began. Her voice sounded as young as her face but contrasted with her older body.

'What work were you doing at Bar Beach?' Aunty Baby said.

The young girl's head dropped. Her fingers returned to the hem of her shirt.

'I was a prostitute,' she said, barely audibly.

Aunty Baby put her arm around her.

'I was working on the beach and one night the police came to raid us. They took us to the police station and said we must bail ourselves. Some of the other girls had money but I had not done any work that night. One girl phoned her boyfriend to come and bail her. I begged her to ask him to bail me too. I promised to pay her back the money the next day.

'When the boy came, he bailed us and took us to his house. My friend went to sleep in the room with him. I slept on the chair in the parlour. Later, he came to wake me up and started touching me. I asked him: 'what about my friend?' He said she was sleeping. I told him I can't do anything with him because my friend is his girlfriend, then he told me that she is not. I begged him to leave me alone because I did not want any trouble but he wouldn't listen.

'He told me to give him the bail money or take off my clothes. I said I would pay him the next day. He said he wanted his money right now so I told him that if he didn't leave me alone I would go and tell my friend. Then he slapped me. I shouted for my friend to come but she did not answer. He started to beat me and try to take my clothes off. I was shouting and struggling with him until his neighbours knocked on the door. They asked what was happening and he told them there was no problem but I shouted that he wanted to rape me. He opened the door and told them I stole his money. I said he was lying but they joined him in slapping me, saying I should take off my clothes so that they could search me. I begged them to enter his room and ask his girlfriend if what he is saying is true but he didn't allow them to enter his room and he then phoned the police.

'I was locked up for five months before they took me to court. Nobody knew where I was. It was at the court, just before my case, that I met Aunty Amaka. She was talking to the police, then she and another lady came to talk to me. They asked why I was in court. I explained everything to them. Aunty Amaka told me that she already knew. She told me that the other lady was my lawyer. The lady lawyer won the case for me. Aunty Amaka asked if I wanted to stop working at the beach so I explained to her that I came to Lagos to work as a house girl. It was when my madam and her family travelled overseas and I couldn't find another job that I started going to the beach. She told me about this place and brought me here. That is how I came here.'

'How old are you?' I said.

'Seventeen, sir.'

'What about your family?'

'My mother is in the village, sir.'

Aunty Baby cut in. 'I call her mother regularly. She is blind. She has cataracts in both eyes. Agnes is saving money for the operation. Her uncle brought her to Lagos to work for his boss's wife.'

'What do you do now?' I asked. I held my breath for the answer.

Aunty Baby replied for her. 'She is in school. Amaka pays for her tuition out of her own pocket. She doesn't do any kind of work. She is focusing on her studies and she is very bright. She says she wants to be a lawyer like Amaka. It is out of the allowance that Amaka gives her that she sends money home to her mother.'

I was embarrassed to find myself almost close to tears. This girl was only a teenager and yet she had worked as a slave to look after a suffering mother, had prostituted herself, had been beaten – probably raped – had been falsely accused of theft, had been arraigned before a court on false charges, and had been locked up for five months.

'This is the life these girls suffer,' Aunty Baby said. She was still holding Agnes, softly rocking the girl in her arms. 'People call them prostitutes but they do not know anything about them. They don't care what happens to them. Can you imagine if

Amaka had not learned about her, what would have happened? She would still be in prison today. Countless times, Amaka has saved girls like her in court. The charity pays for lawyers to go around the courts in Lagos looking for these kinds of cases. It was Amaka's idea. She is truly a godsend.'

Agnes was excused. She went to Amaka and threw her arms around her.

'Please, Guy, tell your people to donate money,' Aunty Baby said.

'Talking about donations, Aunty, do you know any Chief Amadi? He lives in VI. I want to start hitting high-net-worth individuals for donations. The economy is affecting our corporate donors.'

'Chief Ebenezer Amadi? I know him. His house is off Ajose Adeogun. Who told you about him?'

'I'm putting together a list of people on the Island that I can approach. His name is the first on my list. What do you know about him?'

Aunty Baby looked unsure. 'He is a member of Ikoyi Club. He has money.'

'What does he do?'

'Honestly, Amaka, I cannot tell you that I know.'

'Do you think he would be willing to donate to the charity?'

'I hear he is very generous, but why him?'

'Why not him? I have to start somewhere. Do you know any reason why I shouldn't approach him?'

'No. I just think that maybe you should focus on bank MDs, CEOs, people like that.'

'What is wrong with Chief Amadi?'

'Nothing. Nothing at all. He is a very rich man. I think I have his number. I can call him and tell him about the charity. I'm sure he will donate something.'

'I want to meet him myself. Can you organise a meeting?'

'You want to meet him? I haven't spoken to him in a very long time, but these rich people never change their number. I'm sure I still have it.'

'Is it too late to call him now?'

I checked the time. It was just past nine.

'Now?'

'Yes. I want to hit the ground running. If I can get an appointment tomorrow I would be very happy.'

I may have been wrong, but Aunty Baby seemed reluctant to arrange the appointment. Also, I'd noticed the first time Amaka mentioned his name, it gave her pause.

'I don't think you should go and see him,' I said when we were in the car driving back to the island.

'Why?'

'He could be a murderer. What do you hope to achieve by going to his house?'

'I don't know.'

'I really don't think you should go. He could be dangerous.'

'I'll be OK.'

'Amaka, I can't let you go.'

She took her eyes off the road to look at me.

'You can't let me go? And who are you to tell me what I can or cannot do?'

'Amaka, please don't be silly. You know what I mean.'

'No, I do not know what you mean, and please, do not tell me not to be silly.'

'This is about the club, right?'

'This is about you telling me what to do.' She pulled up in front of a wrought iron gate and honked twice.

'Where are we?'

I figured she had driven straight to the party, but if that was the case, then we were first to arrive.

'My house. My parents' house. I need to change for the party and so do you. You are about the same height as my father. I'll find something for you to wear.'

'So, we are going to the party? Because you hope Chief Amadi will be there?'

'Yes.'

I said nothing more. If we continued arguing, she might decide to go alone, which I feared would be worse.

38

A table and a chair were set in front of Catch-Fire's house on the dirt road. A kerosene lantern on the table provided orange lighting. The man sitting on the chair was shouting at a crowd of men who still hadn't managed to form a straight line in front of him. They were being manhandled by other men whose task, it appeared, was to stoke the mayhem.

Under the table was a rucksack full of money. A scrawny man in a yellow LA Lakers shirt was next in line, having fought off challenges from other thugs. He placed an old rifle on the table and folded his arms.

The seated man studied the gun. It was impressively large, but it was rusty and held together with black electrical tape.

'E day fire?'

'Yes. Well, well.'

'You get bullet?'

'Of course.'

'Oya, sound am make I hear.'

The man picked up his gun and raised his right leg, wedging the butt of the weapon onto it to cock it. The crowd retreated. He raised his rifle into the air and fired a shot. The crowd cheered.

The man behind the table dipped into the rucksack and gave the shooter two thousand naira.

Next was a middle-aged man whose protruding belly looked like an engaged pregnancy. He had brought a cutlass, and when that elicited a 'you-must-be-kidding-me' look from the one doling out cash, he poured a sack of charms onto the table. He left with a thousand naira and applause from the onlookers.

Catch-Fire was watching from a window upstairs. He had sent a message to the local thugs and they responded by turning up in front of his house armed with machetes, guns, catapults, and sledge-hammers. They were pickpockets, burglars, extortionists, hired heavies, and general ne'er-do-wells. All they had to do was show a weapon and they would earn the right, and some money, to be forever known in the area as one of Catch-Fire's bodyguards. It was an honour to serve one of their own who had done well.

By the time the money bag was exhausted, there still remained a little crowd of hopefuls, armed with sticks and guns, and even a man who had come dressed in his white, judo uniform complete with black belt. A promise was made to reward everyone in due time; the thugs were assured that this came from Catch-Fire himself.

The men took up positions around the building they had been summoned to protect. The night was, as usual, dark from a power failure. Glowing ends of joints showed the spots where each thug stood guard.

A white van stopped on the other side of the road opposite the house. Moments passed then the side door slid open and two dogs sprang out, growling and racing at the men. The mob scattered.

Knockout jumped out, yelling like a beast, automatic pistols in both hands. He picked his first target: a thug keeping his position, holding his machete up, readying himself to swing it down once one of the dogs got close enough.

Knockout aimed and fired. Red mist sprayed out of the man's head. Knockout turned to the fleeing men and ran after them, screaming and shooting.

The brothers filed out of the vehicle and spread out. They expected a response from the house they had come to raid. When it came, it would be up to them to quell it.

A girl in jean shorts and a red bra came running out of the house holding a pistol. One-Nation pumped a cartridge into his shotgun's barrel and fired. The blast stopped the girl in her tracks, lifted her off the ground and sent her flying back into the house, arms flailing, belly exploding.

Knockout returned panting, his spent guns by his sides.

'What are you waiting for?' he said. 'Let us go and burn down the bastard.'

'We did not come to kill anyone,' One-Love said. 'Each life will cost you fifty thousand naira extra.'

'So? Is that all? Kill all of them.'

Catch-Fire's men, realising that they outnumbered the assailants, marched towards the house. A shot that missed its target brought the approaching army to the attention of Knockout and the brothers. At the same time, shots from the upper windows of the house peppered the ground around the would-be assassins. One-Nation motioned for Oscar, Romeo, and Kekere to deal with the approaching mob. The three clicked their AK-47s to automatic and opened fire. One-Nation and One-Love dealt with the building. As if impervious to bullets, they took their time to determine where the shots were coming from before bathing each hostile window in lead. They dropped spent magazines and clicked in replacements.

Knockout ran to the van planning to arm himself with a more

robust weapon from the brothers' bag, but when he looked inside, a grenade made him smile.

'That will cost you twenty thousand,' One-Love said, mid-volley.

Knockout pulled the pin and hurled the bomb with all the propulsion his short hands could muster.

The intended victims must have thought he had resorted to throwing stones. They ran into the bomb's kill zone and it exploded with an overpowering bang that sent bodies flying, pummelled by hot shrapnel. The remainder of the army lost interest in the battle.

Shots were still being fired from the dark windows. The girls knew what the gunmen would do to them if they managed to enter the house. Their single shots were followed by bursts from the gang's machine guns. A generator roared to life. A second later, floodlights flickered on. The shots from the house became more accurate. Exposed, the gang took cover behind their van, crouching behind the tyres. Small calibre rounds pierced through the car's panels.

'Knockout, the money you paid does not cover all this – oh,' One-Love said. 'Knockout?' He looked around. Knockout was not with them. Head down and body pressed to the ground, One-Love peered under the car. Empty shells glistened on the road.

Knockout had heard the generator and remembered the floodlights in front of Catch-Fire's house. He ran towards the building. He went down the side, bending below the windows that had burglar-proof iron bars on them. The backdoor was made of metal, probably bulletproof. He tried the handle. It was locked. He looked up at the building and his eyes fell upon a drainpipe that ran up the wall to the first floor where perforated blocks stretched the rest of the way to the roof. He gripped the pipe with both hands to test its strength then began to climb.

At the first floor, Knockout peeped through the holes. The passageway beyond was dark and smelt of gunfire. Placing his hands and feet into the holes and holding his breath, he continued climbing, aware that a shot could throw him off at any time. He made it to the top and hoisted himself onto the roof. He balanced by stretching out his hands and walked along a line of roof nails where there would be a strong beam beneath. Picking a spot on the asbestos roof, he leapt into the air, crashed through the ceiling, and tumbled onto the bare floor below. Debris followed him. He was bleeding from peppery cuts along his arms but he scampered to his feet, still clutching the guns in both hands.

Knockout pointed his pistols up each direction of the corridor but no one appeared. He began searching in the rooms farthest from the shooting – a coward like Catch-Fire would not be hanging out at the front line. The first door was locked. He kicked it open; it was a storeroom full of beer cartons. He moved on to the next door.

Go-Slow was by the window in Catch-Fire's room. Catch-Fire was on the floor, his hands wrapped around Go-Slow's leg. Go-Slow's weapon was drawn but he was not wasting ammunition; he was only surveying the situation to see when it was safe to leave. Whatever mess Catch-Fire had gotten himself into was not his problem. He would take the money, kill the crook himself if he objected, or go and kill the Chief if this battle was won by the girls. But ultimately, all that mattered to him was getting out alive.

The handle on the door rattled and the key in the lock dropped. Both Go-Slow and Catch-Fire turned to look. Go-Slow repositioned himself away from the path of any shot fired through the plywood. The door flew open, shattering into splinters at the lock. Knockout sprang in, holding both weapons up and ready. Go-Slow aimed his pistol at Knockout's head. They both stared at one another. Catch-Fire began to cry.

39

Her parents' home was a white mansion on a drive overlooking the lagoon. A policeman opened the gate and peered inside the car at me. There was an old Rolls Royce gathering dust in a corner. I wanted to see it but Amaka was already walking into the building. The policeman kept looking at me.

Inside, in a large bedroom, she measured me with her eyes then reached into a wardrobe and brought out a folded bundle of white clothing.

'Try this on,' she said, and left.

In the mirror over the dressing table something caught my eye. I turned to look. Next to the bed, leaning against the wall, was a double-barrelled shotgun. I heard a door close. I remembered she had gone to get dressed as well. I placed the borrowed clothes on the bed and began to unbutton my shirt.

We arrived at the party dressed alike in white, though Amaka had a huge red headscarf wrapped around her head that looked like an origami flower. She told me it was called 'gele.' Perhaps this meant something, the fact that she'd chosen matching outfits for us.

At the entrance of the Yoruba Tennis Club, people were showing their invitation cards to the police. Amaka put her arm in mine and pressed her phone against her ear. I hesitated when it was our turn at the gate but she tugged my arm and we walked past the policemen unchallenged.

A huge white marquee was set up in the middle of an open field. A live band played just beyond the gigantic tent. Gabriel guided us by phone to his table. He had saved us two seats by placing his wife's handbag on one, and a half-eaten plate of food on the other. He stood to greet us, looking theatrical in a flowing white outfit that at full spread was as large as a duvet cover. He had to keep gathering the excess fabric into folds over his shoulders. All the guests were in white outfits.

'Where is madam?' Amaka said, looking around.

Gabriel pointed out his wife, standing with a large woman who was fanning her face with an embroidered fan.

'She's with the wife of the new NDIC chairman. I told her to introduce you. You'd better run along now.'

She looked at me apologetically and I nodded that I would be fine. She held my arm and squeezed it before leaving. It felt good. Perhaps we were cool again? It occurred to me then that we'd had our first fight.

'Won't you sit down?'

He looked drowsy. There was a glass of wine and an empty bottle on the table. He pushed a glass towards me and poured red wine from a bottle that he brought out from under the table. I took in the crowd with my first sip. The vibrant music, the beautiful people, Amaka as my date – it all felt surreal.

'You look good. Did you have it made here?' Gabriel said.

'Oh, no. It's her father's.'

'The ambassador's? She's dressing you up in her father's clothes now? Interesting.'

'It's nothing.'

'If you say so. Tell me, what's she up to?'

'How do you mean?'

'I know Amaka; she's always on one project or the other. It's either an orphanage she's trying to rescue or a politician she's trying to expose. What is it this time?'

'I wouldn't know,'

'I'm sure you know, but she has sworn you to secrecy. Never mind, she'll tell me herself when she wants to. Sooner or later, she tells me everything.'

'You two seem to be very close.'

'Yup. Like brother and sister. Nothing going on there, my man. No need to worry about me.'

'There's nothing between us,' I said.

'Yeah, yeah.' He took another sip from his glass and started people-watching. 'You know, I know everything about these people. Every single one of them. You see that one there? The woman with the fat ass? Last month, I sold her father's house in Monaco. The man was a civil servant all his life. Head of Service. You have to ask yourself where he got the money to buy a twelve million pounds sterling villa cash down. Her husband used to be a good friend of mine.'

'Used to?'

'Oh yeah, he died. Cancer. We played golf together. He always won; that's how I got him to be my client. I'll tell you a funny story. A few years back, he got her a gym subscription for their anniversary. He didn't understand why she was upset. She made her point by getting him a penis enlargement kit in return. She called me in the States to buy her the stuff.'

We laughed at the story then he pointed at someone.

'See that guy there? The tall lanky fellow? He used to be in the

Navy. He was a commander. Shehu, that's his name. Shehu Yaya. Retired Navy Commander Shehu Yaya. He had a brilliant career. We all expected him to make CNS one day, Chief of Naval Staff, but then he got mixed up in a dirty oil bunkering deal and they quietly retired him. Guess what he does now?'

'Oil bunkering?'

'Nope. I never said he did it. In fact, the deal that got him the sack had nothing to do with him. His sin was actually not looking the other way, but that's another story. What he does now, my friend, is this: he arranges young girls for his rich friends in the Force. Can you believe that? A man, who got kicked out of his job for being straight, now pimps girls the age of his daughters to the same bastards who ended his career. Now what would you call that, poetic injustice?'

I turned to watch the retired commander. He was standing in a group with four other men, all deep in conversation, except for him. He was looking at something. I followed his gaze to Amaka. She was chatting with Gabriel's wife and an elderly woman. Her back was to him. She looked gorgeous. I noticed a few other men checking her out too.

'What about the man she's looking for? Is he here tonight?'

'Who? Malik?'

'No, Chief Amadi. Is he here?'

'Well, I haven't seen him. Why is she looking for him?'

'I don't know.'

'So, why do you ask?'

'I saw the expression on your face when she asked you about him.'

'What expression?'

'You seemed to disapprove. Do you know something about him?'

'Well, you see all these people here? I know how they all made their money – it's my job to know. I need to know who's rich or who's going to be rich, you understand? But that guy, Amadi, he just appeared on the scene out of nowhere. I've asked around and no one knows how he made his money, what he does, or for that matter how much he's worth. I'll tell you a secret. I have people in the banks who tell me how much any one has in their account. I need to know how much you can spend if you're asking about a villa in the Côte d'Azur, you understand? I need to be able to weed out the time wasters. I've asked all my contacts about this geezer and he doesn't have one account in any bank in the country. Not even under a false name. And yet he spends as if he prints money.'

'Drugs?'

'Nah. I doubt it. That racket has become too dangerous to run through Nigeria. I thought he was fronting for someone in government but that would require a registered business, at least. He doesn't have any. I dodged him over a property he wanted to buy in Cape Town last year.'

'Why?'

'If I don't know where the money is from, clean or dirty, I can't weigh the risks.'

'What risks?'

'Money laundering took on a new meaning post 9/11. For all I know he may be conning some Arab nation under the guise of religious advancement in Nigeria. Using funds like that to buy properties abroad may be interpreted by a paranoid CIA agent as funding extremists – however they may arrive at that, you follow? No, thank you. I'll stick to my corrupt politicians and dubious businessmen.'

'What about black magic?'

'What about it?'

'Could that be the source of his wealth?'

He looked at me as if I just said something stupid.

'Guy, don't tell me you believe in that hocus-pocus bullshit. I don't know what he does for his money but I don't think Amaka should be messing with him. Whatever she's up to, please stop her.'

Amaka had disappeared. I saw that a lot of the guests had gathered to dance in front of the band. Dollar bills were being thrown into the sky, or plastered onto the foreheads of female dancing partners. The ground beneath them was covered in notes and young girls were picking them up and stuffing them into empty wine boxes.

40

At the Lagos State Police Command Centre in Ikeja, on the mainland, an incident report officer took a call by hitting a button on the keyboard in front of her.

The caller identified himself as an undercover officer. His call sign and number checked out. The female officer greeted him by the name that flashed up on her screen, above a picture of his face. He was reporting a violent altercation in his assignment area; he'd been part of a group of men hired by a certain crook called Catch-Fire, in anticipation of an attack. He had no information on why Catch-Fire thought he was going to be attacked or who the aggressors were, only that the attack had been imminent.

The offensive happened sooner than expected. A group of gunmen stormed the house. Shots were still being fired. He had never seen anything like it, and he was still there, watching from afar. The aggressors were heavily armed with sophisticated weapons. He recognised a car snatcher that went by the name Knockout – he didn't know his real name.

'Any known affiliates?' she asked, referring to Knockout.

'Go-Slow, his partner, and Chucks of Matori. But they are not here.'

'Any casualties?'

'Not confirmed.'

'Current status?'

'Still hot.'

'Are you requesting backup?'

'No, just reporting.'

'OK. Try not to get killed.'

She had been typing all the time, recording the information on a central database that grew each day but faster by night. She did a quick search to see if there were any patrols in the area of the gun battle; she would warn them to stay clear of the vicinity – warring criminals armed with machine guns were not worth any police officer's life. Next, she checked the names she had typed against the 'persons of interest' column on the details of every police branch in Lagos. The record for Bar Beach police station flagged red. She clicked the row to see what the connection was. The name Chucks appeared on her screen. She saved the details she had recorded and cleared her screen for the next call.

Chucks rode in the back, between two policemen. Inspector Ibrahim sat in the passenger seat while Saliu drove. The officers discussed an upcoming Arsenal match while they drove to a motel room in Alagbado, on the outskirts of town.

'Would you like anything from the kitchen or the bar?' Ibrahim asked.

Chucks shook his head.

'I didn't hear you.'

'No, sir.'

'OK. Please, take a seat. I'll be back soon.'

Two officers sat on adjacent chairs facing him. One of them picked up a thumbed copy of *Vogue* and flipped through it. The other played a noisy game on his mobile phone.

Ibrahim asked the sleepy girl behind the counter downstairs if he could smoke inside. She said he could smoke in his room or outside. In the little compound outside the building he fetched the packet of cigarettes he had sent an officer to buy. It was the first he'd had in six months. He closed his eyes and drew in the smoke. He had promised his wife he would quit. He made a mental note to buy a toothbrush and a tube of toothpaste to keep at the station.

He took Chucks to the motel because he didn't want word of his arrest to get out. He had been instructed to solve the case of the murdered girl and Chucks was his only lead. He would use him to flush out all his accomplices without arousing any suspicion. After his second cigarette, he checked the time. He called the police commissioner, hoping the man would be sleeping. At least then his phone would show that Ibrahim had tried to contact him.

'Hello, Ibrahim, you have news for me?'

'Sir, we have apprehended a suspect who was in possession of the car involved in the homicide.'

'Have you caught the killer?'

'No, sir.'

'Call me when you have.'

Ibrahim returned to the room and his officers stood to attention. Chucks followed suit.

'Please, sit down. How are you?'

Chucks tried to talk but his mouth was dry and his tongue seemed to have glued to his palate.

'I hope you like this room. It was very difficult getting a hotel at this time of the night. Do you like this place? Should we go somewhere else?'

'It is OK, sir.'

'Are you a police officer?'

'Sir?'

'Are you a police officer?'

'No, sir.'

'So, why are you calling me sir?'

'I am sorry, sir.'

'Look, Chucks, I'm sorry that we tricked you in order to bring you here. You have to forgive me. Do you forgive me? You see, my boy Saliu that you have been bribing, he works for me, first. All the money you have given him has been paid into the account of the Nigerian Police Force. You know that bribing a policeman is an offence?'

Chucks swallowed.

'We will come to that later. There are a few things you must know. First, nobody knows you have been arrested, except me, Saliu, and the officers here with us. That means I can release you if I want to and it would be like this never happened. Do you understand?'

Chucks nodded.

'I want you to do something for me, just a little favour. Do you think you can do that for me Chucks?'

'What sir?' He hoped the man would ask him for a big bribe.

'I want you to tell me about the girl killed in front of Ronnie's Bar yesterday.'

'Ehn? Girl? What girl, sir?'

'You know what I'm talking about, Chucks. The girl killed for rituals yesterday.'

'Rituals? I don't know anything about any ritual, sir.'

'Chucks, I'm sure you're a reasonable man. I know you probably had a little part to play in it. It is not you I'm after, but the people you work for.'

'Sir, I don't work for anyone, sir. I swear I do not know anything about any ritual.'

'Come on, Chucks, the car that was used to dump the girl's body was found in your yard a few hours ago. You cannot tell me you don't know anything about it.'

'Sir, I swear on my life, I don't know anything about any girl or any ritual.'

'You don't know anything?'

'No, sir, I swear. I don't know anything about any ritual or any girl. I only deal in cars. Ask Saliu.'

'It's a pity you don't want to cooperate.'

Ibrahim stood and left the room and Sergeant Hot-Temper walked in through the open door.

'Is this the bastard? Bring him.'

Chucks recoiled at the sight of this new person. He was taken down the corridor to another room. Hot-Temper told the policeman accompanying him to leave and took charge of the prisoner. He pushed Chucks into the room, stepped in behind him and slammed the door.

The furniture had been pulled back. The bed had been lifted off the floor and was leaning against the wall. A single chair stood in its place and loose rope lay at its feet. Police officers began rolling up their sleeves.

'Customer,' an officer said, 'come and sit on your throne.'

Chucks balked. Warm urine ran down his legs.

'Please, please, don't do this. I'm begging you in Jesus' name, please don't do this.'

'You don't know me?' Hot-Temper said. 'I am Sergeant Hot-Temper. You must have heard of me. I am not like Inspector Ibrahim. Me, I don't waste time. You will tell me what I want to know, sharp-sharp.'

They gripped Chucks, forced him to the chair and held him down. Ropes fell over his face and tightened around his body. He shook uncontrollably.

The men finished securing him to the chair and stood back to admire their work.

'We are going to play a little game,' Hot-Temper said. 'It is called Know-your-mother. Are you ready?'

Inspector Ibrahim walked in.

'What are you boys doing?' He looked alarmed. 'You don't need to do this, he is going to cooperate.'

'You will cooperate?' Hot-Temper said.

'Yes, yes. I will cooperate. I will cooperate.'

'Oga, let us soften him up a bit,' Hot-Temper said.

'No need for that. Take him back to his room. He is a good boy. He will cooperate.'

Once he started, Chucks didn't stop talking. Yes, the car was stolen, but no, not at his request. The car was snatched by two boys, Knockout and Go-Slow. Yes, he had collected stolen vehicles from them in the past. No, he did not think they were part of a bigger gang.

He paid them two hundred thousand for the car. He had told them he wanted nothing to do with the vehicle but they begged him to take it off them. He did not know if they killed the girl or used the car to dump her body but he would not put anything past them. He knew where they lived. He could take the policemen there.

'What about the blood in the car?' Inspector Ibrahim said.

'I don't know anything about any blood. I haven't even inspected the car. If I'd seen any blood I wouldn't have accepted it.'

Ibrahim believed him. He called the station on his radio.

'Run these names on the system. Knockout and Go-Slow.'

The officer didn't have to. She had been listening to the traffic on the radio in the communications room all night and had received the signal from the command centre. She pulled up Chucks's updated record and gave the inspector a third name, Catch-Fire, then she told him about the gun-fight at Surulere.

Ibrahim asked the officer to stand by. He turned to Chucks.

'Do you know any Catch-Fire?'

'Catch-Fire? No, sir.'

Ibrahim studied him then he continued with his call.

'What is the status at the location?'

'Hot sir. Very hot.'

He turned a nub on his gadget. The radio went silent.

'Chucks, you will do one more thing for me tonight.'

41

Trapped behind their van, the brothers chanted spells and returned to the battle. They could leave, crawl in the open gutter behind them and climb out down the road where they could snatch a car. But Knockout's bill had swollen and he had to pay them tonight. If he was in the building, they had to go inside. They only hoped he was still alive.

Crouched against the wall, under jagged edges of glass, the girls snorted cocaine and took turns to raise their guns above the parapet and shoot into the street below. Catch-Fire had told them that these killers sent for him would kill them too, after raping them with the barrels of their guns.

A girl lay motionless on her back, on a bed of broken glass, gripping her left arm where blood from a gun-shot wound was soaking its way through cloth. She was breathing heavily through her mouth, staring up at nothing. Her sister, sprawled by her side, shook her and shouted.

Another girl, pressing bullets into a magazine, looked at them. 'She need bandage.' She rammed it into the gun. 'Go ask Catch-Fire.'

The sister crawled through the door into the corridor, mouthing the Lord's Prayer, and continued to Catch-Fire's room where she stopped when she heard voices.

'Shoot him, please, shoot him,' Catch-Fire said from the ground. 'Please, shoot him now.'

Go-Slow kept his gun aimed at his friend's head. 'Sharap.'

'What are you doing here?' Knockout said. His pistols were pointed at Go-Slow.

'I came to see Catch-Fire. What are you doing here?'

'I also came to see him.'

'With guns and thugs?'

Knockout had often made his friend angry, so he knew what Go-Slow was like when he was in a temper. He recognised the look on his face and it had nothing to do with anger. He had only seen that look a few times: always when they were about to kill someone Go-Slow would rather they didn't kill.

He held his friend's gaze, slowly moving his finger to the trigger. He knew that if he was too quick, Go-Slow would notice and make his own move even quicker.

Something warm and hard pressed into his neck. Without dropping his hands he saw the gun out of the corner of his eye, and the girl holding it. The rest of them were crowded onto the corridor, sweating, looking vicious, and pointing their weapons at him.

He grimaced, expecting to die from the girl's bullet or from his friend's. But Go-Slow didn't shoot. Knockout could still fire and take the big guy down, but why waste his last shot on a pal? He felt the muzzle press deeper into his throat. He smiled and braced himself for a bullet to tear through his neck, but not before he would swing round and shoot as many prostitutes as he could.

'Everybody, freeze.' The brothers, led by One-Nation, pointed their weapons at the girls.

Go-Slow scooped Catch-Fire from the ground and held him

in a neck choke. He pressed his gun hard against Catch-Fire's head to make sure he got a reaction.

Catch-Fire's body shook. 'You are with them.'

'I am not with them,' Go-Slow said. 'I am not with anyone. I just want to get out of this place alive. Tell your girls to drop their weapons.'

'You want to kill me?'

'Nobody is going to kill anybody. Just tell them to drop their weapons. Now. And you, Knockout, tell your men it is over. We are going to work this thing out.'

'Go-Slow, you too?' Catch-Fire said. 'You are with them. You have also come to kill me.'

'If you want to end this night alive, tell your girls to lower their weapons or I will shoot you myself. You too, Kanayo.'

The brothers, Knockout, Go-Slow, and Catch-Fire (who had Go-Slow's gun against his temple), backed out of Catch-Fire's house, escorted by the girls, who were still pointing their guns at the guns pointed at them.

A boy dozing on a bench on Knockout's road, outside his family's tyre repair business, heard a vehicle approaching and prayed it would drive over one of the rotten oranges he had stuck with nails.

The bus stopped in front of Knockout's bungalow and six men with guns jumped out and ran towards the building. The door yielded to the force of a sledge-hammer and the men rushed in.

In another part of the city, another van arrived at the address they had for Go-Slow: a well-kept block of flats on a tarred road in Maryland. One of them walked to the building. He kept his pistol out of sight under his shirt. He found a sleeping watchman behind the locked gate and rattled the chains on the padlock to wake him.

'Yes? What is it?' the old man said, yawning and stretching while he began to slap at the mosquitoes that had found exposed flesh on his neck.

'I am looking for Go-Slow.'

'Go-Slow? You mean, traffic jam?'

'No. My friend, we call him Go-Slow. He told me to come and find him here when I arrive in Lagos?'

'There is no one bearing that name here. You know his name? The one his parents gave him?'

'I don't remember, but he is very tall, and large. And darker than me but not as light as you.'

'Oh, OK. There is one tall man who used to stay here but they chased him away a long time ago. He was not paying his rent on time. It has been long since he packed out of this building. He didn't tell you he has moved?'

'No. He gave me this address. I just arrived in Lagos this night. I am supposed to stay with him. Can you remind me of his name? The one that moved out?'

'I think it is Ali, or Akpan, or Akin. It is something like that. It starts with A, but I can't remember. But he must be the one. All the other men that stay here are very short, like me. When last did you speak to him?'

'Just yesterday.'

'Why would he lie to you like that when he knows they have driven him from this place? Anyway, I cannot expect anything better from a shameless man that refuses to pay his rent. One pastor is renting the flat he used to stay in. The man is not a nice man; if he was I would have taken you to him so you can explain your situation – maybe he would let you sleep there till morning.'

'No, it's all right. I will be OK. So he left here a long time ago?'

'Yes. If you have his number you can call him. Maybe his new house is not far from here. Maybe that is why he told you to come here. Call him. Tell him Baba Segi is greeting him.'

'I've tried. He's not answering his phone.'

'Why is he doing this to you? I told you, he is a shameless man, if it is the same man we are talking about. Where does he expect you to sleep this night? Do you have any place you can go? Or can you manage here with me?' The old man pointed at his worn mat on the concrete floor behind the gate.

'It's all right, I'll be OK. Do you have any idea where he moved to?'

'I don't know, but if you come back in the morning, the building manager will be around, maybe he would know. Are you sure you don't want to stay here with me?'

'No, thank you baba.'

The man left to converse with his mates.

Once their car was out of sight, the old night guard went up to the building and pressed the bell to Go-Slow's flat.

The men looked under Knockout's bed and in his wardrobe. The bed was undone, there was semen in a condom left on the lid of a bin, and stew in a pot on the kerosene cooker that had not gone bad. Someone lived there, but there were no pictures on the walls or albums in drawers.

Outside, the boy watched. He dialled Knockout's number from memory, waited till the call was answered, said 'They are here,' then deleted the phone's call log.

The brothers got into their van last, after Go-Slow, Catch-Fire, and Knockout. The girls surrounded the vehicle. Kekere sat on pieces of glass and turned the key in the ignition. The engine did not make a sound. He tried again and got a click.

Catch-Fire, sandwiched between One-Love and Go-Slow, was shaking and crying. 'Please, just let me go, please.'

Kekere tried again and the engine roared. The silencers had taken bullets. With two flat tyres and no windows, he began to drive. He struggled with the steering to keep the vehicle straight and he kept his head low, expecting shots.

'We have to get rid of this car,' Go-Slow said from the rear.

'Yes,' replied One-Nation. He turned to Knockout in the middle row, between the brothers Oscar and Romeo. 'And this car will cost you three hundred thousand.'

Go-Slow's phone rang. It was his wife. As he took the call, Knockout's phone also began to ring. Go-Slow returned the phone to his pocket. 'Chineke,' Knockout shouted. 'I cannot go back home. Some men have just gone to my house with guns.'

'Police?' One-Love asked.

'I don't know. I don't think so. I think it is Chief Amadi. He sent me to kill Catch-Fire. He has sent people to kill me too.'

'Chief Amadi sent you to kill Catch-Fire?' Go-Slow said.

'Yes. He said we can join his business once we take care of Catch-Fire.'

'And you believed him?'

'Who is this Chief Amadi?' One-Love asked.

'He is a killer,' Catch-Fire said. 'He tried to poison me today. We must kill him or he will kill all of us.'

'Why does he want to kill you?' One-Nation asked.

'I was doing business with him before, ritual business. Human spare parts. I know all his secrets. That's why he wants to kill me, and kill Knockout. He is a very wicked man. He will find all of you and he won't stop until he kills everybody. We must kill him first.'

One-Love leaned forward and placed an arm on Knockout's shoulder. 'Friend, you did not tell us any of this. This kind of job is worth a lot more than we charged you.'

Knockout did not bother calculating what he now owed. His mind was on how Chief Amadi had made him look like a fool.

'How much did he pay you to kill Catch-Fire?' Go-Slow said.

One-Love turned to look at Knockout. 'We would all like to know. How much did you collect?'

'Nothing.'

'You mean nothing yet or nothing at all?' One-Love said.

'I told you, nothing. He said I should call him after I have killed the boy. Maybe then he would pay me.'

Listening to them discuss his assassination made Catch-Fire uneasy. 'You have to call him now and tell him you have killed me,' he said, then recited a silent prayer to ward off bad luck from speaking about his own death. 'Ask him where to meet him. We will all go there and kill him.'

'That is a good plan,' Go-Slow said.

One-Love thought about it. 'Tell him you haven't killed Catch-Fire. Tell him you have kept him in a safe place and he must bring ten million naira with him or else Catch-Fire will go to the police.'

'How will we share the money?' Knockout said.

'When we have calculated how much you owe us, we will divide the rest equally.'

'But will we kill him?' Catch-Fire asked.

They all turned to look at him, even Kekere who was driving. Catch-Fire wasn't going to get a share of the money, he probably knew that and he probably didn't care so long as Amadi was killed.

'We will kill him,' Knockout said.

42

Ibrahim had not slept in over twenty-four hours. He was tired, he was irritable, and now he was getting frustrated.

An officer had called to tell him that going to the homes of the two criminals had yielded no arrests. It was possible that they had been tipped off. The plan had been to detain their family members to draw them out. He wondered just how many of his officers took bribes.

So far, all he had was Chucks, who clearly knew nothing of the girl's murder, and the two names the crook had given up. He had never heard of them. On another day that wouldn't have mattered: being in possession of the stolen vehicle involved in the crime would have been enough to charge Chucks with the murder and parade him to the press as an example of the police doing their job of apprehending criminals – ritual killers included. But this was different. This had made it onto CNN and that damned British journalist had witnessed it. He had also witnessed the murder of a detainee. That's what he would call it when he reported it: Nigerian Police Kill Defenceless Suspect in Cell. It wouldn't matter that the boy was a member of a notorious gang of armed robbers and possibly a killer himself. Armed robbery carries the death penalty in Nigeria. The boy would have been executed anyway, but that wouldn't matter to Mr Guy Collins of the BBC.

What was Amaka's part in all this? She was going to make him regret being so nice to her and giving her so much freedom.

There was also the small matter of the police commissioner who kept calling for updates. Does the man even sleep?

Thank God he had one more lead to follow. He called his station and left instructions for the men of operation Fire-for-Fire to be ready to move when he returned. A convoy of armoured vehicles arrived on Catch-Fire's street, lights flashing, sirens screaming, and tyres screeching. They blocked off the road by parking zigzag across it. The men took positions behind their vehicles and aimed their guns at the building.

Ibrahim had a bulletproof vest over his shirt. He had armed himself with an Uzi sub-machine gun and the men awaited his command.

A generator was humming in the background. The air smelt of carbide. Spent shells lay scattered on the road, and two dead bodies were sprawled in the doorway of the building. At their feet, two black dogs sat as if guarding the carnage.

The beasts growled at the men, stood, and barked, digging their front paws into the ground and pulling their muscular bodies backwards ready to charge.

Ibrahim pointed to Hot-Temper then to the dogs. The sergeant fired two shots from his Kalashnikov.

Ibrahim held his hand out for a megaphone. 'This is the Nigeria Police. Come out with your hands on your heads and you will not be hurt. This is your first and final warning.'

One of the dogs whimpered on its back and kicked the air with its hind leg. Ibrahim handed back the megaphone and cocked his Uzi. He fired off a bust of bullets punching holes into the dead bodies on the ground and making them jolt like they still had life in them.

Moments later, the door opened. The men got ready to shoot. A girl walked out with her hands raised above her head. She was young, barefoot, and wearing hot pants and a black bra. Sweat had glued strands of her hair to her forehead and neck. She slowly walked towards the men. Others followed behind her.

'What is this?' Ibrahim said. Where were the gunmen? Was this a whorehouse? Had they come to the wrong address?

'To your knees,' Hot-Temper said, gesturing with the barrel of his gun. Officers surrounded them.

Ibrahim waved and Hot-Temper led the men into the house.

'What happened here?' Ibrahim asked the girls. Nobody answered. He tried to make eye contact but they looked away. One girl had clearly been crying. A cloth, wet with blood, was wrapped around her hand. He pointed to her. 'You, stand up. Come here.'

The girl shifted her weight from one knee to the other then turned her gaze the other way.

'Bring her.'

Two officers slung their rifles back and stepped through the throng of girls to fetch her. The rest of the girls stood up and surrounded their friend. They ignored the guns now held with renewed vigour to their faces. On the command to 'stay down,' they began to protest in a dialect none of the men understood.

'Leave them,' Ibrahim said. Other officers were already handing their guns to colleagues to go join in quelling the riot.

Ibrahim handed his Uzi to an officer beside him. He undid the Velcro straps on his body armour and pulled the heavy suit off his head. The officer took it. With the girls still watching, he removed the pistol in his holster and handed it to the officer, then spread his hands and stepped closer to them. 'Ladies, the police are your friends. We are only here to help. I am only concerned because she's wounded. Is anybody else wounded?'

'We are fine,' one of the girls said.

'What is your name?'

'Cecilia.'

The other girls watched her. They let her speak for them.

'OK, Cecilia, what happened here tonight? Who did all this?'

'Armed robbers.'

'Armed robbers? What did they steal?'

'I don't know.'

'Where are you from, Cecilia?'

'From Lagos.'

'I don't think so. I think you are from Togo. Do you have papers to live in Nigeria?'

She eyed him, hissed, and looked away.

'I can arrange papers for you, and your friends.'

'We no need papers, we are not illegal. We are from Lagos.'

'Is that right? Where in Lagos are you from?'

'Surulere, here.'

'And who is the President of Nigeria?'

With the corner of her eyes, she scanned him from his toes to his eyes then back to his toes, like a confident wrestler sizing up a mismatched opponent. She let out a long loud hiss, crossed her arms over her breasts and looked away.

'Cecilia, I just want to talk to that girl. I don't have any problem with you. I just want to talk to her then I'll leave with my men.'

'What do you want to ask her?'

'I would like to ask her myself.'

She looked at him, taking him all in with a single roll of her eyeballs.

'Please,' Ibrahim said.

She turned to the girls. 'Joy. Come.'

Joy stepped out of the protection of her friends. She stopped by Cecilia and looked at her feet.

'Joy, are you OK?' Ibrahim asked.

'Yes, sir.'

'Joy, we are here to help you. Who did this to you?'

'I don't know, sir.'

'Do you know Catch-Fire?'

She looked at Cecilia who shook her head.

'Is he dead? Did they kill him?'

Her eyes turned cloudy and she began to sniff.

Ibrahim stepped forward and put his arms around her, careful not to touch her bandaged arm. He held her to his chest and patted her on the back. 'It is OK,' he said, 'it is OK.'

'It is Chief.' She began to say. Cecilia stepped forward but the officers quickly grabbed her and dragged her away.

Ibrahim held Joy's hand and walked with her away from the other girls. Cecilia shouted something in their language. Joy turned to look back but Ibrahim gently encouraged her on with his arm. Two officers followed them holding their guns ready, their eyes darting around.

'Tell me what happened.'

Tears fell down the girl's cheeks. He pulled out his handkerchief and dabbed her face. 'It is OK. I am here. Everything will be OK. Who is Chief?'

'Chief, he sent his boys to kill our oga. They came with many men and they started to shoot everybody.'

'Catch-Fire, is that your oga?'

'Yes, sir.'

'Where is he now?'

'They took him away.'

'Why did Chief send people to kill him?'

She looked back at the rest of the girls. Cecilia was struggling with two officers trying to force her to her knees. The other girls stayed down under the guns trained on them. 'Oga said it is because of their business.'

'What business?'

'They do human ritual business together.'

Ibrahim paused and took a deep breath. 'Do you know the Chief's name?' he asked.

'Yes. His name is Chief Amadi. Chief Ebenezer Amadi.'

He stopped walking and stared at her. Her hands flew up to shield her face. He looked back at the officers following them. Perhaps they hadn't heard her.

'I'm not going to hurt you,' he said. He checked on the officers. 'You and your friends must leave Lagos tonight. If anybody asks you, you don't know any Catch-Fire or any Chief Amadi. Do you understand? If you don't want to be arrested and deported, you must leave Lagos tonight. OK?'

43

I was nodding, pretending to understand what a sloshed older friend of Gabriel was saying when Amaka placed her hands on my shoulders from behind and said 'Time to leave.' It was almost midnight. Had she found the man she came for? I wanted to tell her about my conversation with Gabriel but I decided against it. In silence, we found her car and in silence, she drove us back to VI.

She pulled up in front of the hotel lobby and left the engine idling. It hurt that she wasn't staying. I didn't get out.

'Aunty Baby called,' she said. 'The meeting has been set for two p.m. I'll pick you up at one thirty.'

'What do you hope to achieve by meeting him? You don't even know if he's the killer.'

'I already told you. He was on my 'Don't Go With' list, and then yesterday a girl calls because her girlfriend hasn't returned. And whose plate number does she give me? His. It's too much of a coincidence.'

'Fair enough, but do you expect him to simply confess to you?'

'No. I'm not stupid. I have a plan.'

'What's your plan?'

'I need to get close to him first.'

'That's your plan? To get close to him? Then what?'

'It's late, Guy, I need to get some sleep.'

Perhaps it was better to wait until the morning to try to change her mind. I considered leaning over to kiss her goodnight. She wasn't even looking at me. I got out of the car and shut the door.

I crawled under the duvet. We had not let the cleaners in so the sheets still smelt of her perfume. I pulled a pillow into my arms and hugged it.

I was slowly shutting down. Flavio's words kept repeating in my head: 'Girls like a man who has a talent. What is your talent?' I did have one talent, or maybe it's more of a skill. I was a darn good researcher. I could find enough material off the web to flesh out any story I was working on. I had perfected the skill at work when deadlines loomed after boozy nights. In the morning, I was going to dig deeper into this ritual killing thing. I was going to learn as much as there was to learn and I was going to impress her with the story I would write. In the space between waking and sleeping, with the latter gaining in the tussle, a thought flourished unchallenged, and emboldened itself into a truth: what if Amaka had only slept with me to get me to do her bidding?

My mind, slowly shutting down, dwelled on this. I thought everything over: how her towel slipped, the kiss in the elevator, how we ended up in bed, what she said afterwards, how she said it. How she wouldn't let me kiss her in public at News Café, how she dropped me off knowing that I would be here waiting to take instructions from her in the morning…

I woke up to my head throbbing with a light hangover and then recalled the night's drinking session with Gabriel. I'd bought a packet of maximum-strength Ibuprofen at Heathrow. The thought of searching my bags for it made my head hurt even more. I made myself a coffee and checked the time. Twelve thirty. I still had an hour before she turned up. I powered up my laptop and lit a cigarette. She would find me working on her story and see how seriously I was taking it.

Habitually, I opened up my emails. The ten latest messages were from my boss. I'd forgotten all about him. The last message was ten minutes old. I read the subject header in his voice: 'Where the hell are you?'

As I opened it, I felt a familiar anxiety that reminded me of my working day back in London. The Walrus was not the most pleasant of men. There was no telling what would set off his temper. Not replying to his emails within minutes was one of the triggers. At least I was not in the open-plan office where he had reduced many colleagues to tears. What was the worst he could do over the internet?

The first sentence was, as I expected, a prologue to justify what would come next: 'Guy, this is the twentieth email I have sent to you in the past twelve hours that you have chosen to ignore.' I didn't bother reading further. I picked up the phone by the bed, dialled zero, and asked the operator to put an international call through.

'Hello?' the Walrus said.

'This is Guy.' I braced for the assault.

'Guy. Where the hell have you been? What happened to your phone? Where are you calling from?'

'I'm at the hotel.'

'I called the hotel. They said you checked out. What the fuck is going on?'

'I lost my phone.'

'You lost your phone? And it did not occur to you to get a new one or send an email to the office?'

'I was going to do that just now.'

'So, what the hell have you been doing? Sitting on your arse? Do you know how much it costs to have you out there? I spoke to your guide, Ade. He's been trying to get in touch with you. Have you spoken to him?'

I'd forgotten about him. 'No.'

'When he couldn't get in touch with you, he was intelligent enough to call me.'

'He's been in Abuja since I arrived,' I said.

'He's back in Lagos but how would you know if you've made yourself incommunicado?' He was doing the thing he did in the office when he spoke slowly as if talking to an imbecile whose brain could not process normal speech.

'I've been working on a story.'

'What story? Ade told me there is no story. The election is going to be free and fair. UN observers are going to be all over it. There's not going to be any rigging and no riots, so there's no story, just boring stuff. He also said he can't guarantee your safety; I can't blame him if it's going to be like having a kid running wild in the circus. I've hired him to cover the damn thing. As far as I'm concerned your assignment is over. Sally will arrange your flight for tonight. She'll send you the details. Check your email and be on that flight. This has been a bloody waste of money.' He ended the call.

I had called his mobile thus denying him the joy of slamming the phone down on me. I wondered if I should give it a few minutes then call him back. I couldn't leave Nigeria. Not now. But if I wasn't on that flight, I might not have a job to go back to. I couldn't afford that either.

I looked through the rest of my emails and saw that Mel had

sent me something. I realised it was the longest time I'd gone without thinking about her since our break-up. I double clicked and questioned my sense of expectation. It was a group email, something about saving London's Africa Centre. I studied the other people copied in; their email addresses all started with G.

Someone knocked. It had to be Amaka. I closed one eye to look through the peephole all the same. She walked in, taller in black stilettos. She was in a black leather skirt that rode high above her knees and a bare-shoulder purple silk top with straps so thin you could hardly see them.

'Hi,' she said. She went to my computer and started typing. 'He wants to meet over lunch. I've been doing some digging around. It appears more than one girl has gone missing with him.'

'How did you find out?' Had she slept at all?

'I called some older girls. But that's not all, I also talked to some business contacts I bumped into at the party – people who know him. I told them I was raising money for my charity and someone had recommended him.'

'And what did they say?'

'Nobody knows how he made his money. He's been trying to join Ikoyi Club for a while but they've always snubbed him.'

'I thought Aunty Baby said he was a member?'

'Well, he isn't. To join, a number of members must recommend you and you have to be above a certain level at work, be director of a listed company, be above a certain rank in the armed forces, something like that. They're very careful who they take. No one knows what he does for a living or how he became so rich, so no one is willing to risk their reputation recommending him. He goes to the club often, though, posing as a member. He probably has friends who are members who sign him in.'

'But you still have no evidence that he was involved in the girl's murder.'

'I don't but he's obviously into something illegal. It could be drugs, he could be laundering money from some people, it could be anything. A bank MD I spoke to tried to convince me not to see him.'

I wanted to tell her that Gabriel shared the MD's sentiments. 'Why?'

'Well, he just said the man is not right for my charity. He was uneasy when I said I was meeting him today.'

'Maybe we shouldn't go, then. I mean, that sounds like a warning.'

'And that is precisely why I am going. The MD is a traditional chief as well. He's involved in the occult. I'm thinking he might know something about him and that might be the reason he doesn't like the idea of me mixing with him. These people know each other.'

'Occult? You mean another ritual killer?'

'Oh no,' she laughed. 'He's a member of the Ogboni. It's more like a fraternity. It's a Yoruba traditional secret society, a bit like the Freemasons. People say they practice black magic but I wouldn't know. The fact that he didn't want me to associate with Amadi makes me even more suspicious.'

'I really don't like this, Amaka.'

'You don't have to. Listen, I've just changed my email password to your name, Guy Collins, one word. I always email myself all the information I get. My database, pictures, movie clips, it's all in there. I've left my webmail open.'

'Why are you telling me this?'

'I've always thought that someone else should have access to it. Just in case.'

'In case what?'

'Just in case. Anyway, you need the information to write your article. I have to go now. Stay in the room, I might need to reach you on the phone.'

'Where are you going?'

'I told you, to have lunch with him.'

'I thought we were going together?'

'It's better that I go alone.'

'Dressed like that?'

She glanced at me. 'What do you mean? What are you insinuating?'

'Nothing, Amaka. Look, I really don't think this is a good idea. At least let me come with you.'

'I have to do this alone. Your part is to tell the story. And besides, nobody must be able to link us to one another. Do you understand?'

'But what do you expect to achieve by going to see him?'

'I told you, I don't know. We'll just have to wait and see.'

She got up to leave. I watched her walking away and decided I had to tell her how I felt. I caught up with her and held her by the arm. 'Amaka, I don't want you to go because I care for you.'

She stopped but she did not turn round. 'You care for me?'

'Yes. I do. I really do.'

'And why would that be?'

I didn't have an answer. 'I just do. And I don't want to see you get hurt.'

'Hurt? By who, you or the person I'm going to see?'

'You know what I mean, Amaka. I think you're really in over your head with this one. You don't have to do this. This man might be dangerous. Amaka, what I'm trying to say is…' The timing was wrong. 'Look, I don't know how I got involved in this mess but all I know is that there are evil people out there and this guy might be one of them.'

She turned her head sideways and looked at me from the corner of her eye. 'You got involved in this mess, as you put it, because you went out looking for black pussy, remember? Well, congratulations, you've had one. Don't tell me you care for me. You don't know me and I don't know you. You will return to your girlfriend in England, and then what?'

I shook my head. 'Amaka, it's not like that.'

She turned to face me. 'No? And how is it? Tell me? How is it? All I am to you is some black adventure. I know your type. You people come here thinking you can just tell a girl that you care for her and she'll melt into your arms – as if you're doing her some kind of favour. I don't want to regret what happened between us. Please, don't make me.'

She left, leaving me stunned. Where did all that come from? I knew I shouldn't have told her about Melissa, but what the hell? I couldn't worry about that now though, because more importantly she had just left to go and meet a potential killer. I had to do something.

I went through my inbox searching for an email. I found it and used the phone in the room to call the number I knew it would contain.

'Hello? Ade? It's me, Guy.'

'Guy? You are still in Nigeria?'

'Yes. I'm at the hotel. I need to see you now.'

He asked for my room number.

'Don't leave the room,' he said. 'I'm coming now.'

I wondered how much I would have to tell him.

44

'Please, we have to go back for my dogs,' Knockout said again.

They ignored him. They had driven through the night to the brothers' hideout: a room in a trucker's motel in Badagry.

Catch-Fire told them what they needed to know about Chief Amadi: he would ask to meet at a secluded place, probably at his secret bungalow off the Lekki expressway. He would have no problems paying the ransom. He would ask for assurance that Catch-Fire was dead, then he would try to kill Knockout as well. They had to kill Chief Amadi.

Go-Slow came up with a plan. Knockout would call Chief Amadi and ask to meet alone. If Amadi asked where Catch-Fire was, Knockout would tell him that his men, who were waiting for him to return with the money, were holding him. If Knockout failed to return on time, the men would drop Catch-Fire at a police station where he would tell them everything he knew. Knockout didn't know where Catch-Fire was being held, only where to return with the money. If on his return the men suspected something was afoot, they would take Catch-Fire to the police. If he returned without the money, they would also take Catch-Fire to the police.

'No,' Catch-Fire said. He had been silent, listening to the rest of them making the plan. Now they all looked at him.

'What?' Go-Slow said.

'Not just the police. He always brags that he knows every oga of police. Tell him that you will invite the media to come and hear me confessing how I used to drug people and kill them with him. That would scare him more. If you say you are taking me to the police, he will tell you to do your worst.'

Go-Slow and the twins exchanged nods.

'Tell him we are taking his boy to the police headquarters at Panti, and that we have told radio and television reporters to meet us there,' Go-Slow said. 'Tell him we have recorded his confession and we will send the video to saharareporters.com.' He asked Knockout to recite the instructions one more time before calling the Chief. Knockout swore at him. One-Love asked him to repeat the instructions three times. He did.

45

Amaka realised that she knew Chief Amadi's house when Aunty Baby described it to her. Her family had lived on the same street years ago. She remembered the building being a colonial-style bungalow before someone bought it and tore down the old house, replacing it with a mansion. As she drove into his compound, she took note of the cars parked under canopies. She recognised some of the licence plate numbers and memorised the rest.

A security guard showed her where to park then he held the door open for her. She saw him trying to look down her skirt as she climbed out of the car.

'Welcome, ma. Chief is waiting for you.' He bowed and held his hand out in a way that reminded her of a waiter showing her the way to her table.

She paused at the sight of an elderly Chinese man in chef whites who opened the door.

'Welcome. Please, come.'

As she stepped into the foyer, she observed the statues on small plinths, oil paintings on the walls and the carved wood banister of the staircase that curved up to the next floor.

Her host appeared at the top of the stairs. He was in a purple silk tunic that stretched to his toes. He took his time descending, his hand sliding on the banister. At the bottom, he stretched out his hands and waited for her to come to him.

'You must be Amaka. You are on time, I'm impressed.'

He wrapped his arms around her and held her tight. She was about to ease out of his hold when he let go.

'We are twins,' he said, pointing at their outfits.

It took a moment for her to realise he meant the colour. She smiled politely, noting that the charm offensive had begun.

'Come. I can't wait to hear all about your charity work.'

He led her into a huge dining room. The long table had been set at the middle with two chairs on opposite sides. He led her to what he had decided was her side and pulled the chair out for her before walking the long distance round to sit opposite her. The old Chinese man waited by his side.

'Tom would like to know what you are having for lunch.'

She did not have an appetite. 'Oh. Erm, what's being offered?'

'Tom?'

Tom fetched a folded sheet of white paper from his pocket. He unfolded it and presented it to her with both hands. She did not know anybody in Lagos who had a Chinese cook.

'Shrimp dumpling soup sounds good,' Amaka said, returning the menu.

'Make me the usual,' Chief Amadi said and the chef left.

'Tell me everything about your charity work. Why should I donate my money to you instead of an orphanage?'

'Well, for one, the work we do ensures that fewer babies are dumped at orphanages.'

Fifteen minutes later she was running out of things to say when he raised his hand to stop her. 'Darling, I'm sold,' he said. 'This is the kind of thing I like to get involved in. The truth is I'd rather support this kind of work than pay tithes to a pastor.

I'll write you a cheque for five million naira today and see what I can do later.'

'Wow. Thanks. I don't know what to say. I've never raised that much money for the charity so quickly. I mean, with the corporate sponsors, our big donors, I have to write proposals and attend meetings, and even then it still takes months before I see a cheque. This is a record. Thank you, sir.'

'You are welcome, ma. Your corporate sponsors do it for publicity. I do it because I genuinely want to. And it's not because a pretty girl is the one asking me.'

'I really don't know what to say. Five million is a lot. Thank you. Really, really, thank you.'

'Stop thanking me, please. You're going to make me blush with my black skin.'

'Do you mind if I ask you something? What exactly do you do?'

'Do? You mean, business wise? The question you want to ask is, what don't I do?'

'OK. What don't you do?'

'Steal. Anything else that brings good money, I've either done it, I'm doing it, or the profit is not big enough. I've done all sorts. It's the Igbo in me. I've done container business, frozen fish, tokunbo cars, cleaning business, even government contracts. Any clean business that brings good money.'

'You call government contracts clean?'

'You are funny.'

'Where do you draw the line?'

'What line?'

'You said you'd do any business except steal.'

'No. Any profitable, clean business. Stealing is not a business.'

'But where do you draw the line? What makes one business

clean and another not clean?'

'This sounds like an interview.'

'I'm just curious.'

'You are in my house and we are talking about me. It's making me look pompous. Let's talk about you instead.'

'I've told you everything about myself.'

'No. You've told me everything about the charity. What about you? Who is Miss Amaka?'

'Well, let's see, Amaka is a professional, single, female Nigerian who enjoys swimming, travelling, oh, and clubbing. Like last night, I was in a club on the island. What did you do last night?'

'Last night? I was in my bed, darling. Sleeping alone.'

'Really? What about your wife?'

'She's in America.'

'You were in this house all through the night?'

'Yes. Why are you asking?'

'You know this is Lagos, and Lagos men are allergic to sleeping alone.'

'You are very funny. Are you sure that's the only reason you're asking?'

'Yes. What other reason would there be? I'm just a curious girl.'

'I'm also curious now. Maybe you think you saw me somewhere? Maybe the club you went to?'

'No. I was just asking.' Amaka looked around. 'You have a lovely home.'

'Thank you. You know what? While we wait for Tom, why don't I take you on a tour?' He got to his feet without waiting for a response and skipped round the long table to fetch her.

He took her through each room on the ground floor and had a story to tell about everything. He had bought the grand piano because his daughter saw it in a shop window in Switzerland and she wanted to play it. The crystal chandelier was a gift from a business associate and the Le Corbusier chaise longue was bought on a whim.

They climbed the staircase to the first floor and through another series of rooms. He opened the door to his bedroom last.

'And like they say on MTV, this is where the magic happens.'

His phone rang. He groaned. 'Sorry, darling, this is business. I have to go downstairs to my study, do you mind?'

'Nope.'

'OK, please feel free.' He waved at his room.

Just as she expected, he had led her to his bedroom. Men. She shook her head and waited till she saw him disappear down the stairs, then she walked to the chest of drawers with family pictures arranged on top of it and pulled out the top drawer. She had no idea what she was looking for; she simply hoped to find something – anything.

46

I checked to see who was knocking. A man's face, rounded out of shape by the curved lens of the peephole filled my line of sight.

'Guy, it's me, Ade.'

I opened the door and finally met my elusive minder. He was shorter than I'd expected. We shook hands in silence, then he apologised for being in Abuja and asked that we go down to the poolside. On the way there I brought him up to date with what had happened. I started at the beginning with Ronnie's Bar. He wasn't fazed when I mentioned the dead body in a gutter. I said it appeared to be a ritual killing and he nodded. Then I told him about the horror at Inspector Ibrahim's police station and how Amaka deceived the police inspector into releasing me. Lastly, I told him how a girl had called Amaka because her friend had gone missing after being picked up by a man the night before. Amaka checked the man's licence plate on her records and Chief Amadi's name came up. She was sure the missing girl was the body in the gutter, and Chief Amadi had something to do with it.

I'd told him about Amaka's records before I remembered it was a secret. Thankfully, he seemed as disinterested as I had been when she first told me about them.

He listened without interrupting. We might well have been

talking about the weather. At the bar near the pool, he ordered a bottle of Star for himself and a gin and tonic for me.

'What do you know about ritual murder?' I said.

'Nothing. It's just one of those things that we still need to eradicate from our society.' He sounded disinterested.

'What I don't get is how this can still be going on today. It should be obvious to anybody that black magic is bollocks. How come people still believe in it?'

He checked his watch and looked over his shoulder at the lobby.

'Are you expecting somebody?'

'No. So, your friend Amaka has gone to the Chief's house?'

'Yes. I tried to convince her not to go. Won't it be something if she single-handedly exposes him?'

'Yes, it would be something. Please excuse me. I need to use the toilet.'

I pointed the way. He started to make a call as he walked.

47

Amaka's heart was beating so fast that she felt short of breath as she opened drawer after drawer, probing into each with her fingers, careful to leave everything as she found it. She pushed the last one in and stopped to listen. She went to the closet, opened the first door and reached in. Each time she parted neatly hung clothes, the thought of discovering a skull on top of a hidden shrine held her back a moment before she looked. She turned to the drawers at the dressing table and cringed as she slowly drew each one out. She rifled through jewellery and odd bits inside but found nothing.

Amaka stood looking around the room. It was sparse but neatly furnished with few places to hide stuff. Her eyes rested on the huge bed, the only place she hadn't searched. She pulled up the covers. She cocked her head to hear if someone was coming then she bent down and reached with her hands under the bed. There was a black bag. Her fingers touched the leather exterior. She found the handle, gripped it, and dragged the bag out from under the bed. It was heavy. The type that lawyers carry. She placed her thumbs on each of its brass locks and pushed. It clicked open. The bag was full of dollars. She gasped. On top of the neatly arranged bundles of one hundred dollar bills was a small black book, like a small diary.

48

When Ade returned from the bathroom, he asked if I was enjoying my time in Nigeria. Had he not heard anything I'd said? Had he become so used to the madness in this country that he had become immune to it? He checked the time.

'Do you have to be somewhere?'

'No.'

'She has gone to his house.' Did he miss that bit about the guy possibly being a killer?

'What does she expect to find at this Chief Amadi's house?'

'I don't know. I've been doing some research into ritual murder in Africa but I haven't found any solid information. What exactly do they do with the organs they take from their victims?'

'All sorts of charms, I guess.'

'Money rituals? I read about that too. Exactly how does it work?'

'I really wouldn't know, Guy.'

'They seem to have a preference for human heads but I also read that they sometimes take eyes and tongues and breasts?'

'Yes,' he said and sighed. 'That is what the papers report. They take virtually every organ in the body: heart, lungs, livers, kidneys, even testicles.'

'So, you do know something about it?'

'Well, I'm a journalist. I've come across several similar cases. What is reported in the papers is not always what actually happened. I once saw a corpse that had its liver removed. It had been lying in the bush for some time and animals, maybe birds, had eaten its eyes. I read in the papers the next day that the man had been killed only for his eyes.'

A member of hotel staff walked up to us. 'Mr Collins?'

'Yes?' I vaguely remembered the chap from my first day at the hotel.

'You have a call at the lobby, sir. Miss Amaka.'

'Oh.' She'd asked me to stay in the room and I'd forgotten. Ade followed as I went to take the call.

'Do you have a pen?' she said. She was whispering.

I got a pen and a writing pad from a receptionist behind the counter.

'Where are you?'

'I'm in his room. Listen, I think I found something. It looks like a code. Take down these numbers.'

'Where is he?'

'Downstairs. Guy, I have to be quick. It's in a diary he hid under his bed. See if you can figure it out.'

She began to read out the numbers. 'Amaka? Amaka?'

The line was dead. The phone showed the caller ID and I dialled the number. It rang but she didn't answer.

'What happened?' Ade said.

'She's in his room. She found some numbers in a diary. She thinks it's some kind of code. She wants me to try to figure it out.'

'Let me see.' He took the pad I'd been writing in.

I went over the conversation I'd just had with her, trying to remember if I heard any sounds or anyone else when she ended the call. I tried her again. The receptionist eyed me as if I should have asked before making a call.

'These are flight numbers,' Ade said. 'Virgin Atlantic international flight numbers. See this? This is the date of the flight, and this part, this is the flight number. He has written them all together without spaces. That's why it appears like a code.'

'Flight numbers?'

'Yes. They normally start with V S but he has left out the letters and the dashes between the dates. Maybe the man is only into drug trafficking. This could be the flight numbers and arrival dates of his couriers.'

'Drugs? No.'

Since I'd been researching the killings, a thought had been forming at the back of my mind. I'd not been able to pin it down but it had stayed with me, tugging at my consciousness. It all came together.

'I knew this juju thing didn't make sense.' I said.

'What?'

Livers, kidneys, hearts, and now flight numbers. It all suddenly made sense.

'Don't you see? They are selling body parts. Think about it. You said they take livers, kidneys, hearts. Back in the UK, people spend years on waiting lists for an organ transplant. Why wait to die when you can get a bent surgeon to find you the organ you need on the black market? In Nigeria. I bet you, if we cross-check the medical records of people on those flights with these so-called ritual killings we would discover a strong tie. They are killing people for transplants.'

He cocked his head to one side as he looked at me.

'That's all it is, Ade, we've cracked it. They are selling organs to rich foreigners.'

'Guy?'

'Yes?'

'I need to use the toilet.'

The receptionist had moved the phone away. I ignored her eyes and pulled it back to me. I wanted to tell Amaka what I'd discovered. I wanted to tell her that she could leave his house now.

I was still waiting for her to answer the call when Ade returned.

'What's wrong?' he said.

'I think she was sneaking around his stuff when she called. I think he might have caught her.'

'So, what do you want to do about it?'

'I have to go there. Do you have a car?'

'Yes.'

49

Amaka heard footsteps. She dropped the diary and pushed the bag under the bed.

'Food is ready,' Tom said from behind the door.

She adjusted her hair in the mirror on the dressing table and waited until he had left. Then she picked her phone from the floor by the bed and walked out of the room. She tucked it into the strap of her skirt behind her back. It vibrated silently. She knew it was Guy calling back but she couldn't answer it. She had come so close to being caught.

The Chinese man walked ahead of her down the stairs. Had he seen her getting up from beside the bed? Amadi was standing at the bottom with a man whose back was to her. He smiled at her and the man turned. It was Inspector Ibrahim. Amaka held the oak banister for support.

'Amaka, come and meet my friend,' Amadi said.

Ibrahim looked straight into her eyes.

50

Ade's car was an old Toyota Corolla. He climbed in and opened the passenger door from inside. The stifling heat of the car combined with the overwhelming, obnoxious scent of air freshener made me cough.

'Do you have his address?' he asked.

Till that moment I hadn't thought of that – I just wanted to get to Amaka. I felt stupid. His hand was at the ignition, ready to go.

'Chief Amadi is a popular Lagosian,' Ade said. 'I think I know where the house is.'

He drove out of the hotel. Stationary cars stretched both ways on the dual carriage road, bumpers almost touching. He inched forward but no one let us through. Traffic lights kept changing colours unnoticed. What was a two-lane road had gained a third lane. Rickety commercial buses, packed with squeezed-in passengers, rode with one set of wheels on the pavement. Their 'conductors' hung from open doors, calling out destinations, soliciting for more passengers amongst the people walking the pavement which they made unsafe.

Added to the chaos were scrawny bikers stubbornly trying to navigate their beaten okada through the jam, their passengers perched on the brink of disaster behind them, enduring jerks and jolts as the drivers tried steering through the impossible maze.

Horns of all tones and pitches bleated. I wondered why they bothered to honk. No one could move. It was bedlam.

51

'Amaka, meet Ibrahim, my friend.'

Ibrahim squeezed her hand. 'We know each other very well. We even have a mutual friend,' he said, looking into her eyes and not letting go of her.

'It's a small world.'

'Yes. And it's getting smaller all the time.'

She felt numb. Ibrahim had probably found out that she lied about the minister. Had he also found out what she was up to? They say that every big criminal in Nigeria has police protection.

'Well, since you know each other perhaps you should stay and join us for lunch.'

Her heart pounded. Ibrahim's grip was getting tighter. How could she have missed this? How could she have failed to check whom Amadi knew in the police? All she had to do was ask around and someone would have told her. Guy warned her not to come and now she had walked into a trap.

'I have to go and take care of something,' Ibrahim said. He released her hand. 'Chief, let us continue our discussion outside.'

'OK, I'll see you off. Amaka, please, give me a minute will you?' They left together.

Tom was standing in a corner, watching her. She remembered the guard that had let her in. Who else was in the house? She looked around. The paintings stared back at her like extra guards.

Amadi returned. She was standing in the same spot. She searched his face. What had he learned about her?

'Don't let us keep Tom waiting,' he said. He placed his palm on her back and her body shuddered.

Her legs were moving but she did not feel them. She was walking where he led but it felt like floating. The table came towards her. Her chair slid out. She sat but everything kept moving. He was talking but she couldn't hear him. Tom appeared by her side, placed a napkin on her lap, and vanished. Everywhere she turned, Tom was there, keeping watch over her, making sure she could not escape. She felt dizzy.

'Amaka.'

Everything slowed down. The beating of her heart faded to the tick-tock of a wall clock behind her.

'Amaka.'

She focused.

'Amaka. What's wrong?' His face became clear again.

'Are you all right?'

'Yes. I'm fine. I think I sat down too quickly.'

'Are you sure? Should I get you something?'

'No. Really, please, sit down. I'm OK.'

'You scared me for a moment there. I could already see the headlines: 'Last Seen Alive Entering Chief Amadi's House.' '

It was a cruel joke. He knew everything about her. He knew what she had come to do.

'And what would they say Chief Amadi did with Amaka?'

He laughed. 'Oh, what wouldn't they say? A pretty girl in a rich man's house with his family away? They will put two and two together and arrive at five.'

'Would it be because that is what rich men do with pretty girls or because that is what you do with pretty girls?'

'Girls? I don't do anything with girls. I am a one woman man, I swear. Only one girl at a time. After another.'

He laughed. He was enjoying this. Should she run? And if so, where to?

'But I hear you like having two girls at a time. I almost didn't come to see you because I didn't have a friend to bring along.' She placed a palm on her chest and drew her fingers down, dragging her top with it.

He stopped laughing and watched her hand. She dragged her nails over her cleavage.

'Well? Is it true that you only like two girls at a time, or is one enough for you?'

He looked down at the table and straightened the cutlery in front of him. He looked at the perfectly aligned silverware for a few seconds then clasped his fingers over them, shut his eyes, and slowly shook his head.

'Amaka, you are something.'

His phone rang.

'I have to take this. Am I excused?'

'You are.'

Her plan, that she had not finished putting together, was to lure him back into his bedroom, away from the watchful eyes of his servant. Once that first stage was over, she would think of the next step.

As he went to take his call, he stopped at the door where Tom stood, and placed a hand on his shoulder. 'Don't let her go anywhere,' he said. He turned and smiled at her then walked away, bringing the phone to his ear.

52

The brothers, Catch-Fire, and Go-Slow, stood around Knockout as he dialled Chief Amadi's number for a third time.

'Hello?'

'You are a dead man. Hello, are you there? Chief, you are dead.'

The thugs lunged at him but Go-Slow shielded his friend and put a finger to his lips.

'Are you there? You are a wicked man. So you sent people to my house to kill me? I thought you were a gentleman. I did not know that you are a liar and a bastard. Bastard. I have your boy, Catch-Fire. I will release him to the police if you don't bring me ten million naira now.'

'Who is this?'

'Please. I beg you. No need for all these James Bond moves. I am alone. I am still alive. The boys you sent to kill me have failed. You cannot capture air. I am telling you now, last warning, bring me ten million naira or else I will go to the police with Catch-Fire.'

'I do not know who this is or what you are talking about.'

'Look, it is me, Knockout. You know who I am. There is no need for all these games you are playing. I am telling you, I have Catch-Fire, and if you don't stop all this nonsense and talk to me, I will just release him to the police now-now. Hello? Hello?'

'You are Knockout?'

'Yes, I am Knockout. This is me.'

'And you have Catch-Fire?'

'Yes.'

'And you believe I should give you ten million naira?'

'Yes.'

'I really can't talk now. I will call you back.'

'No. If you cut this phone, that is the end. I will take your boy to the police station now-now.'

'OK. I don't know who you are or what you are talking about, but supposing you and I do have some outstanding business arrangement, don't you think ten million is a lot of money? Where do you expect me to get that right now?'

'I don't know and I don't care. You are the one that does money juju. Go and do your magic and bring me the money. Hello? Hello? Chief? Hello?'

He realised the line was dead. He held the phone in front of him, looking at it as if it had done something wrong.

'What happened?' Go-Slow said.

'The phone cut.'

'The phone cut or your credit finished?'

He checked how much airtime he had left. 'The phone cut.'

'Network problems?' One-Love said.

'No,' Go-Slow said, 'He dropped the phone. You were not in charge.'

'What do you mean I was not in charge?' He redialled the number.

'Kanayo, talk like a human being.'

The phone rang out, then he tried again.

'Send him a message,' One-Love said, 'say that we have invited reporters to meet us at Panti.'

Go-Slow shook his head. 'No. First, tell us what he said.'

'He said he would call me back.'

'If he says he will call, he will call,' Catch-Fire said.

'You think he will bring the money?' Knockout asked.

'He has more than that,' Catch-Fire said. 'I tell you, ten million is nothing to him. He normally pays me cash anytime I deliver someone to him. He always has plenty, plenty money all the time. If he believes you, he will bring the money but he will make sure he kills all of us. We have to kill him.'

53

Amaka looked at Tom. He turned to look at her. She smiled. He smiled back. She got her phone and called the hotel, keeping her eyes on Tom. The phone rang out so she composed a text message to Aunty Baby.

Amadi walked in. 'I'm so sorry about that. I promise you, no more calls until we've had our meal.'

She pressed the send button and deleted the message she had sent.

He settled back into his chair and inspected his cutlery. He adjusted a knife using the tip of his forefinger, looked at it, and adjusted it again.

'Where were we?'

'You were about to tell me what you do with pretty girls.'

'Well, my dear, I don't know what you think you know about me, or what gossip you might have heard, but I assure you that I am the gentlest man you will ever meet.'

'Is that right?'

'Yes, that's right.' His phone vibrated on the table. He ignored it. 'My dear, you seem to believe you know something about me. Why don't you tell me what you've heard and I'll tell you whether it's true or not?'

His phone beeped twice as a message arrived. He read the text.

'My darling,' he said without glancing up from the phone,

'I have to see to this right away. I'm so sorry we keep getting disturbed like this.'

'I thought you promised no more interruptions,' she said. Her mouth was dry.

'I know, I know. Please forgive me. Some things just need to be dealt with immediately.'

As he left, he patted Tom on the shoulder and turned to wink at her.

He went to his study and closed the door behind him before making a call.

'Hello?'

'Yes, Chief, my message scared you, abi? I am on my way to Panti now. All the reporters in Lagos will be there to hear how you kill innocent people and use them for juju.'

'I thought you said you were professional.'

'I am very professional. That is why the boys that you sent to my house couldn't kill me.'

'I did not send any boys to kill you. I don't even know where you live.'

'Please don't lie to me. Catch-Fire has told me all your tactics.'

'Where is he right now?'

'Catch-Fire? He is with my boys. I have told them to take him to Panti if you try any nonsense games. You think you are the only one who has sense? We have invited all the radio and television people, dem. They are just waiting to know what we want to expose to them. It is finished for you.'

'That was not our agreement.'

'So you now think it was not our agreement? After you sent your boys to kill me?'

'Look, I don't know what you're talking about, but if Catch-Fire talks to anyone, even you will not be safe.'

'Me I will be safe. Don't worry about me. Worry about yourself. You murderer.'

'Calm down.'

'Don't tell me to calm down. Who are you to tell me to calm down? Just bring me my money.'

'Where are you now?'

'You think I will tell you where I am so that you can send your boys to kill me? Tell me where you want me to meet you and I will be there. If anything happens to me, my boys will take Catch-Fire to the radio station then they will take him to Panti. Even now-now, reporters are waiting for them there. We have even recorded him. He has confessed everything. I have the video.'

'I don't have ten million naira with me. I have dollars. I will give you a hundred thousand dollars, that's more than you asked for. But you must give me proof that Catch-Fire is dead.'

'Dollars is good. Just bring it. After I collect the money, I will return to my people and we will kill the boy.'

'OK. Listen carefully. I did not send anybody to you. All I wanted was for you to take care of Catch-Fire. I don't know what he has told you or how he has convinced you that I tried to kill you, but I will give you the money only on the condition that you do what we agreed and kill him.'

'No conditions. And stop trying to mess with my brain. Just bring the money and don't try any of your tricks.'

'OK. I will get the money ready and I will call you back to tell you where to meet.'

'One hundred thousand dollars?'

'Yes, one hundred thousand dollars. And there is more where that is coming from. Wait for my call.'

Chief Amadi had hoped Catch-Fire would be dead by now, and with him, the problem he posed. But now there was no telling who the idiot had spoken to, or who he was still speaking to. If Catch-Fire as much as mentioned Amadi's name to the police, or to hungry reporters, all sorts of digging would be done. He had known this day would come and he was ready for it. The Voice had made sure of that. He knew exactly what to do.

He went to his room and closed the door. By his bed he got on his knees and reached for his bag. He opened it and paused. The notebook was no longer in the middle, perfectly aligned with the neatly stacked bundles of cash.

54

We were never going to get onto the road. Ade revved, shot forward, and applied the brakes before we knocked into the Mazda in front of us. The driver spread his fingers at us. Ade inched even closer. The car behind the Mazda didn't look like it would stop for us either. The traffic moved the distance of a car and Ade lurched forward again. The man behind the wheel had no choice but to let us through.

The car beside us was being pushed along by a woman and two young boys. Behind them, three men were pushing a pickup van. A bonnet popped on another car.

'Overheating,' Ade said.

'How far is it to his place?'

'Not far. Once we get out of this.'

But we were never going to get out of 'this'. Perhaps I was overreacting. Maybe we would get to his house and she would have a go at me for turning up.

Up ahead in our lane, some men climbed out of a four-by-four. Another group got out of the minivan in front of them and they all began arguing. Someone pushed someone and fists formed and flew. The cars ahead of the fracas began to move but the fight had now drawn a crowd and we were stuck.

Cars began to pull out of the lane. Ade pointed the nose of his car into the traffic coming from behind. I heard the screeching of tyre locked on tar before I saw a body flying across our bonnet: one of the motorcycle taxis had driven into us and the driver was now deposited somewhere on the road ahead.

55

Tom looked straight ahead. Amaka slipped a knife off the table. He didn't see her. She tucked it under her lap and looked at him. Amadi appeared in the doorway. When their eyes met, he broke into a smile.

'You can excuse us now, Tom.'

Tom bowed and left.

He walked up to Amaka, stopped behind her chair and began massaging her shoulders. She stiffened. He placed his hand on her chest and spread his fingers across the base of her neck. She tucked her hand under her thigh and touched the knife with the tips of her fingers. He pushed his palm into the cup of her bra as he shifted the other into a side pocket of his garment. She lifted her leg to grip the knife. He clasped a cloth onto her face and gripped her head against his body. Her hands flew up and grabbed his. She tried to scream but instead inhaled chloroform vapour and then everything went dark.

56

Ade got out and went to inspect the damage. He didn't bother to look at the person on the ground. The destroyed motorcycle lay on the road on its side, its tyres still spinning, fuel leaking from its small tank, and debris forming a trail behind it.

Other motorcycles began to park up around us. Someone helped the injured boy to his feet. He held his bleeding elbow. He didn't have a helmet. I wanted to get out of the car but decided against it when Ade slapped the boy twice in quick succession. He was outnumbered twenty to one; what was he thinking?

The boy said something and Ade slapped him again, grabbed him by his shirt and dragged him to the door.

A huge fellow who had just arrived on his own motorcycle stepped in front of Ade. They started shouting at each other.

The argument grew louder. The mob grew. I got a few menacing glances myself. Ade opened the door and leaned in. He was sweating and he had a spectacularly vicious look on his face.

'Hand me the bag in the glove compartment,' he said.

I reached in and found a small leather bag. He opened it, counted out a few naira notes, and returned to the waiting men.

He handed the money to the boy who was still writhing in pain then he slapped him one more time before climbing back into the car, grinning.

By this time the traffic had subsided. He fired the engine and drove at the mob, scattering them and stirring up shouts and obscene gestures in our wake. I expected a stone or some other improvised missile to come crashing through the window.

57

Amadi held Amaka until her hands fell away from his and dangled by her sides. Tom stood up from the breakfast table as Amadi walked into the kitchen.

'I want to wash my hands.'

He walked to the tap and Tom squeezed some liquid soap onto his palms and turned on the water.

'You will go to the house in Ikeja. The driver will take you. I'm expecting guests there later tonight. Take the gateman with you. He will help you dust the house.'

Tom nodded.

Amadi picked a napkin from a stack on the island in the middle of the kitchen.

'Follow me.'

He led Tom out the front door. The gateman jogged up to them.

'Go and get Eremobor. You are going with Tom to Ikeja. He'll tell you what to do when you get there.'

The boy sprinted round the house to fetch the driver.

'Take the Range,' he told Tom. He entered the house, walked into the dining room and watched Amaka for a few seconds before going upstairs to his room. He lifted the black bag onto his bed and retrieved his passport from under a vase in a corner.

Amadi pulled off the purple kaftan and opened his closet. He squeezed into a pair of black jeans and a dark blue polo shirt, fetched a pair of worn trainers hidden away in the corner, then looked at himself in the mirror. He rummaged through a drawer for the spare keys to a Peugeot 504 that Eremobor sometimes used for errands. He had bought the car from an army auction, and he had kept its dark tinted windows and deep green military paint. He had never driven it himself and it had a manual transmission, no power steering, and no air conditioning, but it had a huge boot and its military appearance meant that the police would hesitate to stop it.

He returned to the ground floor, placed his bag by the front door, and went to the dining room. Looking at Amaka, he pulled out his mobile.

'Hello?'

'Hello.'

'It's time to move to Ghana,' he said.

The Voice paused for a few moments. 'OK. Have you taken care of the house?'

'I'm going there now. The next time we speak I'll be in Accra.'

'Good. I'll be waiting.'

He made another call.

'Knockout? I have your money. Ask Catch-Fire to tell you where he takes me to in Ajah. Meet me there.' He switched off the phone.

He was fleeing the country, possibly never to return. People would miss Chief Ebenezer Amadi, but nobody would notice the disappearance of Okafor Bright Chikezie. Knockout didn't matter anymore, but Catch-Fire still did. If Knockout showed up at the bungalow, it meant Catch-Fire was still alive. If he didn't show up, Amadi could dream of one day returning to the country and the city he loved so much; the city that once condemned him to a life of poverty, only to spare his life and open the doors of opulence to him.

After loading the boot of the car, he opened the gate and returned to the Peugeot. The old motor responded with a roar and a puff of black smoke. Amadi drove out onto the road, pulled up by the fence and got out to shut the gate.

'Good afternoon, sir.'

He turned and saw his neighbour's teenage daughter. Nobody could see him leaving.

'How are you?'

'I'm fine, sir.'

'And your parents?'

'Fine, sir.'

'Where are you going?'

'I'm going to Lekki, sir.'

'Lekki? Are you walking there?'

'No, sir. I'm getting a taxi.'

'I'll drop you off. A young lady like you shouldn't be taking public transport.'

'On no, sir, I don't want to take you out of your way. I'll get a taxi on the main road.'

'Don't be silly. What will the ambassador say if he hears I let his daughter take public transport?'

He was one of the wealthiest people on the street but her parents had never invited him to their Sunday lunches. He finished locking the gate and walked round to her. He placed an arm on her shoulder to lead her to the door.

'Thank you, sir, but I'll be fine.' She tried to move away and felt his hand firmly gripping her shoulder.

'Look, you are being very rude now. Why don't you want me to drop you? Are you going to see your boyfriend? Are you going somewhere your parents shouldn't know about?'

'No, sir, I'm just going to see a friend.'

'OK then, get in.'

She looked up and down the street. She didn't want anyone to see her getting into his car. He was not like the other neighbours. He brought young girls to his house and none of the friends of her parents visited him at home. She climbed in.

He got into the driver's seat next to her. 'Use your seatbelt, darling,' he said. 'OK. I am at your service, ma. Where exactly in Lekki do you want me to take you to?

'Phase One, sir.'

'All right.' He engaged the first gear. 'So, how old are you?'

'Sixteen, sir.'

'Sixteen? Whoa. You seem so mature. That boy you are going to see is very lucky.'

She smiled and looked away when she saw the way he was looking at her. She couldn't wait to tell her friends how an older man had hit on her.

58

Take away the traffic and you realise that VI is not that big. We were soon driving on quieter roads having left the madness behind. We turned onto a tree-lined street with large compounds and big houses set back far away from the fences. Ade slowed down, pulled to the side, then stopped altogether. I looked at him for an explanation. He was watching something. I followed his gaze. A man had just climbed into an old green car parked in front of a house ahead.

'What?'

'Strange.'

'What?'

'That was Chief Amadi. There is a girl in the car, but unless I'm mistaken that is an army car.'

'A girl? Amaka?'

'I don't know. She just got into the passenger seat. Didn't you see?'

I looked. The car was driving away. It had tinted windows so I couldn't see inside.

'We have to follow them. Ade, we have to follow that car. Now.'

'Sure, sure.'

We drove past the house and I caught a glimpse of Amaka's Jetta through slits in the fence. It was his house. The gate had a padlock on it. It had been locked from outside. Where were they going?

The car pulled onto a side road. When we turned into the same road it was gone.

'We've lost them,' I said.

Ade floored the accelerator and I jerked back into my seat. At the end of the road, we screeched onto an adjacent road just in time to see the car turn down another street.

Ade raced forward, only slowing when we came to the turning.

'Get closer,' I said.

'If we get too close they will see us.'

He allowed the car to gain some distance on us. I didn't like his strategy. I didn't want to lose them. Next thing I knew he was making a phone call. It was a short conversation in a local language.

'Who was that?'

'My next appointment today. I was telling them I'll be late.'

He had taken his eyes off the road to answer me and missed the car turning again.

'They went that way,' I said.

He nodded and accelerated.

Amadi drove fast, taking back roads to avoid traffic. He took the narrow road by the Mobile building to get onto the Lekki expressway. The exit to Lekki Phase One was just ahead.

'I am off to America tonight,' he said. 'My family is there on vacation. They have insisted I should join them. Have you ever been to America?'

'Yes.'

'Lovely place, isn't it? I'm going to the airport after I drop you.

Would you like me to bring you something when I get back? I should be back in about a week.'

'Thank you, sir, I don't need anything.'

'Don't be silly. What is your dress size?' She felt uncomfortable.

'You don't have to worry, sir, mum buys all my clothes.'

'At your age? Big girl like you? OK, what about an iPad? Do you have one?'

'Yes, sir, I do.'

'The latest one?'

'No, sir.'

'OK, I'll get you the latest iPad. I see your mum often at the neighbourhood meetings. Will you tell her for me that I had to travel so I won't be attending the next meeting?'

'Yes, sir.'

'Don't worry, I won't tell her I took you to your boyfriend's house. It will be our little secret.'

She smiled.

'Tell her you saw me in front of my house when I was packing my bags to go. When I get back I'll watch out for you so I can give you your goodies, OK? Remember to tell her I've travelled. I've never missed any of the meetings without informing the secretary in advance.'

If anyone came looking for him they would ask around and be told he had gone to America. They would either wait for him to return or they would simply forget about him.

Amadi took the second exit at the roundabout and drove onto Admiralty Road. He owned a property there that he had never visited since he bought it. He didn't even remember the way to it. The girl directed him onto a narrow, cobbled stone road then onto an even smaller one. When he stopped the car she quickly got out.

'Remember to tell your mum I left for America today. Here, take this for your taxi back home.'

He gave her ten thousand naira in new notes.

59

We lost the car again. We had followed it off the roundabout but were stopped by security personnel at the gated entrance to Lekki Phase One. They wanted to know who we were visiting. Ade gave them a name and they waved us on. Several cars were now between us and the green car. We saw Amadi indicate off the road but by the time we got to the turning he was nowhere to be seen.

Ade drove slowly, looking down each side road. We got to the end and discovered that it was a close. Ade did a three-point turn and ahead of us, at the top of the street, we saw the green car reappear and turn onto the main road. Ade stepped on the accelerator.

The gang chartered taxis to Epe and found a buka where they would wait for Knockout to return. Catch-Fire had told Knockout how to get to Amadi's bungalow in the bush; an okada would take him the rest of the way.

When he could see the building, Knockout asked the motorcycle driver to stop. He continued the journey on foot, his pistol in his hand, his senses alert.

The building looked empty. Knockout walked up to it. He

dusted his clothes off and walked round the bungalow searching for a way in. Metal bars protected the doors and the windows. He returned to the front and banged on the door. No one answered. He dialled the Chief's phone one more time but it was still off. If Amadi failed to show up, he would take Catch-Fire to the police himself, he thought as he sat down on the floor in front of the door.

Several roundabouts later the Peugeot turned off the expressway and down a narrow untarred road that led to an even narrower sandy one. We had left the city far behind and were now driving through what looked like a village, complete with thatched buildings and goats roaming free. We were the only two vehicles on the road. Ade let Amadi gain on us, and as much as I didn't like it, I saw his point. Now, more than before, it would be obvious we were tailing him.

The car slowed to zigzag through the sand, looking for firm ground underneath for the tyres to grip. Ade turned down a path to someone's compound. We couldn't see the Peugeot but we could hear it and it sounded like it was struggling.

'Where is this place?' I asked.

'Ajah.'

'Are we still in Lagos?'

'Yeah.' He shifted into reverse just as the owner of the house appeared from his half door. As we backed onto the dirt road I tried to calculate how far ahead of us the green car would be, but what really bothered me was where he was going, and who might be there.

We drove four yards forward then the wheels started spinning and spraying sand.

Knockout heard the sound of an engine and stood up. A car appeared on the road leading to the house. Catch-Fire had described all of Chief Amadi's cars to them. This was one of them. He drew his pistol.

Amadi pulled up close to the door then killed the engine. He looked at Knockout's weapon and got out of the car.

Knockout pointed the gun at Amadi and took a couple of steps backwards. 'Don't try any games,' he said.

Amadi walked to the boot of the car and opened it.

'Come and help me with this,' he said.

Knockout approached slowly. He took one look in the boot and withdrew. 'What is this?' He brought his gun back up, level with Amadi's head.

'What does it look like? Put that thing away and help me carry her inside.'

Amadi went to the house and began to open the locks on the door. Knockout stood by the trunk. Was he about to witness a money ritual?

'What are you waiting for?' Amadi said. 'Let's get her inside.' He reached in and placed his arms under Amaka's armpits.

'What about my money?'

'Get her legs.'

Knockout hesitated. He tucked his gun into his belt and grabbed Amaka's bound legs. Together they lifted her out of the car and half-carried, half-dragged her to the house.

They stepped into a narrow corridor with three doors off it. Stacks of heavy-duty car batteries were lined up against one wall, all connected by thick cables that led into a metal box. Amadi was in front; he kept them moving towards a door that he pushed open with his back. They carried Amaka inside. What looked like a hospital bed stood in the middle of the room. Aluminium cabinets lined the walls.

'We are putting her on the bed,' Amadi said.

'Untie her.' He turned and walked to a cabinet by the wall, took a syringe and returned to the bed. Placing his fingers on her neck, he found a vein and pressed the needle into it. Her body shuddered. He returned to the cabinet with the spent syringe.

Knockout looked at the girl before him. Her face held his eyes. His hand glided over her. He put a finger under her nose and felt her warm breath. He placed his palm on her breast and squeezed. He thought of rescuing her from the hands of this evil man. He undid the cloth used to bind her feet then turned her on her side to work on her hands tied behind her back.

His body jolted suddenly and his muscles contracted involuntarily. Amadi kept the taser pressed to Knockout's neck, sending fifty thousand volts through the crook's little body until his feet gave way and he collapsed.

Amadi walked back to the cabinet and picked out a sterile knife. He shoved Knockout's body away from the bed then he knelt across him. With his fingers, he felt between his ribs then he lifted the blade and brought it down in a strong blow that tore through Knockout's chest cavity and lodged in his heart. He pulled the knife out and stabbed again. He continued until he had exhausted himself then sat away from the dead body and wiped away the blood that had sprayed onto his face. He turned the butchered corpse over, took the gun tucked into the belt, then stood up and spat onto Knockout's lifeless body. 'Bastard,' he said.

60

Ade's car wailed as he tried to get us out of the sand and we attracted the attention of some teenage boys. They were mostly bare-chested, skinny, but toned, and they had planks and sticks.

'Ade,' I called his attention to the approaching gang. He handed them some money and they began to dig us out, placing their planks under the rear tyres so we could reverse out of our trap. The boys pointed out safe paths to take and we were off; but the green car was gone. Ade drove fast at the edge, close to grass, onto another sandy road; the forest grew larger around us. He slowed down and gazed ahead, then without warning, he downshifted and the car leapt forward.

We followed the road to a compound and pulled up behind the Peugeot. The trunk was open, as was the door to the house. We went inside. I led the way. A door in the corridor was open. I went to it and called out Amaka's name. Nobody answered. Suddenly, a loud bang erupted from inside the room. Ade yanked me away from the open door and onto the ground. He had a pistol in his hand. He signalled for me to stay down, then he crept towards the door, fired two shots into the room and withdrew. There was no response. He stood up and approached the door holding his gun in front of him. 'Drop it,' he said. Silence.

I thought of Amaka. I got up and joined him at the door. A

largish man – it must be Chief Amadi – was holding her to his body. He had a knife pressed against her neck. Her eyes were shut. He had a gun in his other hand, pointed at Ade. A bed and a bleeding body on the ground separated us.

'Let her go, you bastard,' I said. I ran at him and he fired. I dived the rest of the distance, crashed onto the bed and rolled to the ground before reaching him. I saw Adè fall backwards. He had been hit. The man dragged Amaka with him through a door.

I scampered to my feet and followed. The next room was like the first – a crude kind of surgical suite. I dashed past an operating table in the middle and sidestepped a trolley with medical instruments set on top of it. A door leading out of the room swung shut and I bounded towards it. Two shots splintered the wood. I ducked, waited a couple of seconds then launched through the door. It led to a passageway and on to an open door at the end. Beyond that I could see the forest. I ran forward hoping his next shot would also miss its mark.

I stepped into the backyard and saw only trees. A branch snapped back to hide a flash of colour. I ran towards it. My feet sank into vegetation. I grabbed at shrubs and pulled. Amadi levelled his gun at my head. I fell forward and he shot. He had Amaka with him: her torso drooped over his arm. He fired two more shots. I hid behind the nearest tree and he started to move again but Amaka was slowing him down. By now he was dragging her by her neck. He looked over his shoulder, tripped and Amaka fell away from him. I bounded forward and launched at him. We rolled around in the foliage. He elbowed me in the neck. I coughed, choking. He pushed me off and reached for his gun but I caught his leg and dragged him backwards. He grazed the side of my face and I grabbed his belt, pulling him onto his back.

I forced my hands under his shoulders and looped them back to clasp my fingers over the back of his neck. With all the strength I had left, I pressed his head forward and straightened my elbows. I wanted to dislocate his shoulders if I could.

Amaka staggered to her feet. She put a hand to her head. She looked like she was going to fall.

'Run!' I shouted. I didn't know how much longer I could hold him. He pushed with his feet, rolling his body until he was on top of me, crushing my back into the thick undergrowth. I couldn't see Amaka.

'Run,' I shouted.

He headbutted me. The pain seared through my face. He freed himself and rolled into the bushes, crawling towards his gun. Amaka was trying to steady herself, her hands searching empty space for support.

'Run!'

But she just stood there, looking at him, not me. By now he had picked up the gun and was climbing to his feet. I rolled over and kicked his leg as hard as I could. He fell and his gun fell away.

'Amaka, run!' I shouted again. I jumped onto him and felt his fist in the side of my belly. I wrapped my arms around him before he could manage another punch. Amaka picked up his pistol, almost falling over as she did. She held the gun in both hands and tried to aim. The pistol waved dangerously from my head to his head and back.

'Drop it,' someone shouted. I turned to look but I didn't loosen my grip. It was Inspector Ibrahim, dressed in his uniform, holding a sub-machine gun, which was aimed at Amaka.

'No!' I screamed. I let go and launched at him.

He let out a burst of shots before I wrapped my arms around his legs and tackled him to the ground. He had shot her. I screamed so loud that I didn't hear the sound of my own voice. I was on top of him laying my fists into his face. Someone caught my arms from behind and yanked me away. I kicked at him then the barrel of a gun pressed against my temple. I didn't care. I kept kicking. They dragged me away. Ibrahim was getting to his feet. I lurched forward then a pistol was placed sideways against my head and a shot was fired. My head felt like it had exploded, then there was silence. I couldn't hear a thing. I saw Ibrahim stand upright and straighten his uniform.

'You bastard!' I screamed. 'You bastard!'

He spoke to the person holding me. I couldn't hear but I read his lips: 'Let him go.'

I did not want to look but I turned to see what he had done to Amaka. She was still standing, pointing her gun at Amadi. He was sprawled face down, his head at her feet, a tiny pistol in his open palm, blood turning the leaves red around his body.

61

Police officers were all around us. I recognised them. They were the men of Fire-for-Fire I'd seen at the police station. An officer gave his weapon to a colleague, and with the cautious movement of a bomb disposal expert, he slowly took the weapon from Amaka's hand. She swayed and I moved towards her but someone stepped in front of me and pointed his rifle at my belly. It was a face I would never forget: Sergeant Hot-Temper.

'Let him go,' Inspector Ibrahim said. Although my ears were buzzing, I heard him this time. The killer cop lowered his gun, grinned toothily and winked, as if he had been joking with me. I stepped past him and reached Amaka, catching her just as her knees crumpled. She looked at me through almost-closed eyes.

'Guy,' she whispered, and her lids shut before she collapsed into my arms.

I lifted her off the ground and looked at her face. She was breathing.

'Let's go,' Ibrahim said to his men, then to me: 'Mr Collins, it's time to leave.'

An officer moved to help me but I didn't let him take Amaka from me. I carried her out of the forest and back to the bungalow.

Armed officers stood everywhere. The chatter of police radios was going off all around. About five police vans were parked in front of the building, their doors open. I saw Ade getting his arm bandaged by an officer. The body I'd seen inside the house was being wheeled out on a trolley.

Two men came to take Amaka from me.

'They are doctors,' Ibrahim said. 'They will take care of her.' He had been walking by my side all the time. I watched as they lay her on the ground. They crouched, one on each side of her. One of them held her wrist in his fingers and watched the face of his clock.

'That bullet was meant for you,' Ade said. I turned and saw his smiling face.

Ibrahim saluted him. 'Guy, meet Commander Mshelia.'

'Did you think we'd let a foreign journalist go chasing after killers? I'm with the DSS,' Ade said. 'You know, like the FBI. Ibrahim asked me to keep you out of trouble. I thought it was going to be a walk in the park, as you say.'

It took a second for what he said to sink in. 'You are a policeman?'

'You could say so. Undercover, but my cover is blown now.'

'You are a policeman?'

'Yes.' He winced as the officer tending to him wound another length of bandage round his arm. 'I'm not Ade. But I wasn't spying on you or anything like that.'

'So, where is Ade?'

'Oh, Ade, he sends his apologies. He had to jet off to Abuja.'

Mshelia explained that Ibrahim was in his office inspecting my phone when the real Ade called. As Ade's number was the only contact stored on the phone, Ibrahim figured he could use him to flush me out. He sent Ade a text message supposedly from me, asking to meet at the Eko Hotel lobby. He found Ade there, looking impatient, and he calmed him down by showing him his badge and placing him under arrest.

Ibrahim wasn't sure what to do with the journalist so he took him to the Navy Dockyard, to his friend in the secret service, Commander Mshelia. Together, the two officers began to interrogate Ade but the journalist was just as eager to impress them with his knowledge of his rights and what the law was pertaining to those rights. Commander Mshelia offered him a deal: spend the next few days in detention at the Navy Dockyard while the police continued investigating the murder that the Briton might be involved in, or, cooperate and help us find the foreigner before he gets himself into even more trouble.

Weighing the charge of conspiracy in a murder against his freedom and some time in a crowded cell, Ade chose the latter. He confided in the officers that he had never trusted the man's story, anyway. A UK-based Nigerian journalist, an old acquaintance, had found Ade through the Associated Press and offered him the task of looking after the British journalist, but as far as Ade knew, the entire setup could be a CIA thing. For this reason he had stayed away from Guy from day one: this reason and the fact that only once Guy was airborne did he learn that he wasn't even getting paid for the job. He had never even met the man before. He didn't even know what he looked like.

Ibrahim took over. According to him, Mshelia was first to get the idea of impersonating Ade, but he, Ibrahim, preferred a different approach. Ade had told them that he was in touch with Guy's boss. They made him call England and explain to Guy's boss that he could not find Guy. Ibrahim wanted Guy to come to him. Amaka, he could only assume, was still with him; she just might suspect something if Mshelia turned up pretending to be a journalist. Ade gladly made the call but soon started ad-libbing. Guy's boss swore and shouted when he learned that Guy had not bothered to meet up with his guide, and then he asked Ade to do him a favour and tell the fool that he was fired – if he managed to speak to him.

'That's how the call ended,' Ibrahim said.

They both paused to look at me, unsure if they'd just given me bad news. I nodded and Ibrahim continued.

They released Ade, who said he had to return to Abuja, and Mshelia became a journalist. My phone showed that I'd sent several messages to Ade and tried to call him a few times. They decided to gamble on me getting in touch again; that way, I wouldn't be suspicious when Ade suddenly became available to meet.

'Ibrahim wasn't sure how you got yourself mixed up in this mess,' Mshelia continued, 'but he was afraid you were sniffing around and endangering yourself. My job was simply to steer you clear of trouble so that he could do his job without having to worry about a white boy getting himself killed on his watch. By the time you told me your girlfriend had gone to the suspect's house, we were already aware of Amadi's involvement in the crime. I called Ibrahim from the hotel and updated him. We agreed that he should go to the suspect's house to make sure Amadi knew that he knew Amaka, and that he knew she was at his place. That way, we believed, he wouldn't dare harm her. I guess we were wrong.'

'Commander Mshelia texted me the flight numbers Amaka found and he told me what you came up with,' Ibrahim continued. 'I obtained the flight manifests from the airline and requested the medical records of everyone on board who wasn't based in Nigeria. He was updating me by phone as both of you tailed Amadi's car. It appeared as if the man was making a getaway and taking Amaka as hostage, so we decided to strike.'

'It looks like you might have exposed an international syndicate, Guy,' Mshelia said. 'You and your girlfriend, Amaka. From the way that this place is setup,' he pointed his good hand at the bungalow, 'it appears they were probably doing operations in there. Very crudely.'

'So, you are with the secret service?' I said.

'Yes.'

'And you followed us?' I was looking at Ibrahim.

'Yes. I had enough evidence to make an arrest. And I was concerned over your safety, and Amaka's.'

'So you didn't want to kill me?'

'Oh no. Why would you think such a thing?'

'So I'm not under arrest?'

They both laughed.

'By the way,' Ibrahim said, 'take your phone. I've been trying to return it to you since yesterday.' He held it out to me.

I hadn't expected to see it again.

'Where are they taking her?' Amaka was being placed in the back of a police car.

'She needs medical attention. They are taking her to the clinic. Maybe you should go with her.'

'I should.'

He looked past me at her. 'She's made quite an impression on you,' he said.

I didn't know how to respond to that. I got the feeling she'd made quite an impression on him too.

Mshelia groaned to remind us he was still there. He waved away the hand of the officer seeking to inspect his bandage. 'Well then, go,' he said. And as I turned to leave: 'And listen, if you break her heart, you'll have us to answer to.'

I stopped to shake hands with both men. 'Sorry about that,' I said to Ibrahim, holding my hand to the side of my face. He smiled.

Amaka was still out of it. I got in the back with her, placed her head on my lap and began pulling shreds of cling film off her neck. Sirens went off as we left the little house in the bush.

We went to the medical clinic at Wilmot Point, the naval base on Ahmadu Bello Road, close to Inspector Ibrahim's police station. Navy nurses took her and wouldn't let me follow them. I waited in the corridor, breathing in antiseptic cleanser. A woman in a naval uniform brought me a chair. I thanked her but continued pacing the corridor. Men and women in military or medical gear walked past me, coming and going through double doors, but not from where they had taken Amaka. Then, about an hour later, three women and two men, all in white coats, hurried to the room she was in. I froze in front of the door.

Fifteen minutes later a doctor appeared.

'Are you Guy?'

'Yes.'

'Please come with me.'

I was afraid to ask him anything. He took me into the room and asked the nurses standing round Amaka's bed to excuse us. They had been taking tubes out of her arms. Her eyes were closed and she wasn't moving.

'She's still slightly sedated but she asked to see you,' he said.

'She's OK?'

I walked up to her side and placed my hand on hers. Her fingers curled around mine and squeezed. Her eyes opened and I felt tears burning behind mine.

She didn't talk. She stared into my eyes and held my fingers even tighter. The doctor drew a chair up to me and I sat by her side. Her eyes closed.

Aunty Baby arrived with Flavio by her side. She asked the nurse at the reception to take her to Amaka.

Inspector Ibrahim walked up to her and introduced himself. He explained that her friend, Guy, had found her number on Amaka's phone and asked him to call; he was with her now.

Apart from a headache and a sore throat, Amaka had recovered and she insisted on being filled in on everything that had happened. She wouldn't let go of my hand, and I couldn't let go of hers.

Inspector Ibrahim and Commander Mshelia walked into the room and behind them, Flavio and Aunty Baby.

I looked up and saw the expression on Aunty Baby's face; I smiled to let her know everything was OK.

She and her husband joined me at the bedside. I stood to let her sit and she placed the back of her palm on Amaka's forehead. Amaka smiled. They wanted to know what had happened. After that, I didn't get any time alone with her but I was happy just to see her smiling and talking again, alive and well.

I stood back and watched everybody: my contact who turned out to be a spy; Ibrahim to whom I owed my life; Aunty Baby and Flavio who had been as worried as I was; and Amaka, weak but still here.

'Guy mentioned a database,' Ibrahim said. 'I would like to see it if you don't mind. It could really help us flush out more of these bad guys.'

Amaka looked at me. She smiled to let me know it was OK.

'Yes. I would love to hand it over to you. Guy has it.'

'He also told me how you use it to keep girls safe. Would I be asking too much if I request that you keep doing this? We will only use the information as leads, we will keep it secret, and we will give you a few officers to work with, if ever you need them – women you can trust.'

'Thank you. That would be helpful,' Amaka said. 'There's another thing you can do for me.'

'What is that?'

'There is a man, Malik…'

'Amaka,' I said.

She turned to me. We looked at each other while everyone waited. Even on a hospital bed, she still had her unyielding look; the look that says, 'There's nothing to discuss. I'm having my way.' I held my ground in the high stakes game of 'first to blink'. This was not the time to worry about Malik or a dozen other Amadis. She could have died. She needed to rest and recover.

'It can wait,' she said, still looking at me. Then she smiled and held out her hand.

The doctor returned to check her with his stethoscope and to look under her eyelids. He said she had been drugged with something that sounded too strange for me to remember, but she was OK now and could go home. She needed to rest and drink a lot of water.

Inspector Ibrahim assigned a police car to us. Amaka, Aunty Baby, and Flavio went back to the hotel with me to pack up my things; I still had a flight to catch.

According to the ticket Sally had emailed to me, my boarding time was in a few hours. Lagos traffic necessitated setting out early. I didn't want to leave but Amaka insisted I go.

Aunty Baby and Amaka talked all the way to the airport while Flavio kept nudging me and nodding towards Amaka, and grinning.

I had not spent a moment alone with Amaka since she regained consciousness. Everyone followed me to the gate. I wanted to say something to Amaka but I didn't know what would be appropriate, or even acceptable.

'I can curl my tongue.'

'What?' she said.

'I can also sleep with one eye half open. And I once won an egg-and-spoon race in primary school.'

'What are you talking about?'

'Someone told me that if I had a talent I would stand a better chance of being noticed by you. I'm sure I have an impressive talent hidden away somewhere. Maybe one day I'll discover it and then you'll notice me.'

'You already have a talent, Guy Collins.'

'I do?'

'Yes. You are good at tracking down killers and rescuing Amaka.'

She put her arms around my head and pulled my lips to hers. We kissed in the crowded departure lounge, oblivious to watching eyes.

'Now that you've saved me from the evil dragon, are you going to come back soon to claim your princess?'

We kissed again.

Epilogue

Ibrahim still had to write his report before he could finally go home to his wife and kids. He had always had his suspicions about Amadi: the way he courted him and went out of his way to shower him with unrequested gifts. The dollars from the Victoria Island Neighbourhood Association meeting were still in his pocket, but there was no way he could have known that the man was killing people. Who would believe him anyway? It wouldn't be too hard to find out that the police inspector and the dead killer were friends and they would assume that Ibrahim was his police protection. And the fact that he was the one who shot the man would only be interpreted as disposing of the evidence.

Before Amadi's body was taken away, Ibrahim removed his wallet, money, and phone from his pockets. It was the phone he was interested in most of all; it would have his number on it, and calls from him, evidence that he was close to the suspect.

He locked himself in his office and left instructions not to be disturbed. He stared at his notebook for several minutes, rolling his pen in his hand and wondering what to put in his report. The more he considered the problem, the more he realised that the solution lay with Amaka. She alone, as far as the case was concerned, could prove that he knew Amadi. Mshelia would understand his predicament, but Amaka would wonder why he wanted her to lie when it came to writing a statement. But she owed him her life; if it came to it, perhaps she would remember that. He made up his mind: he had never met the suspect before. Before he committed anything to paper, he wanted to test it out on someone. He called the commissioner of police.

'Hello, Ibrahim? Any news?'

'Yes, sir. We have found the culprit, sir.' He held his pen tight in his free hand.

'What? You have to speak loud. I'm at a wedding.'

'We have found the culprit, sir.'

'Who?'

'I do not know, sir.'

'What do you mean?'

'Sir, we followed a lead. The suspect abducted another lady and we trailed him. We ended up exchanging fire and he was fatally wounded.'

'He is dead?'

'Yes, sir.'

'What is his name?'

'Sir, I do not know, sir.'

'What are you saying? How can you not know?'

'Sir, there was no identification on him.'

Ibrahim listened to the noisy music on the line, resentful that while he had foregone his sleep, the man who had been on his neck all day had the time to attend a party.

While he waited for the commissioner to walk away from the noise, Amadi's phone began to ring. He picked it up and looked at the screen: 'Boss.' It stopped ringing then it started again. He lowered his phone and answered the call. He heard music playing. He lowered the phone and put his own back to his ear, then he lowered his and listened to Amadi's again. To be sure, he placed both phones to his ears. The same music played through both phones. He ended the call on Amadi's phone and listened to the live band playing while he waited for the commissioner.

He wrote into his notepad: 'I did not mention Amadi.'

Amadi's phone began to ring again.

The police car dropped Amaka at home. Aunty Baby and Flavio wanted her to stay with them but she insisted on going back to her place.

She filled her bathtub, picked a CD from a rack, then shed her clothes, slid into the warm water, and closed her eyes. She lay there until the water turned cold, then she climbed into bed and tried not to think of anything. But she couldn't stop thinking of Chief Amadi, the bungalow, her girls. And Guy Collins. She couldn't get him off her mind.

Later, she turned in the bed and buried her face in a pillow. She did not like feeling like this; it made her feel vulnerable.

She tossed and turned until she could only stop herself from screaming. Guy promised to call once he'd landed. She struggled to sleep but she was kept awake by her thoughts alternating between longing for him to call and wishing he wouldn't.

She kicked the sheets away in exasperation and got out of bed. She checked the time again, got dressed and snatched her car keys off the dressing table. She left her phones behind, something she never did.

She did not have a planned destination when she climbed in her car; she just drove, trying not to think of Guy. At the Awolowo roundabout where she had three choices, she flipped a mental coin and turned left onto the bridge to VI.

She came off the flyover onto the Lekki expressway. The sun blinded her and she flipped the visor down and hissed at forgetting to take her sunglasses. She was close to the home of some family friends but she did not want to turn up without calling first – and she had left her phones at home. She had done it in defiance;

a statement that she was in control. But now, the act itself felt like confirmation that she wasn't. Why was she afraid, anyway? He liked her, and she liked him too. She really liked him. She shook her head and smiled. She did a U-turn at the next exit and tapped the accelerator pedal to force the automatic gearbox down a gear. She raced to beat the traffic lights ahead.

Her phone was ringing when she walked back in to her house. She rushed into her room and snatched the phone from her bedside stool.

'Hello lover,' she said. She lay back onto her bed and closed her eyes, smiling and feeling embarrassed.

'Hello Amaka,' a man said, but it wasn't Guy. She opened her eyes. The voice was deep and low, and the 'Hello' was drawn out. 'I hear you've been looking for me. My name is Malik.'

Acknowledgement

From the first draft to the finished product, a lot of people have helped and contributed in many ways. Special thanks to Souraya Ali Choukeir, Lola Shoneyin, Sofia Alexandrache, Tracy Mann, Bisi Ilaka, Sybilla Wood, Gabriel Gbadamosi, Peter Lawson, Jeremy Nathan, Julian Friedmann, Tolani Ibiduni, Osaretin Oswald Guobadia, Chiekezi Dozie, Najite Dede, Onome Onuma, Cynthia Ogunedo, Yejide Kilanko, Chinapa Aguh, Owi Ochoche, Dipo Agboluaje, Jeremy Weate, Alex Hannaford, Siddhartha Mitter, Kate Haines, and Bibi Bakare-Yusuf, amongst many others.

Title: Easy Motion Tourist
Author: Leye Adenle
Editors: Alex Hannaford & Jeremy Weate
Copy Editor: Kate Haines
Proofreading: Anthea Gordon